"I need Angela's [pacifier in her?]
room. Would you [get it, Regan?]

Regan raced into Ethan's room and found the pacifier. She saw that his bed wasn't made and a couple of dirty shirts lay where he'd dropped them. Dust had collected on his dresser. His room had been immaculate before the babies' arrival. Ethan clearly needed a housekeeper. *Or a wife.* That last thought pulsed in Regan's head as she dashed down the hall and handed him Angela's pacifier.

"Thanks," he whispered, still rubbing the baby's back. Smiling up at Regan, he asked unexpectedly, "Have I thanked you for all your help over the past couple of weeks? If not, I want you to know I couldn't have done this without you. I *said* I could, but I was wrong."

He looked and sounded so serious, all Regan could do was nod. She wanted to hug him back and somehow wipe away the signs of fatigue. If only she could turn back the clock—to the last time he'd proposed. She'd accept the second he got the words out. The realization hit her like a load of bricks. She'd just admitted to herself that she wanted to marry Ethan Knight.

And not just because of the babies, either. Not at all...

Dear Reader,

Since I'm blessed with several police officers in my extended family, you might think a "cop story" would be easy for me to write. Not so. You see, my sources come from different aspects of police work—state, county and city bike patrol. Also the SWAT team. While generous with their information, these fine keepers of our peace don't always agree!

Like many of my books, *The Baby Cop* began with a couple of small news clippings. In this case, they concernerd horribly abused quadruplets, plus a hiker lost for several days in our mountains. Add to that a lot of library research on Child Protective Services. But the book is wholly a work of fiction. (Up to and including the totally fictitious mention of a not-so-nice group of cops attached to the Phoenix police. Trust me, Phoenix has a super contingent of hard-working officers!) Oh, and I can't forget Internet research on search-and-rescue dogs.

Any errors or discrepancies are strictly mine.

Cops, babies, dogs—I guess you'll have to read the story to see how I got all of that to come together in a romance novel. I hope you like the way Ethan Knight and Regan Grant cut through a heap of personal and professional problems to find lasting happiness—the bottom line (so to speak) of what love stories are all about.

I enjoy reading from readers. Write me at P.O. Box 17480-101, Tucson, AZ 85731.

Sincerely,

Roz Denny Fox

The Baby Cop
Roz Denny Fox

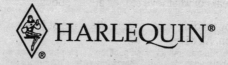

HARLEQUIN®

TORONTO • NEW YORK • LONDON
AMSTERDAM • PARIS • SYDNEY • HAMBURG
STOCKHOLM • ATHENS • TOKYO • MILAN • MADRID
PRAGUE • WARSAW • BUDAPEST • AUCKLAND

ISBN 0-373-70999-4

THE BABY COP

The Baby Cop

CHAPTER ONE

ETHAN KNIGHT tried to block out the chirp of his cellular phone. He'd just gotten to bed after forty-eight tense hours dealing with a hostage situation—armed robber holding a mother and child. He sighed; the inconsiderate caller showed no sign of giving up. Rooting around under his pillow, Ethan found the phone and flopped over so his ear fell across it. "'Lo," he muttered. His free hand batted at the cold wet nose of his big Alsatian, Taz.

"Sorry to bother you, Detective," said an anxious voice. "You probably barely hit the sack. It's Sergeant Vince Paducah. We need you here, man. Our team rolled on a routine nuisance call. We walked into a helluva mess." The sergeant rattled off a street address and an apartment number.

Ethan reared up from his crumpled pillow and snapped on a light. Before his eyes focused, he'd scribbled the information on the ever-present notepad sitting on his nightstand beside a locked box holding his police revolver. Cursing, he shoved his legs into dirty jeans. "I know that address, Vince. What is it this time? Did Brucie-boy tie one on again and beat the crap out of his poor wife?"

Detective Knight shrugged into his shirt and tucked it into his jeans while reaching for his boots. The caller's voice dropped. "Way worse. The worst." Vince uttered a string of codes—department lingo for domestic violence resulting in murder.

Pain exploded in Ethan's head as his fingers closed around his standard issue Smith & Wesson .38. Damn, his body was getting too old to handle the increase in after-hours cases—especially bad ones like this. "The kids?" he asked softly, trying to quell the flow of acid pumping into his gut. The team might want him ASAP, but Ethan figured he'd have to comb his hair and run a razor over a prickly chin or risk scaring two already frightened children with his wild-man look.

"They're spooky kids. No hysterics, no tears," Vince said. "Have you got a good safe place for 'em?"

"Yeah. Of course." Closing his eyes and taking a steadying breath, Ethan pictured a four-year-old girl with huge blue eyes and her stoic six-year-old brother. Two children who'd witnessed more violence in their short lives than any human beings in a civilized society ought to see. Only that was the problem; some people weren't civilized. Bruce Hammond ranked high among the least civilized SOBs.

"I'll make some calls on the way, Paducah." Ethan checked his shield and slid it into a jacket pocket. "I'll be there inside fifteen minutes."

"Good." Paducah expelled a relieved sigh. "My partner said that since Anna M. passed on, you probably don't have the same deal with the new supervisor. He said to phone the Child Help Center direct. But I've heard Anna's replacement is a regular battle-ax."

Ethan had received a memorandum announcing that a Regan Grant was taking over Anna's post. He'd never met this Grant woman, nor would he add to unfounded rumors. He merely grunted a noncommittal response and reiterated his estimated time of arrival as he hung up and stowed his phone in the pocket with his badge.

While he did a cursory shave, Ethan thought about his fifteen-year tenure on Desert City's police force. For more than half of those years, he'd been called the Baby Cop. It was a nickname that had nothing to do with age but with his far-reaching connections in the city and outlying communities, which allowed him to instantly place kids who needed temporary shelter in loving homes. Homes where the adults cared more about a child's welfare than the money the state paid every month for that care. Ethan had started by educating his eight brothers and sisters about the need in the community for safe homes. What had begun as a small network expanded over the years to include the families of police buddies and other friends. He'd convinced all these people—anyone of good heart and moral character who could offer a bed, food and TLC to traumatized kids—to license their homes for care. He'd done all this with the assistance and support of Anna M., the previous Child Help supervisor. Although he was a bachelor, even he was approved to provide emergency housing. An erratic work schedule precluded his taking a kid for longer than a night or two, but there had been times he'd used his vacation hours to turn up a safe house for a child.

Ethan's grandfather, the first Knight to be a cop, had willed Ethan his rambling four-bedroom home. The old man's charge to Ethan had been to fill the house with a passel of noisy kids. Of course, he'd meant that Ethan produce a family in the normal way. Ethan's failure there hadn't been for lack of trying, he frequently assured his nagging parents and siblings. He just hadn't managed to connect with the right woman.

Running a hand over a now-clean jaw, Ethan turned

his thoughts from his family to his job. He had worked out a good system with the compassionate Anna Murphy. Her unexpected death of a heart attack last month at only fifty-five had caused a lot of hardened men on the force to shed tears as they bore her casket to her final resting place. None shed more than Ethan. Anna had been one of a kind. Not a bureaucrat like the majority of city caseworkers who made police officers wade through miles of red tape in order to help victims of violent crimes. Anna's focus from the outset had been to do everything possible to speed the care of innocents. Especially kids hurt by family disputes. Or kids who lost their next of kin to accidents and random crime.

Anna had trusted Ethan to take care of the children first. She allowed him to file the reams of messy paperwork once things calmed down and he had time to concentrate. Ethan would then supply Anna with the name and address of a foster family, and she'd do her requisite visit, making it appear as though she'd placed the kids all along. There was nothing wrong with their procedure except that it was backward. Unorthodox in the eyes of some Family Assistance personnel. Namely Nathaniel Piggot, the CHC director.

Fortunately for the kids, Anna Murphy had said screw protocol—and Director Piggot. Her first priority had been to ensure a child's safety. To alleviate a child's heartbreak.

"Anna's and my method was the only sensible one," Ethan grumbled as he let Taz into the front passenger seat of a perpetually unwashed Suzuki SUV. Flipping his headlights on high, Ethan headed into a dark moonless January night, determined to do his part to help two sweet kids make the transition into a cold cruel world that no longer held their anchor—a mom who'd served as punching bag for the scum she'd had the misfortune to marry.

Ethan hauled out his cell phone and called his cousin, Jessica Talbot, a woman with a tender heart. She'd never yet turned away a child in need.

"Jess, it's Ethan. Sorry to wake you. Listen, have you and Dave got any vacant beds? I'm looking for two. Got a four- and six-year old." Without waiting for a reply, he continued, "Didn't I hear the judge gave custody of Megan and Caitlin Porter to their maternal grandparents? Figured that meant you had a couple of free beds."

In the background, Ethan heard clothing rustle and a murmured deeper voice. "Apologize to Dave," he said. "You guys know I wouldn't call this late if I wasn't desperate."

His cousin, who'd finally collected her wits, responded as Ethan had predicted. "Bring them. But I swear, Ethan Knight, you have an unbelievable pipeline in this community. I barely washed the sheets on Meg and Cait's beds." Jessica chuckled, then yawned. "Dave's already on his way to an all-night market to pick up extra milk and more kid-approved cereal." Sobering, she asked Ethan, "How bad? Do these kids need medical attention?"

"I'll arrange for psych counseling tomorrow." He condensed an explanation of the circumstances as he turned down the street leading to the cordoned-off complex. He could see twirling red and blue lights grotesquely outlining huddled residents in nightwear. All were in the throes of interrogation by uniformed police. Two rows of yellow tape secured the crime scene.

Concluding his business with Jessie, Ethan angled the SUV next to a patrol car. He saw the heads of two small figures pressed ear to ear in the back seat. Exiting his

vehicle, he popped the rear hatch and chose a soft white
fuzzy bear and one dressed in Paddington rain gear from
a laundry bag full of stuffed toys. Too well versed in
the routine, Taz closed his teeth gently around both bears
and trotted, ears erect, to the car where the children
clung together. Ethan opened the cruiser door for him,
and Taz approached the kids.

They recognized the dog at once. The girl, Kimi, dis-
engaged from her brother and snatched the white bear,
which she cuddled close to a thin chest. Mike, whose
pinched face reflected both pain and fright, couldn't
seem to accept Taz's offering. His vacant eyes were beyond seeing toys denoting childish endeavors he might
never again pursue. Ethan understood. He'd handled too
many of these cases not to gain some insight into the
roller-coaster emotions that followed acts of violence.

"I'm Officer Friendly. Remember me visiting your
class at school?" Ethan spoke directly to Mike in clear
yet mild tones. "And you know Taz. We've come to
take you somewhere safe, like the last time Taz and I
came to your apartment."

Kimi pulled the comforting thumb out of her mouth
and erupted in tears. "I want Mom-meee," she wailed.

Her brother stared mutely at Ethan from war-glazed
eyes. Bending, Ethan lifted the little girl and cradled her
close. He stretched out a hand to the boy. "You both
need sleep now, Mike. I know a nice lady who has a
couple of soft warm beds. Tomorrow we'll talk about
what happens next. I promise. Vince," Ethan called to
a broad-shouldered, uniformed cop talking to an elderly
couple, "I've got the kids. Okay?"

Looking up, Vince nodded grimly and gave a thumbs-
up.

A WEEK AFTER the sad incident, local newspapers still treated the story as front-page news. In that time Ethan made a drug bust, accompanied Kimi and Mike to the psychologist and attended their dad's initial hearing. He also placed another child in a safe home, this one a ten-year-old girl who'd been repeatedly molested by an uncle. Sometimes there seemed to be a rash of bad calls. And Ethan had to step outside his job and remind himself that for a city of almost half a million residents, a population that doubled when winter visitors and other transients migrated here for the sun, crime statistics weren't particularly high—no more than average for a community of this size. Still, it was easy to lose a sense of proportion when, day in and day out, you dealt with the dregs of society. For Ethan, a new perspective came through volunteer work with a county search-and-rescue unit.

In fact, over the weekend, Ethan and Taz had been airlifted to Canyon De Chelly, where they'd helped locate a lost camper.

Four o'clock Monday afternoon, Ethan finally had a breather. He sat at his battered desk in the department, typing a report for CHC on the Hammond kids and on Marcy White, the ten-year-old.

Finishing his two-fingered pursuit at last, he stapled vouchers to both reports and re-tallied receipts accounting for monies he'd advanced in each case. He'd paid for the first psychologist's visit for Kimi and Mike. And for Marcy's initial Emergency Room care. He and Anna had designed this arrangement because it expedited services that would otherwise be a long time gaining approval. Authorization came much faster after the fact.

Checking his watch, Ethan decided to drop the forms off with the new CHC supervisor before meeting his

partner, Mitch Valetti, at a stakeout planned for 6 p.m.
He and Mitch hoped to nail the next level up in the latest
chain of drug dealers to plague the local high schools.

Whistling for Taz, who slept under Ethan's desk, the
two left the police station. Rather than drive the three
blocks to the Family Assistance building, Ethan jogged.
Two weekends from now, he and Taz were registered
for a classic Schutzhund competition. They'd partici-
pated in the skill events with regularity ever since Ethan
had collected Taz from a breeder in Holland, a breeder
known for producing obedient, trustworthy, intelligent
dogs with the stamina needed for lengthy search-and-
rescue missions.

Police work paid Ethan's bills. Search-and-rescue was
his most passionate hobby. Between the two, they took
up most of his time. Not that he complained. Ethan loved
every minute of both. Though Schutzhund events, orig-
inating in Germany, were geared to show a dog's skill
in tracking and searching for hidden objects placed in
rough rugged terrain, handlers had to be in pretty good
shape, too. Which Ethan was, if the admiring look be-
stowed on him now by Nicole Mason, the CHC Department receptionist, was any indicator.

Ethan returned the appreciative glance. A healthy
thirty-six-year-old male, Ethan liked pretty women. And
he hadn't seen Nicky since Anna's funeral. He would
have taken a minute to flirt and maybe ask Nick a few
questions about Anna's replacement. But the pert redhead was tied up at the switchboard. A casual wave suf-
ficed as Ethan's greeting.

Taz, too, glanced longingly at Nicole. Normally she
gave his soft brown ears a rub. As if he understood she
was too busy today, Taz trotted past the switchboard and
on down the hall, several feet ahead of his master. He

turned the corner leading to the administrative offices and sped up. Taz knew Anna Murphy kept doggie treats in the bottom drawer of her desk. She had never failed to give him one.

The fact that this ritual would have to change didn't register with Ethan. Not until he reached the open door of Anna's old office and saw pure terror leech all color from the face of an attractive blonde seated behind the desk. Ethan thought the woman was going to scream, but instead, her eyes—so light a blue as to appear transparent—rolled back in her head. Her entire body went limp, although she made a vain effort to hang up the phone before she lost consciousness.

Shocked, Ethan could only follow well-honed instincts. Dropping his reports, he leaped forward and grabbed the woman seconds before she tumbled to the floor.

His boot barely missed Taz's tail. The dog had nosed open the drawer. He'd rooted under a purse and tossed to the floor what looked to Ethan like several packages of unopened nylon stockings.

Not finding his doggie treats, Taz flopped down on his stomach with a disgusted sigh. He stared at Ethan and the woman with an injured air.

Ethan had his hands full. The Grant woman was no lightweight, even though she appeared to be nicely put together. Ethan knew she was Anna Murphy's successor. She wore a name badge pinned to the breast pocket of a navy pin-striped suit. Her breathing seemed normal. At least, her badge rose and fell steadily.

Calling on his first-aid training, Ethan grasped the narrow chin between his thumb and forefinger. He shook her gently but firmly and spoke her name. "Ms. Grant, open your eyes. Tell me what's wrong. I'm with the

Desert City police. Are you in need of medical help? Are you diabetic? Was that a threatening phone call?'' Shifting her weight, Ethan spared a cursory glance at the dangling phone receiver. Lunging for it with his free hand, he realized there was no caller at the other end of the buzzing line. Still confused, he slammed the instrument back into its cradle and gently slapped her cheeks.

Light-colored eyelashes with sooty tips flickered, finally rising a fraction to reveal eyes dilated in confusion. Huge dark pupils stared past Ethan's broad shoulder and promptly grew wider. This time the woman shoved Ethan. So hard he landed flat on his butt on her carpet. She sprang away and tried to hide in the corner next to two tall filing cabinets. ''Ge…get th-that be…beast out of here,'' she gasped, her fingers clawing the wall behind her.

Her ranting made no sense to Ethan. He deduced that by beast she meant Taz. A dog now lying in perfect repose except for the occasional flick of one ear.

Nevertheless, it was clear that Regan Grant was too terrified to think straight about anything. She probably hadn't heard Ethan say he was a policeman. Headed as he was for an undercover assignment, he looked pretty casual.

With a hand signal and two words of softly spoken Dutch, Ethan banished Taz to the hallway. Rising, he dusted off his jeans. ''My dog is outside, Ms. Grant. Do you think you can relax now?''

She uncurled a little at a time, unconsciously clamping a hand over an almost invisible scar that started at the base of her jaw and ran the length of her neck. It was one of several jagged scars long since repaired by plastic surgery. Regan had some wounds that could never be repaired.

Forcing her hand and mind away from bad memories, Regan ran shaking fingers through her heavy mop of corkscrew curls. Her sun-streaked hair had fallen into her face when the clip restraining it had somehow become dislodged. Seeing the silver clip lying on the floor, she bent to retrieve it and felt woozy. Her heart beat so hard and fast she doubted she could calm down. It'd been two years since she'd had a fear attack this bad.

A few weeks ago, when she'd been out jogging, Regan had actually passed a woman walking a Scottie. She hadn't crossed the street to avoid them. A feat so rare Regan had patted herself on the back. Her hope then was that it meant she was conquering her phobia. Obviously not.

Ethan took heart as a bit of color crept into Regan Grant's chalky face. Familiar with the private bathroom in this office, he took the liberty of drawing her a glass of water—which he extended slowly to the woman he'd come to meet. While he was at it, Ethan grabbed the opportunity to make his own assessment of someone secretly labeled a battle-ax.

Ethan would guess Regan Grant's height to be five-five or -six. He'd pass on weight. She looked trim. Vroom-vroom, in fact. When he'd held her briefly, he'd had a sensation of holding something solid—not just skin and bones. Her taffy-streaked blond hair was cut in one length to her shoulders. A million curls picked up rays of afternoon sun and danced around her narrow face like a jagged halo. Any normal man would give her face a second look—or a third. If her generous mouth didn't draw a guy's interest, the arresting pale-blue eyes certainly would. Ethan knew he could never call anyone who looked like Regan Grant a battle-ax.

Regan stared for far too long at the unwavering water

glass held by a bronzed masculine hand. She licked her lips, wanting the water. But she was still shaking so badly she thought she'd spill it if she accepted the glass. What must this man, this stranger, be thinking of her? And who was he? Her last appointment of the day had been Mrs. Campbell. She'd been gone more than an hour.

With the hated dog out of sight and her thoughts returning to work, Regan managed to accept the glass. "Thank you," she murmured, motioning her Good Samaritan into a visitor's chair while she returned to her desk. Only after she was seated and the water had eased the tightness gripping her throat did Regan examine her unannounced visitor.

She had no doubt her staff would consider him "hot." She frequently overheard co-workers rating men who visited the CHC offices. This one had appealing black curls falling over straight black eyebrows. And eyes so dark, so rich a blue, they were almost black. He was a little too tall and muscular for Regan's taste. But he had a nice smile. And he smiled it at her now. Waiting.

She set the glass down with a thump and, with an effort, refrained from straightening her blouse and checking the status of her suit jacket. "Uh, I'm, Ms. Grant, supervisor of the Family Assistance Department's Child Help Center. Nathaniel Piggot is our director, Mr....?" Regan reached a hand across her desk. Her firm clasp demanded the man seated opposite her supply identification.

Ethan's stomach turned when he heard Nathaniel Piggot's name. He could only hope Ms. Grant wasn't taking a page out of the director's book. Left up to Nathaniel, all needy kids would eventually be phased out of the system to sink or swim. He guarded the department's budget as if it were his private fortune. Piggot didn't believe in providing what he termed "frivolous" services. Basic needs, in Ethan's estimation.

"Sorry," Ethan said, realizing he'd taken too long to give her his name. "I'm Ethan Knight, Detective, Desert City PD. That's my partner, Taz, out in the hall. One of them, at least. Mitch Valetti is the other." Grinning, Ethan turned briefly toward a huge black shadow visible through the frosted glass panels that flanked Regan's door.

She followed his movement and barely suppressed a shudder. Her lips tightened and her earlier welcoming voice became decidedly cool—due only in part to the hulking animal. Regan erased her first favorable assessment of Ethan Knight. Policemen didn't rate high on her list. In fact, she'd taken this job to forget a messy breakup with her fiancé. Jack Diamond, a captain with the Phoenix force had the same outward charm as Detective Knight. Too late, Regan had learned that Jack spread his charm around to every woman he met, including some he arrested. They'd lived together a short time, yet she'd been the last to find out Jack had a problem keeping his pants zipped. His pals on the force all knew, but not one had clued her in. In Regan's estimation, policemen were vermin scraped from the bottom of the barrel.

She clasped her hands on top of her desk and leveled at Knight the sternest look she could muster. "I've read your name on case files processed by my predecessor, Detective. While you may have worked directly with Anna, I have a different policy. All new cases go straight to Level-one Intake. There they'll be read, ranked and assigned to available caseworkers on a needs basis set up by Director Piggot."

Ethan, who'd gathered his reports from the floor during her terse little speech, slapped the stack in front of her on the desk. "Well, I've saved you the trouble of ranking Mike and Kimi Hammond, as well as Marcy White."

Regan's narrowed gaze went from the man's thinned lips to the papers still fluttering on her blotter. She didn't like Ethan Knight's belligerent stare or his arrogant attitude. "Wh-what do you mean, saved me the trouble? Ranking cases based on service requirements is what we do at CHC. Reports come to us from several sources. Police intervention is one, but minor in the larger scheme, I assure you. Take these forms to Sandy Burke, three doors down. Oh—should you need to see me again, please leave your dog outside. I assume there's a rule excluding animals other than seeing-eye dogs from government buildings. If not, there should be, and I'll certainly make a request to have one implemented."

"Really?" Ethan leaned forward, supporting both arms on the desk. His nose nearly touched Regan's. "My dog has better manners than a lot of people you'll meet, including some who work here. I don't know where you got your training in social work, Ms. Grant, and I don't give a damn. But in Desert City we take care of our needy or abused kids at the time they require help. We don't send them up dead-end channels never to be heard from again." Rising to his full six foot two, Ethan glared down into her pale features. "These kids have been processed. All my reports need is your look-see at the foster homes and your signature. It's fine by me if you shred the vouchers. The kids got the medical care when they needed it. That's what counts in my book."

Regan picked up the top set of papers and scanned the page until anger blurred her vision. Her jaw sagged, but her head shot up and she impaled Ethan with a scowl. "I can't *believe* you have the gall to step on our toes so blatantly and then come here and deliver me a lecture, as well. What credentials do you have? What gives you the right to decide who in this town is qualified to care for a troubled child?"

"Three children—this time," Ethan said in a low, dangerously soft voice. "I suppose you could say my credentials come from working Desert City streets for fifteen years."

Regan drummed her fingers on the paper she'd let fall. "No degree in psychology or sociology?"

"Criminal Justice," Ethan snapped.

"I see." She waved a hand vaguely in the direction of the back wall. "I have a master's in child psychology and one in social work, Mr. Knight."

"Detective," he said curtly. "A rank I earned working with the scum of society while you sat in civilized classrooms and studied in quiet libraries." Damn, but something about the snooty tilt to this woman's chin irked him.

Regan pursed her lips. "I don't have to defend myself to you. I think you're well aware that you've exceeded your authority, and to what extent. I want it stopped here and now." She stabbed a finger at Ethan's painstakingly typed reports. "Otherwise, Detective, I'll initiate a formal reprimand and personally place my complaint in the hands of your commander."

Ethan felt heat claw its way into his throat. Suddenly the term battle-ax didn't seem so far out of line. Rising stiffly, he inclined his head in a curt movement, his back teeth clamped too tightly to manage any sort of formal leave-taking. For a moment he was tempted to whistle Taz back into the room to give the psychology expert another taste of the type of fear kids experienced when their worlds were turned upside down. But he was more humane than that.

Yet it went against Ethan's grain to leave, allowing the supervisor to think he'd heeded her threat. Other social service agencies in town lauded the system he and Anna Murphy had built. If Ms. Power Suit Grant assumed he'd turn away from a suffering child rather than risk a reprimand from the chief, her degree in psychology wasn't worth crap.

Bringing Taz to heel with a flick of his finger, Ethan strode from Regan's office. Still fuming, he collected his vehicle from the station, then drove to meet Mitch.

"Wow," Mitch said a few minutes after Ethan and Taz joined him in the unmarked car they'd been assigned. "Who climbed your butt?"

Ethan, who'd thrown himself into the passenger seat, aimed a glower at his closest friend. "What makes you think anybody did, cowboy?" Mitch was known as the Italian Cowboy around the department for two reasons— he was of Italian extraction and he owned a small horse ranch.

"I wonder." Valetti laughed. Brown eyes sparkled with humor. "I've got it." He snapped his fingers. "You got taken down a peg or two by the heir to Anna's throne. Your message on my voice mail said you were going to drop some reports off to her. So—" Mitch waggled his dark eyebrows "—rumors must be true. Grant is a certifiable bitch."

Ethan winced. "Where do rumors like that start? If you've never met her, Mitch, why would you pass on such garbage?"

"Ah. So she's a fox?"

''Screw you, Cowboy. Quit trying to put words in my mouth.''

''Ouch.'' Mitch's grin spread from ear to ear. ''The lady really messed with your head, didn't she, my friend.''

Ethan mind flashed back to the pale delicate face made stark by terror. His fault for surprising the lady with Taz. Her terror had been real. So Regan Grant had a vulnerable side. A weakness he could exploit if he cared to blow the incident out of proportion and let Mitch add to the rumors. Or he could keep it to himself and try to create a working relationship with her.

Using the time it took to pour coffee from a thermos, Ethan dragged his mind back to Mitch's remarks about Anna's replacement. ''Ms. Grant's going to be a stickler for following rules Anna bent a little.''

''From what I hear, that's putting it mildly. Did you set this new supervisor straight?''

A smile tugged at one corner of Ethan's mouth. ''Not exactly. I didn't overwhelm her with my charm and personality. In fact, she said if I don't go by the book when it comes to placing needy kids, she'll institute a formal reprimand against me and hand-deliver it to the chief.''

Mitch's jaw dropped. ''You're kidding! No, you aren't,'' he muttered. ''That goes with what Brian Fitzgerald said about Grant. Fitzgerald's fiancée, Danielle Hargreaves, is the last caseworker Anna hired. She's working on her master's. Has to finish her thesis and do her orals. According to Brian, Grant had a hissy fit because Piggot told her all caseworkers were either MS's or PhDs.''

''Did she fire Dani?''

''Still deciding, I guess.''

''It'll be a loss to the department if they let Dani go.

She's got a great rapport with rape victims.'' Ethan sipped from his cup.

"Yeah. And she needs the job to pay off six years of college loans. Brian said they'll have to postpone their wedding if Dani loses her income. Some of the guys were thinking you might put in a good word for Dani with the Grant dame. Guess not, huh? Doesn't sound as if you two hit it off.''

Ethan shook his head. ''The way it stands, my speaking up might jeopardize Dani's position even more. Is her potential job loss why all the guys at the station are grousing? I mean, is that what started the rumors about Grant?''

"There's more. Grant instituted a dress code for caseworkers. Slacks and ties for the men, dresses or suits for the women. Like people who need the services of a caseworker cares how they're dressed!''

"Dress codes are a nuisance, but most areas have them. You know how the chief is about white shirts and no loose ties unless we're undercover.''

"Yeah. Well, that's not all. Anna didn't pay attention to quotas. She apportioned cases out based on criteria other than straight numbers. Your Ms. Grant has decided everyone ought to have a equal number of cases, and it doesn't matter if some involve a family of ten and others a single mom with one kid.''

"She's hardly *my* anything, Mitch. Maybe if she makes enough waves and ticks off enough people, Piggot will get rid of her.''

Mitch shook his shaggy head. ''Don't think so, Ethan. Rumors also say Nathaniel brought her in from out of town, selecting her over qualified in-house candidates.''

"I don't know if I'd repeat that rumor, Mitch. Regan Grant has impressive credentials. From a strictly technical point of view, I can't think of anyone in-house who's as qualified to replace Anna.'' He shook his head. ''Let's face it. *No one* can replace Anna. She poured her heart and soul into the job.''

''Anna was a gem.'' Mitch poked Ethan in the ribs before settling back to watch the house they were staking out. ''The guys at the station used to say it was too bad Anna M. was old enough to be your mom. Otherwise you'd have made the perfect couple.''

Ethan's ears burned. He'd been teased a lot about his open admiration for Anna Murphy. ''Tell you what, Valetti. If I ever find a woman my age who has half of Anna's intelligence and compassion, I'll snap her up in a flash.''

''I'd give a lot to see that, my man. In the almost seven years we've been partners, I don't think I've ever seen you with the same woman twice. At least not at any official functions.''

''If I did that,'' Ethan said dryly, ''my family would book the church and start planning wedding showers. Being a middle child, I saw how the Knight railroad worked. Anybody dated someone twice, and first thing you knew, Mom invited them to dinner. Or Grandpa took them to the club for a friendly round of golf. Or Dad just happened to run into them on the day of a family barbecue. A guy or gal doesn't marry *one* Knight, they marry a family. I plan to be damn sure I'm dating Ms. Right before I let the clan get their hooks in.''

''Too bad you're not getting any younger, big E. By the time you locate Ms. Right, you'll be bald, fifty, and flabby.''

Ethan sputtered that no man in his family went bald and he was far from flabby.

Mitch, who seemed to enjoy the heck out of needling

his friend, sobered soon enough. "Frankly I hoped Anna's replacement might be the woman for you. Too bad she turned out to be a butt-faced ogre."

Ethan lifted a brow. "Anybody who tagged Regan Grant with *that* description hasn't seen her."

"Really? Then she's a looker?"

Ethan recapped Ms. Grant's attributes to himself. Damn, he'd never hear the end of it if he let on to Mitch that he found Regan Grant attractive. He also had to admit she had the proper credentials. One degree more than Anna had, to be exact. Lifting a shoulder, Ethan casually let it drop. "She's okay," he said without inflection. "Isn't it time we gave this topic a break and worried about who's in the car that's pulling into our suspect's driveway?"

CHAPTER TWO

REGAN SAT IDLE at her desk for long minutes after the detective stormed out. She was shaken by the encounter with his dog and also by the harsh words she'd exchanged with the man. It wasn't like her to raise her voice to someone she'd just met. Especially someone she might have to work with again.

Her reaction was obviously related to the last ugly scene she'd had with her fiancé. She had taken a friend to help move her furniture and personal belongings from the apartment. They'd arrived midmorning on a weekday and discovered that he'd had the locks changed. When Regan phoned asking him to come let her in, Jack's language had become abusive. As well as calling her names, he'd said she could forget about taking even one thing from the place.

Regan regularly counseled women about their rights in just such instances. Yet she'd been unprepared for the way Jack's treatment had made her feel. He'd caused her knees to shake. Put her stomach in turmoil. And those physical feelings were secondary to her sense of being used. Until she realized she wasn't totally defenseless. She'd lived in the building for five years before Jack moved in, claiming he loved her. The hard reality had suddenly smacked her in the head. Jack had never loved her.

Once she'd accepted that, Regan hadn't argued. Instead, she'd hung up on Jack and gone straight to the building superintendent. Mr. Thornton said he'd always hoped she'd come to her senses and dump Jack. The old man hadn't thought twice about letting her into the apartment.

Although she'd been careful to take only what belonged to her, Jack had had her arrested at work for breaking and entering. It was a nasty scene. As a cop, he'd had the muscle, literally and figuratively. He didn't want an amicable settlement. He wanted to humiliate Regan for daring to cross him. Thanks to the pull he had in the courts, she'd lost everything except her jewelry and clothing.

The experience had left her bitter. For weeks she'd doubted her ability to help other women faced with similar situations. In the midst of her confusion, Nathaniel Piggot had phoned and offered her the supervisor's job in Desert City. A couple of years back they'd successfully collaborated on a state grant project. The faith he expressed in her was exactly the encouragement she'd needed. Piggot's career offer gave her a valid reason for leaving Phoenix and a job where she'd constantly be running into Jack and his buddies. In time she hoped to put the episode with Jack completely behind her. Except that she was afraid she'd let her anger at Jack spill over into her dealings with Detective Knight.

But perhaps her reaction was justified. While it was true that Ethan Knight looked nothing like Jack Diamond, except in the swagger shared by all police officers, he exhibited the same annoying "my way or the highway" attitude.

Grimacing, Regan admitted to having gone ballistic over the dog. She regretted that—although maybe she shouldn't. Knight had broken the rules. A lot of rules. And from the sound of it, he had no remorse.

Regan didn't for one minute believe he'd gone to all that trouble for those kids out of the goodness of his heart. It'd be news to her if policemen had hearts. Jack had stolen her furniture simply because he could. Because Regan couldn't produce proof that she'd bought the living-room and bedroom sets, or the various kitchen appliances she'd acquired over ten years. Who kept receipts for that long? But that was beside the point, she reminded herself firmly. Her fight with Jack shouldn't reflect on new relationships with police officers in an entirely different city.

All policemen weren't necessarily jerks just because Jack Diamond and his pals on the force came from one insufferably arrogant mold.

"Ms. Grant." The interruption to Regan's self-analysis followed a soft knock on her door. A cascade of long black hair appeared first in the narrow opening.

"What is it, Danielle?" Regan shook herself out of her stupor. She dropped her hands from the temples she'd been massaging and grabbed one of the files Detective Knight had tossed on her desk.

At her response, a young woman's head and shoulders emerged. Bright eyes peered furtively around for a moment before her red lips formed a disappointed pout. Regan could think of no other way to describe the look.

"Nicole told me Ethan Knight was in your office. I'd hoped to catch him before he left. M-Ms. Grant, is everything all right? You don't look well."

"It's nothing. I'm fine." Regan didn't realize she was crumpling Knight's carefully typed report in one fist. When Danielle Hargreaves's gaze drew Regan's attention to the fact, she quickly dropped the paper and smoothed it out.

"I'm sorry if you had personal business with Officer Knight, Danielle. As you can see, he's gone. And I really mustn't take time to chat."

"It's Detective Knight, Ms. Grant. And my business with him isn't personal. I need to give Ethan my sister-in-law's name and address. She's been approved to provide foster care for up to three kids. I'll have my fiancé, Brian, pass the word to Ethan. They work out of the same police unit." The dark head started to pull back and the door began to close.

"Danielle, wait!" Regan issued a rather sharp call to the newest caseworker in the department. She and Danielle had inadvertently gotten off to a bad start. Now it seemed the young woman blamed Regan because her predecessor had broken the hiring rules. The irregularity had come to light when Nathaniel collected all the employee records to discuss each one with Regan before she took over Anna Murphy's old position. In actuality, Regan had begged Nathaniel to give her time to evaluate Danielle's performance, rather than outright fire her. He'd refused.

Unfortunately there was no way to tell Dani that Regan planned to drag her heels about the firing until after Dani had completed her thesis. Regan could scarcely admit to a subordinate that she'd started her tenure by going head-to-head with their boss.

As the weeks went by and the rumors circulated about Regan's hard-line approach, she'd tried to ignore the talk.

Dani stepped nervously back inside the office. "Yes, Ms. Grant?"

"Please, when we're one on one, call me Regan."

She smiled, hoping to put the young caseworker at ease. Danielle's work was exemplary from what Regan had been able to judge by follow-up visits to Dani's clients. Regan was sure that once she clarified the rules regarding the chain of command in all foster placement cases, Danielle would understand.

Appearing extremely uncomfortable, Dani focused on her watch. "I have a client to visit at four, Ms. Grant. It's three-forty-five now."

"It's Regan, remember? And this won't take a minute." She motioned to the chair recently vacated by Ethan Knight. When Danielle remained standing, Regan cleared her throat. "Apparently Detective Knight had some type of arrangement with Mrs. Murphy to circumvent normal placement procedures. As of today, children in need of foster care will go through accepted channels. It's a universal method of placement used by Family Services in nearly every city in the U.S. Your sister-in-law's name will reach our intake office on a computer printout. She, in turn, receives a placement when her name rises to the top of the list."

"But...but..." Dani's brow furrowed.

Regan injected a little steel in her voice. "That allows our department to function as a well-organized team, Danielle. It gives the assigned caseworker time to examine a prospective home, as well as evaluate all children in need of placement. A good match ensures a positive experience for both foster child and foster family. Go on to your appointment," Regan said more gently, making a shooing motion with her hands. "If your sister-in-law is desperate for the monthly stipend allotted to foster families, she shouldn't have to wait long. Mr. Piggot sent me a memo yesterday indicating that demand for foster families outweighs applicants."

"Maddy doesn't care about the money!" Danielle blazed. "She signed up because she cares about kids—and...and as a favor to Ethan. Because he likes to know his abused kids will be going to loving homes. That's Ethan's whole intent, Miss Grant. He wants the kids to be more important than the dollars they generate for the foster families."

Regan's mouth fell agape. She quickly closed it, then again smoothed the pages of Ethan Knight's report. Pages fast representing a thorn in Regan's side. "Surely you understand that our department is a minor part of a massive state operation, which receives federal funding." Turning, she pulled two fat books from the floor-to-ceiling bookcase behind her desk. "Each and every office is governed by the same rules. Rules established by supervisors who have served countless hours in the placement and entitlement of families in need. Nowhere within these guidelines is there any rule remotely pertaining to what Detective Knight does or does not want."

Regan noticed that her voice had risen.

"Yes, ma'am. I understand what you're saying. Um...I really have to go to my appointment, Ms. Gr—Regan. I'm meeting a client at her job. She only has a twenty-minute break and I don't want her to lose her job on account of me."

"No, of course not. I'm glad we had this opportunity to talk, Dani. If other caseworkers have sidestepped rules to accommodate Detective Knight, please set them straight. Or better yet, ask them to pay me a visit. As I said in our first group meeting, I have an open-door policy. One that allows us to iron out differences before they become insurmountable."

Nodding, Dani backed out of the office, quietly closing the door behind her.

Regan stared at Dani's petite shadow on the frosted glass until it disappeared. She shuffled the Knight reports to the bottom of her stack of current cases, all the while thinking Anna Murphy must have been ill for some time before anyone had ever realized. Otherwise her department wouldn't have fallen into such disarray. Anna's name had been practically a byword in the hierarchy of the state Family Services system for as long as Regan could remember. That was a big part of why she'd accepted this assignment. Not that she was having second thoughts now. And yet, Regan did wonder how much had slipped by Anna M.

She tapped the eraser end of a pencil on the pile in which she'd placed the Knight reports. In an earlier examination of the department's active cases, Regan recalled seeing Ethan's name on countless records. Maybe she ought to pull them all and have a second look. Regan sighed. What she supposed she should do was pay a visit to every foster home where Knight had placed a child.

"Oh, brother," she muttered. But it was the only way she'd know for sure that the department was in good shape.

Picking up the phone, Regan called Records and asked to have all the currently active case reports transferred to diskettes. "I want to take them home to study on my laptop," she informed the clerk.

She sighed again. There were many evenings of work ahead.

ETHAN DRAGGED into his office sometime after midnight. He'd been down at the jail for two hours trying to sort out the legitimate arrests he and Mitch had made from the innocent kids accidentally caught in their raid on the drug dealers' house. The young kids who were buyers needed help. But no officer on the Desert City police force believed they'd get the right sort of help if they were tossed into juvie. Mitch's specialty was getting these kids into programs where they'd learn productive ways of spending their free time. Mitch was a whiz at wangling slots in already overloaded boys' and girls' clubs and sports centers. That was why Ethan let Mitch go to visit the parents, while he stayed to word their reports in such as way as to put the scum responsible for selling drugs to thirteen-year-olds behind bars for the maximum sentence. Or so he hoped...

Sinking into his swivel chair, he booted up his computer and went into e-mail to retrieve his messages. Using his free hand, he filled Taz's bowl with kibble. Ethan kept a sack in his desk drawer; it saved taking time to run by his house on days when one shift overran another.

Thirty-four messages. Ethan groaned.

"Damn, damn, dammit all," he swore roundly. The first two messages informed him that two of the scuzzballs whose paperwork he'd completed were already out on bail. The next thirty-two were from family and friends telling him Regan Grant had phoned making appointments to visit his network of foster homes.

"It shouldn't worry me, Taz," Ethan said, pausing to rub dog's neck. "All those folks are doing an A-1 job. Everyone Grant's called, the kids are settled in fine. Better than fine," he said with satisfaction.

Before Ethan finished his sentence, a dark shadow fell across his computer. He glanced up, giving Taz one last pat. "Hiya, Fitzgerald. Chief demoted you to graveyard? What did you do to piss him off?"

"Manny Garza's wife went into labor at noon today.

His partner and I agreed to split Manny's shift for the next few days.''

"That's great. Everything all right with Mary Garza? Isn't the baby early?'' Ethan asked when Brian Fitzgerald looked puzzled.

"Time flies when you're having fun, Detective,'' Brian said around a cockeyed grin. "It's been nine months since Manny strutted around the office bragging that he was going to be a first-time dad. He told us the minute the rabbit died.''

"What cave have you been living in, Fitzgerald? Rabbits no longer have to kick the bucket. Now they have this innocuous little strip of litmus paper that turns a different color if the lady's pregnant.''

"Have a lot of experience checking those strips, do you, Knight?''

"The sum total of my experience comes from having six sisters, Fitzgerald, five of whom married. Plus, one of my brothers has a wife. So get outta here. You must have reports to write or something.''

"Always. But I actually stopped in to pass on some information. Dani asked me to tell you that her brother's wife, Maddy Hargreaves, has been approved to take up to three foster kids.'' He dug in his shirt pocket, pulled out a pink message sheet and slid it across the desk to Ethan.

"Good for Maddy. She and Greg have that great old six-bedroom house down in the central area. Their Josh needs to be around other kids. Did Maddy tell Dani what ages she'd prefer?''

Brian shook his head. "Oh, wait. Dani said something about preschool or kindergartners. Her message was a little garbled, what with all the complaints about her ogre of a boss.''

"Regan Grant?" Ethan stopped folding the message and pinned Brian with a wary look.

"One and the same. I hear you've met Her Royal Battle-ax. I probably don't have to tell you that rumors say she's gunning for Desert City's favorite shining knight."

Ethan flushed. If he had to have a nickname, he preferred the Baby Cop. "Word travels," he murmured. "Guess Mitch shot off his mouth about me tangling with her, huh?"

"You duked it out with Grant?" Brian's eyes widened. "Wow. Is that why she climbed all over Dani about making sure Maddy's authorization for foster care goes through the proper channels?"

Ethan shook his head grimly. "Kick me for finding anything attractive about the new supervisor. I'll take someone with Anna's lived-in face and big heart over Regan Grant's angel looks anyday. She's got a rule book in place of her ticker."

"She pretty?"

"Who?" Ethan asked idly as he tucked the message into his jeans pocket.

Fitzgerald threw up his hands. "Battle-ax Grant. Who were we just discussing?"

"Huh. She's easy enough on the eyes." Ethan rolled his own upward, too clearly recalling the tumble of blond curls that—more than once—he'd pictured tickling his naked chest. Ethan had resented the fantasy, since the woman had torn a strip off him. And she'd given him no reason to think she wouldn't do it again if the opportunity presented itself.

"Hmm. From the way Dani talks about her, I figured Grant's got fangs, claws and one beady eye, all wrapped in a package of green scales."

"Hardly," Ethan snorted. "If you're just looking, she's a babe." His description of Regan Grant was punctuated by a huge yawn. "Babe or not," he muttered, pushing back a sleeve to check his watch, "I can't sit here all night discussing her. Tomorrow Taz and I are visiting the elementary schools. I've gotta be one of the good guys. Can't go in with bloodshot eyes."

"How many years have you been putting on a uniform and going into the schools? Don't you get tired of answering the same questions over and over?"

Ethan leaned back in his chair and laced his hands behind his neck. "I took over the Stranger Danger program when Granddad retired. Must be ten years ago. And no, I never get tired of it. Those little kids are cute as buttons and clever as the dickens."

Fitzgerald grunted. "So where do we go wrong? How come I'm hauling so many of their smart-asses in for B & E's, carrying concealed and worse?"

Snapping forward in his chair, Ethan walked his computer through shutdown. Then he stood and shrugged into his leather jacket. After waking the slumbering Taz, he accompanied Brian to the door. "Somewhere between cute and clever and those smoking guns lurks a string of bad role models. How many kids see Dad drunk and disorderly or beating up on Mom? Sometimes both parents work sixty hours a week. Home gets lonely, so they find friends on the street. Sometimes it starts with empty kitchens and emptier bellies. The first thing they swipe is a piece of fruit or a can of soup. Kids don't go bad by themselves, Brian. They have help."

The younger policeman sighed. "Now you sound like Dani. She's a big one for pointing out why kids go bad. Maybe I need to switch jobs. I see so much juvenile crime, I'm not sure I want to bring a kid into this world.

You've got twice the years on me in law enforcement, Ethan. Is that why you haven't gotten married and had kids? 'Cause you deal with so many screwed-up families?''

Ethan slowed his walk. "My own family isn't screwed up. Like I said, five of my six sisters are married and so's my brother Matt. All happily. So, no, I'm not afraid of having kids. I think I'd be a good dad."

"Then why are you still single?"

"Good question. If you ask my mom, she'll say it's because I'm too busy trying to save the world." A grin altered Ethan's tired features.

"Yeah. Relationships take a lot of time and energy," Brian agreed. "Sometimes I go two weeks without seeing Dani. Both of us have hectic jobs and erratic hours. I've started to wonder if we're crazy to get married."

Ethan clapped a hand on the younger man's back. "The wedding is what—three months away? You probably have prewedding jitters. Right now Danielle's working hard to get her master's. Once she's finished with that, you'll have more time together."

"Thanks for the encouragement, Ethan." Brian hung back and let Ethan proceed alone through the busy central office.

Ethan couldn't say why, but after he'd climbed into his SUV and headed home, he felt unsettled and vaguely jealous of Brian's impending marriage. Headed home to a large empty house. A house once filled with the laughter of a boisterous family. A house always in need of cleaning because Ethan rarely spent enough daylight hours there to see how the dust had gathered.

"Why *aren't* I married, Taz?" Ethan often had conversations with his dog. He could count on Taz to be a

I think Taz makes her nervous. Could you shut him in the backyard?''

A sullen frown marred Jeremy's sweat-sheened brown forehead. ''What's she want here? Let's sic Taz on her so she'll go back where she belongs.''

''Easy, kid. It's a routine visit. Remember, Anna died before she could petition the court to let you change your name to Knight—after your birth mom nixed the folk's adoption request. Maybe Ms. Grant will carry on where Anna left off.''

Jeremy had a wonderfully sunny smile when he turned up the wattage. It broke free now as he hurried to take Taz as Ethan requested.

Regan had leaned over the passenger seat and rolled the window down an inch. ''I don't know why you're here, Detective Knight, but please restrain your dog. I have a four-o'clock appointment at this home, and I'm already late.'' She fumbled in her briefcase and pulled out a card. ''My appointment is with Elaine Knight. Oh.'' She leveled her gaze on Ethan. ''Is Elaine your wife?''

Ethan laughed wickedly while blotting sweat from his brow. ''Elaine is my mother. I'm not married,'' he said, slanting her a glance to see if the news of his single status affected her. If it did, she covered well. He was almost disappointed. ''Have you always been so skittish around dogs?'' he asked bluntly.

''Dog is man's best friend. Not woman's.'' Regan peered up the driveway and in both directions along the street. ''Is he gone or merely lying in wait somewhere?''

Swiveling, Ethan saw Jeremy close the side gate and head toward them again. ''Taz is confined, Ms. Grant.'' Jogging across the driveway, Ethan assisted Regan from her car. ''I'm no psychologist,'' he murmured, feeling her arm tremble. "But you seem beyond skittish. More like phobic, I'd say." He had a niggling urge to bedevil her. Bending close to her ear, he whispered, "Well, Ms. Grant, oh, great master of sociology and psychology, have you ever sought counseling for your problem?"

She jerked from his hold so fast Ethan didn't know exactly what he'd done wrong. But he felt bad for razzing her.

"If you're hoping to divert my attention and keep me from examining this foster placement, I assure you it won't work. I found Jeremy Smith's case history most interesting." Squaring her shoulders, she started up the walkway.

Curious, Ethan followed. "Interesting how?" he challenged. "Because of the way he's done a one hundred percent turnaround in the time he's lived with my parents?"

Her hand raised to knock on the door, Regan glanced back, giving Ethan a cool look. "Interesting in that I watched students in this neighborhood get off the school bus a while ago. It made me wonder why you would place an African-American child in an all-white neighborhood."

Ethan, who'd just leaned forward for a better whiff of Regan Grant's spicy exotic perfume, stopped dead. "What exactly are you trying to say? It doesn't take an Einstein to note the marked decrease in Jeremy's encounters with the law since he came here." He glowered at Regan, then spun to see that Jeremy hadn't heard her statement. Fortunately the kid had found another basketball and was practicing free throws.

"You mean it never occurred to you that the boy might be intimidated at being ripped from his ethnic roots?"

Ethan's arm tightened on the ball he still held. Of all the things she might have taken him to task for—like the flouting of procedures or the nepotism angle—the battle she actually chose floored Ethan. Almost as suddenly as he'd tensed, he felt an urge to laugh. He couldn't wait to see how she'd react when Jeremy set her straight.

"Well, nothing to say for yourself, I see." Regan again raised a fist to knock. "Those are the types of considerations trained social workers know to look for when deciding on placement. We take the whole child into account."

Ethan blocked her knock by reaching over her shoulder to shove open the unlocked door. "Mom," he yelled. "I'm showing Ms. Grant into the living room. She's here for your Family Assistance appointment."

"I like the foster families I work with to call me Regan," she said while attempting to shut Ethan outside. "I'll wait right here in the entry until Elaine comes," she told him.

Her obvious efforts to get rid of him didn't deter Ethan. "In this house, Family Assistance appointments involve everyone, Regan. I see my dad has driven in. He'll bring Jeremy." Ethan's smile was charming if not slightly provocative. "I'm so glad you want to use first names. Calling you Ms. Grant sounds so stuffy. And now you'll call me Ethan, of course." Taking her arm, he propelled her into a homey room that held two leather couches, each with a matching chair. A large beehive fireplace took up all of one corner next to an arched north-facing window, which let in the afternoon sunlight. Family pictures covered the largest wall and spilled over onto every available surface in the room. School photos, mixed with graduations, weddings and christenings. At least four school pictures of Jeremy hung among the others.

Regan, who'd grown up in a divorced family, estranged from her mother all these years, found the Knights' gallery fascinating. Her dad, who'd had custody of her, was a busy executive. Regan had spent her formative years in boarding schools. Summers she lived with Great-aunt Roberta, a terribly allergic soul who kept a pristine dust-free house. Possibly why Regan herself maintained an orderly apartment.

Elaine Knight and her husband, Joseph, walked in together. Short and plump, yet still youthful-looking at fifty-eight and after bearing nine children, Elaine immediately noticed Regan's interest in the photographs. She passed the coffeepot and plate of cookies she was carrying to her husband, who hadn't changed out of his county sheriff's uniform. Hooking an arm through Regan's, Ethan's mother proudly walked her through a family rundown.

"Hey, cool, Mom. You made my favorite cookies," Jeremy announced, lumbering across the living room in his untied size-thirteen sneakers.

Elaine glanced over her shoulder and smiled. "There's milk and juice in the fridge, Jeremy. I also left an entire plateful of cookies on the kitchen counter just for you." Turning back to Regan, she said, "Otherwise the rest of us wouldn't get any. My three older boys could take or leave raisin-filled cookies. Jeremy would have me make them three times a week."

Turning from the wall of photos, Regan set her briefcase on the coffee table. "I only see three boys in your family portrait, Elaine. Have you lost a son?" she asked softly, her eyes filled with sympathy.

Elaine's brow crinkled in consternation. "Why, no.

We've been exceptionally blessed in that way.'' Her husband, too, appeared puzzled.

Ethan, busily pouring coffee into the mugs his dad had set on the table, smiled as he handed Regan her cup. ''I think Mom meant three boys older than Jeremy.''

Lips pursed, Regan accepted the cup and sat. ''Jeremy isn't your son.''

Joseph Knight, a big man who wore his uniform well, ran a hand through his full head of still-black hair. ''He's been our son for the last five years. And we're as proud of him as we are of Matthew, Jacob and Ethan,'' he said, reaching out a hand to catch Jeremy's wrist. The gangly boy tumbled down on the couch beside him.

''The folks wanted to adopt Jeremy,'' Ethan said, passing Regan the plate of golden-brown cookies.

''Really? I didn't see mention of that in the file.'' She bit into the cookie as she removed a folder from her briefcase and flipped through it.

Ethan studied Jeremy a moment. The boy had begun to crack his knuckles. ''Maybe Jeremy ought to supply the particulars.''

''My mom…my real mom, she threw a royal fit. She don't want me, but she don't want nobody…uh… anybody else to adopt me. Mom and Dad Knight made me understand how she might not want to turn loose of me. And Anna…uh…Mrs. Murphy talked to her about me legally changing my last name to Knight. As kind of a compromise, she said. Anna was gonna file the papers, but then she died.''

''You want to change your name?'' Regan scribbled on the file. ''I take it you'd like to live here permanently despite the racial incompatibility in the neighborhood?''

''What racial incompatibility?'' Elaine, Joseph and Jeremy said simultaneously.

They looked so genuinely stupefied by her question that Regan, who choked on her cookie, turned to Ethan for clarification. He, in turn, deferred to Jeremy.

"But...but all my friends are welcome here," Jeremy blustered. "Besides, Tony Garcia lives three houses away. And Bill Washington's on the next block."

Joseph Knight leaned thick wrists on his knees. "Either Ethan or I take Jeremy to the Boys' Club once a week to mingle and play basketball. The school he attends is nicely integrated. And our daughter Erica has an adopted Vietnamese daughter."

Regan held up a staying palm. Yet it was to Ethan that she looked when she stammered out an apology. "I'm sorry. But...but...such issues matter in some placements. Jeremy is obviously happy here and quite well-adjusted." She closed the file, tucked it into her briefcase and snapped the locks. Rising, she thrust a hand toward Joe and then Elaine. "Those cookies were the best I've ever tasted. I don't blame Jeremy for wanting them three times a week." Regan extracted a business card from her purse and passed it to Elaine. "If you share recipes, I'd love a copy."

Ethan's mother beamed and so did he. His dark eyes roamed over Regan's face and settled on her lips, where a cookie crumb still clung. He tucked the fingers of both hands into his pants pockets to keep from dusting off the crumbs. "Before I leave today," he blurted, "I'll write the recipe out. I'll drop it by your office tomorrow."

Surprised and flustered by his generosity, Regan stammered her thanks. Then she remembered he didn't travel anywhere without that huge dog. "Uh, don't put yourself out," she said in a changed voice. "I prefer my staff not deal with personal business on company time. I need to set a good example. Jeremy," she said abruptly, careful not to glance toward Ethan. "I'm also giving you one of my cards. I'll follow up on your name-change request. But should you ever need me for any reason, I want you to feel free to call. My home number is the second one."

Almost before Ethan got over the sting of her obvious rebuke, she'd gone. All that lingered in the room where he stood alone, the others having trailed her to the door, was a cloud of her perfume. He sniffed the air, telling himself he didn't give a damn what made Regan Grant run hot and cold. Only, the heightened beat of his pulse told a different story.

"Too bad she doesn't conduct personal business at the office," Ethan muttered under his breath as he made his way to the kitchen, determined to copy his mom's raisin-filled cookie recipe. He found a pencil, then dug the recipe out of a gaily flowered box and sat on one of the counter stools. As he painstakingly listed ingredients, Ethan groaned. He could well imagine what rumors would fly if the guys at the station ever got wind of this. A detective trading recipes. He'd never hear the end of it.

CHAPTER THREE

OFFICE MACHINES hummed and staff chattered around Regan as she unloaded file folders from her briefcase and stacked them on the counter.

"Are you completely finished with these, Ms. Grant?" a young clerk asked. "I can tag them for holding if you think you'll be using them again."

"I've dictated follow-up reports on this batch. I can't see any reason to keep them out. Oh, wait." Regan thumbed through the stack and removed the file on Jeremy Smith. "The foster family for this young man said Anna planned to petition the court for a change of Jeremy's last name. Is there a second file or some other record of how far along his request has gone?"

"I'll check. I shouldn't be long." The clerk—Abby, according to her name tag—took the file and disappeared into the record room.

A caseworker who'd been talking with two colleagues broke away from the group and approached Regan. "Last night I received calls from two of our foster parents. Both felt unprepared for your impromptu visits yesterday."

Regan tapped her fingers on the counter. "I gave everyone the standard two-hour notice. Some families actually had more than two hours, because I phoned everyone before I left the office. Nothing was out of order. Why would they feel a need to complain, I wonder?''

Terry Mickelson leaned on the counter and lowered her voice. "I didn't mean to imply they'd complained. More like they...sounded curious. Perhaps you weren't aware that Jennifer Layton and Erica Barnard aren't run-of-the-mill foster moms.''

"No?" Regan began to feel she'd stepped on a treadmill somewhere that had no off switch. "What are they, then?''

"They only accept kids through a temporary urgent-care safe-home section of the program instituted by Anna and Ethan, you know." She smiled and gave a dainty shrug.

Regan crossed her arms. "I'm afraid I don't know. Enlighten me, please. By Anna and Ethan, I assume you mean my predecessor and Detective Knight of the Desert City PD.''

"Uh...yes." Terry glanced worriedly across the room at her friends who'd stopped talking to listen. The office fell silent enough to hear the tick of the wall clock. "Our records probably don't indicate that Jennifer and Erica are Ethan's sisters. Jen is a commercial artist who works out of her home. As does Erica. Work from home, I mean. She's a CAD engineer. Computer aided design," Terry supplied when Regan lifted one eyebrow.

"Detective Knight's sisters? I don't believe that came up in our conversations. We briefly discussed their occupations. Relative to how they combine full-time careers with providing state-supported child care. Like I said, they passed admirably." Regan allowed a smile for the first time. "In fact, I wish there was a way to videotape one of their average days to use as a training film for prospective foster parents. It's a shame they only provide temporary urgent care for us.''

Terry relaxed a body grown tense. ''Erica and Jenny are great, aren't they? Mostly I think their concerns stemmed from the fact that you seemed to single out their family for review. Elaine Knight is their mother. Lexie Knight's a sister-in-law, and Jessica Talbot is a first cousin. I believe that today you're scheduled to see Melissa Fogerty and Elizabeth St. George, two more of Ethan's sisters.''

''As they all seem to be related, I suppose it does appear I've chosen to pick on the Knights.'' Regan raised her voice enough so that the staff straining to hear could do so without effort. ''I'm planning to review all families who came into our program unconventionally. The people you named and some whose files I still have in my office skipped the application process—an aberration we'll avoid in the future. I'm quite sure our caseworkers know proper procedure, but it never hurts to have refreshers. To that end, I'll be addressing the topic on Monday at our regular meeting, and the people under review may be asked to make proper application.''

There was a collective gasp from Terry's co-workers. She was first to express her shock in words. ''It would be a horrible mistake to trash Ethan's efforts to save Desert City's abused kids.''

''Is that so?'' Regan's light eyes darkened. ''Pardon me, but I labor under the impression that saving this city's abused kids is *our* responsibility.'' Stretching across the counter, Regan tapped a fingernail on the title stamped above Terry Mickelson's name badge. ''Child Help Center. That's us, correct?''

A once-retired caseworker, Odella Price, materialized from the records room along with Abby, the clerk who'd gone to help Regan. Odella had left the department six years previously but had returned part-time at Anna Murphy's request. For more than a year now, Odella's part-time load had totaled fifty hours a week. There were employees like Terry Mickelson and others who thought Odella should have been given Anna's job, even though she had no administrative experience. A fair share of the staff let it be known in unsubtle ways.

Odella Price had grown up the daughter of parents who ministered to the poor. She was intelligent and well-educated. Empathy oozed from her pores. Around the office, she assumed a role of unofficial negotiator.

A tall woman, Odella stood five foot ten inches without shoes. She carried no spare ounce of flesh beneath her smooth mocha-colored skin. Outside of tiny laugh wrinkles fanning from rich brown eyes, few who met her believed she was sixty years old, as she claimed to be.

Moving fluidly, she glided between Regan and Terry. A gregarious smile displayed even white teeth, only close friends knew they'd been crooked until Odella turned twenty-four, when she got her MSSW and subsequently her first paycheck in a field she loved. Now she spoke through that dazzling smile. ''Abby tells me you inquired about the status of Jeremy Smith's request to change his last name, Regan.'' Odella was probably the only staff member, other than Piggott, who dared call Regan by her first name. Nathaniel liberally used given names, but he allowed only a chosen few to call him anything besides, Director or sir. Since Odella's return to the workforce, she'd placed herself on Piggot's short list. More to annoy the man than to align herself with him.

Switching her focus from Terry Mickelson to Odella,

Regan concurred with a slight nod. "I was told Jeremy desired adoption, but his birth mother refused. They believe she agreed that he could legally take the Knight name."

"That was six months ago. Shontelle's status changed just this week. I pulled off a fax yesterday informing us that she's being held in a Utah prison pending murder charges. She's alleged to have knifed her current boyfriend."

"Excuse me? Who knifed whom?"

"Shontelle Waters. Jeremy's birth mom. In the time he's lived with the Knights, she's been married and divorced twice. At last report, she'd left the state with a new man—the one she reportedly murdered. I've considered contacting her court-appointed attorneys in Utah. It occurred to me they could attach a clause in a plea bargain that'll free Jeremy up for adoption."

Regan stared into the guileless brown eyes, feeling a muscle jump in her jaw. She'd heard a rumor to the effect that Odella's mission in life was to see all children in the foster-care program adopted into good homes. An impossibility, of course, for any number of reasons. But a worthy endeavor. One to which Regan subscribed— the operative word being *good*. She might add *loving* and *nurturing* to that. "Hmm, Nathaniel mentioned how successful you've been, Odella, in acquiring adoption permission for formerly unadoptable foster kids. Do you have a minute to step into my office to discuss that in general and, more specifically, Jeremy's case?"

"I'd love to." The older woman gave Regan time to collect her briefcase, and the two strolled out leaving the other caseworkers grumbling over Regan's proposed lecture on Monday.

Once they'd entered Regan's office, Odella asked her

a personal question—something no staff member had done since Regan assumed her post. "I used to see you jogging in Riker Park each morning. Have you stopped or are you going there earlier? I hope you're not going before daylight. Riker isn't the safest park in the city."

Regan bit her lower lip. "I've switched to the track at the high school. It's closer to my apartment. Plus, there are fewer people to contend with. I'm sorry, I don't recall seeing you in the park." Regan felt bad about not recognizing Odella, although she rarely noticed people when jogging, unless they had dogs. It seemed the majority of joggers in Riker Park did have them. Big ones. Now that Odella mentioned it, her decision to change locations probably had to do with the safety issue.

Odella laughed heartily. "The morning-me in no way resembles the workplace-me. When I'm running, I wear baggy sweats and have my hair tucked under one of my husband's old army caps. Add to that a set of earphones and dark glasses the size of saucers. You, on the other hand, could pass for Barbie's sister in your matched pink baseball cap, spandex bike shorts and T-shirt."

Regan flushed at the apt description.

"That was meant as a compliment, Regan," Odella said as they each claimed a chair and sat. "You looked fashionable, and I envied you. I'm such a mess in the mornings. Oh, and you have a great jogging pace. You don't run like I'm almost sure Barbie—or any member of her family—would run."

That garnered a laugh from Regan. "My former fiancé ran five miles every morning before he went to the gym. He couldn't stand the thought of me sleeping in while he went out to sweat. I learned to keep up. It was either that or forever after listen to how weak women are."

"Nice guy. Is that why he's your *former* fiancé?"

Realizing she'd let something private slip, Regan dropped her affable manner. "I believe we came here to discuss Jeremy Smith's situation and that of other children stalled in the foster-care system."

The glimmer of interest aimed at Regan stayed in Odella's warm brown eyes for another moment. "Before we get down to business, let me extend an invitation to meet me anytime to jog, hike or bike. My kids are grown. They're all too busy with their own lives to join me anymore. Roger, my husband, said he had to punish his body every day of the twenty-five years he served Uncle Sam. Now that he's retired, he prefers getting his exercise pruning our cactus. I guess you know how slowly cacti grow."

"I don't enjoy hiking alone," Regan murmured. "In Phoenix I had friends who regularly hiked Squaw Peak. Or sometimes we'd drive to Prescott on the weekend to climb Thumb Butte. I haven't inquired about trails here."

"There are some nice ones in the Catalina Foothills. Mount Lemmon offers more strenuous routes." Odella pulled a business card out of her suit pocket and shoved it across Regan's desk. "I won't bug you. But here's my home phone number if you're ever in the mood. And, Regan, for the record, I leave work at the office."

Regan turned the business card over in her fingers several times before relaxing enough to tuck it into her pocket. "I've missed hiking. The weather lately has been perfect for it. There's something about mountain air—it refreshes the mind and rejuvenates the soul. We'll have to set something up for a weekend soon. I've been spending far too much time inside since I moved to Desert City."

"Good." Odella leaned forward. "Now, about Jeremy's current status—'' She was interrupted by a heavy footfall outside the door, followed by feminine giggles and deeper male laughter.

"Let me shut my door so we'll have more privacy, Odella." Regan rose and circled her desk. She'd gripped the knob, starting to pull the door inward when pointed black ears, a dark muzzle and lolling pink tongue appeared in front of her. Regan felt the floor shift and spin. Her legs refused to carry her backward as her mind screamed at her to do it and do it quickly.

Odella, who'd rotated in her chair, clucked happily. "Well, if it isn't the Tasmanian Devil himself." Climbing to her feet, she hastened across the room to rub the dog's head and pat his wriggling hindquarters. "Is that your handsome master causing a ruckus in the hall? Where Taz is, Ethan's not far behind," she said, aiming a broad smile at Regan. Her eyes encountered a blank stare and a body so stiff it could have been carved from marble.

"Regan?" The question fell on deaf ears.

Ethan had paused across the hall at the open lounge door to chat with Nicky Mason, who was on her way out with a full cup of coffee. He spun when he heard his name. Realizing Regan's door stood open, he excused himself from Nicole and called Taz sharply to heel.

The dog appeared on cue and sat. But rather than a furious Regan Grant flying out of the supervisory office, Odella Price emerged wearing a panicked expression. Ethan knew what had caused the look, and he suffered a stab of guilt. He'd intended to leave Taz in the SUV. He'd forgotten and had let the dog follow him inside the building out of habit.

"Nicky, could you keep Taz at the reception desk

while I complete my business with Regan? I won't be long.'' In truth, Ethan couldn't remember why he'd come. He'd been visiting schools today…. Oh, yes, the recipe she wanted. Yet he certainly hadn't planned to make a special trip to CHC for that. He could, he supposed, blame it on a slow morning. Mitch had an early-morning court appointment to testify in the case of a local car salesman who'd been jailed for being drunk and disorderly. The guy had smacked his girlfriend around a bar parking lot. It was the joker's third arrest in six months for the same thing. Different girlfriend, same charge. Mitch hoped to accomplish more than put the jerk on probation this time.

"Sure, Ethan. I love Taz. Hey—I heard you and Taz are participating in another endurance test.'' Her red-slicked mouth formed a pretty pout. "If it's this weekend, I'm free to be your cheering section.''

"Uh…it's not that soon.'' Ethan stumbled over his tongue. By now he'd reached the doorway where Odella stood. Behind her, Ethan saw the white-faced woman he'd considered inviting to go with him to Taz's Schutzhund. Ever since Regan had refused to get out of her car until he'd restrained Taz, Ethan entertained a crazy notion that watching the dogs work might shake Regan Grant out of her nutty fear.

Observing her statuelike pose and her sightless eyes, Ethan quickly dismissed his plan. Nutty her fear might be to someone like him, but Regan's terror was certainly real to her.

Ethan moved in close to her rigid body. Not positive she'd heard Taz's receding pad-pad as the dog followed Nicole around the corner, Ethan felt a need to reassure Regan. "It's okay. He's gone. The dog left.'' Ethan spoke softly and touched her chin, bringing the glassy blue eyes level with his own.

Regan identified Ethan Knight through a haze of fear. Her right hand curved tightly around her neck, hiding the thin scar she knew tended to stand out more when color flooded her face. She knew because Jack said people wouldn't notice her disfigurement if she didn't draw attention to it. It wasn't until after their split that Regan realized Jack Diamond surrounded himself with perfection. She did owe him something. If not for his constant badgering, she'd never have had the last plastic surgery. Thanks to new laser techniques, what had once been ugly red welts were now faint white lines. But not even lasers were effective against unseen damage.

Her feelings surrounding the long-ago incident left her weak and vulnerable in areas she didn't wish exposed to co-workers. Or to the likes of Ethan Knight. Wearing his uniform today, he looked especially imposing and very male. Too male.

Collecting her wits, Regan released her grip on the doorknob. She stepped back in an attempt to gather her tattered nerves. "Who's gone?" she queried coolly. "Odella and I were trying to have a private conversation. Your dilly-dallying in the hall with Nicole disturbed us. If you'll excuse us, we'd like to get on with our business." Edging him into the hall, Regan began closing Ethan out.

He and Odella exchanged questioning glances. "I, uh, thought you might be concerned about seeing Taz close-up again."

"I don't like to be sniffed and licked, that's all."

Ethan donned a reckless seductive grin. Ignoring Odella, who watched his antics with interest, Ethan propped a broad shoulder against the door casing, crowding Regan in a way that was masculine and intimate. "Now if that was a true statement," he said pleasantly, letting a lethally hot gaze follow the tip of his forefinger as he dusted the top three pearl buttons of Regan's white blouse, "you wouldn't buy perfume designed to turn a man's insides out. Or man-tailored blouses that leave a guy itching to know what's underneath."

Despite the tight rein Regan had clamped on her nerves, she wasn't able to prevent a surge of heat from racing to her stomach. For all that she didn't miss about her former fiancé, she'd enjoyed the sex. Or she had until the extent of Jack's infidelities came to light, forcing her to undertake the humiliating experience of explaining to her doctor why she needed HIV testing. If seeing her name on the vials of blood wasn't sobering enough, the weeks of waiting for the tests to come back clear should have made her swear off men. Especially men whose egos seemed to need proof that they could conquer every woman they met. And policemen headed the list. Hadn't Ethan Knight just been in the hall putting moves on Nicole Mason?

Commanding her own racing blood by issuing a dismissive gesture, Regan marched to her desk and sat in her swivel chair. "It may come as a shock to you, Detective, but not all women buy perfume and clothing to tempt men. I buy what pleases me. If you can check your juvenile hormones at the door, you might find what Odella and I were discussing to be of interest."

"Yes, ma'am. But don't forget that I grew up in a household of six women. Seven, counting my mom. I'd say I have a fair insight into what motivates a woman's purchases." Finding Regan's prim speech amusing,

Ethan winked at Odella as he shut the door behind them and pulled out her chair.

"Six sisters?" Regan wore a surprised, almost wistful expression.

"Yep. And two brothers." Ethan dragged his own chair closer to Regan, spun it around and straddled it. "Never a dull moment in the Knight household. I miss it sometimes," he said reflectively. "All except the part about taking a number to get your turn in the bathroom."

Odella chuckled. "That also happens when you only have four kids. And whoever said boys take less time primping for dates than girls was dead wrong. When my oldest boy hit puberty and started taking forty-minute showers every morning, Roger called a builder and added a master bath off our bedroom. Smartest thing the man ever did, outside of marrying me."

Regan smiled, finding pleasure in listening to them talk about their families—until suddenly Ethan pinned her with a searching look. "Feel free to jump in here and complain about your siblings, Regan."

Wiping the smile from her lips, Regan fiddled with the ruby ring her father had sent her the Christmas she turned eighteen—one of the many holidays she'd spent alone at boarding school. It wasn't that he didn't love her, but after the split with her mother, he needed to keep busy in order to forget the divorce. After five years of burying himself in the consulting firm he owned, Gerald Grant found a new love. Dee Dee was closer to Regan's age than Gerald's. At the beginning, she didn't want any reminder of her older husband's first marriage. Once they had Blair, Dee Dee started inviting Regan home to baby-sit.

"Well, are you an only child or what?" Ethan prodded.

"I have a stepsister. She just turned sixteen. I'd left home long before she began dating or primping in the bathroom. Anyway, the house my dad bought when he and Dee Dee got married has five bathrooms."

"Five," Odella breathed in awe, at the same time as Ethan exclaimed, "My house is big and I only have two bathrooms. You must have grown up in a damned hotel, Grant."

Regan flushed. "I didn't grow up there. Anyway, it isn't a house that's important, but the people living in it." Nevertheless she made a mental note to phone Blair after work—just to see how she was getting along. Straightening, Regan swung her gaze from Ethan's frankly curious look to Odella. "Inform Detective Knight of what you told me about Jeremy Smith's mom."

"It's Ethan," he reminded her. Then, turning to face Odella, he frowned. "Don't tell me Shontelle's back in town. Jeremy's only started to relax in the last few months—since she quit showing up at his school, high, soused or hitting him up for money."

Odella explained about the fax the department had received. She asked what Ethan thought their chances were of freeing Jeremy up for adoption in a plea bargain.

"The folks are still eager to adopt Jeremy. But you know my dad had a mild heart attack five or six months ago. He's only just gone back to work full-time, so I'd hate to cause him stress if the adoption didn't pan out— again"

"I'd heard," Odella murmured sympathetically. "Roger and I were so surprised. We thought Joe was about as fit as any man we've met."

Regan flipped open Jeremy's file. "There's no notation here about Jeremy's foster dad suffering a heart ailment.''

"Is that something you usually log in a foster kid's record?"

"Yes. Especially something that major. An effective caseworker is on top of any situation that may force a change in a client's living conditions.''

"Change, how?" Ethan stretched out one leg and began to drum his fingers on his knee. "Even if, God forbid, my father had died, Jeremy would still have a roof over his head, food in his belly and a loving mother to listen to his woes.''

Regan reacted to the agitation she heard in his voice. "You can't guarantee that. If your mother became suddenly widowed, or if your dad had a series of heart attacks leaving him in need of nursing care and unable to work, Elaine might not have time for Jeremy.''

"Bullshit." Ethan scooted to the edge of his chair and leaned belligerently forward, bracing one hand on a tense thigh. "You have some funny ideas about a person's commitment to family. If something had happened to either Mom or Dad while any of us nine kids still lived at home, do you think the surviving parent would have thrown us out?''

"That's hardly the point. Jeremy isn't of their blood.''

"Gosh, you'd better tell them that. I don't think they've noticed. He's been there five years, after all.''

"You may find this something to joke about, Detective. I don't. Odella, please hold off talking to the attorneys about the possibility of Jeremy's adoption until after I've had a chance to run this by Nathaniel. Serious illness of a foster parent throws a different slant on this case. I'll ask you to keep news of the fax to yourself for the time being, Detective Knight. I'd hate to needlessly raise Jeremy's hopes.''

"Ethan. Call me Ethan.'' He uncurled his long frame from the chair. His badge caught a shaft of sunlight streaming in the window, causing Regan to wince. "I'd cringe too,'' Ethan snapped, "at the prospect of sitting down across from Piggot while he rides the fence on an issue that means everything to a kid. You disappoint me, Regan. I'd pegged you for a woman like Anna. One with the confidence to make her own decisions and the guts to advocate for kids who have damned few champions.''

"With this position come certain difficult responsibilities,'' Regan pointed out. "There are proper channels to navigate. Established rules to follow.''

Ethan sent her a pitying look from the door where he stood, tugging on the hat he'd removed on entering her office.

He looked imposing in his khaki uniform. Regan glanced away to avoid the censure she knew lurked in his expressive eyes. Why was she always trying to please men who didn't think she quite measured up to their expectations? Among them, her father, Jack Diamond and now Ethan Knight. But that was silly! She barely knew Ethan Knight. What did it matter whether he approved of anything she chose to do?

Odella seemed torn between staying to talk further with Regan and walking out with Ethan. In the end she got to her feet and trailed after him. "I'll touch base with you tomorrow, Regan,'' she said. "Need I remind you that timing is critical here? If Shontelle's attorney is going to offer a plea bargain in hopes of getting her sentence reduced, he'll do it soon after the arraignment. That's Monday, according to the fax.''

"Save your breath, Odella,'' Ethan advised loudly

enough for Regan to hear. "Crossing all the *t*'s and dotting every *i* takes time. If you miss the boat while Regan's dithering, no one'll fault you. I mean, you were just *following the rules*." He shut the door with such force the glass panel shuddered.

So did Regan. Damn, but that man rubbed her wrong. He had some nerve implying that taking the proper steps meant Jeremy might lose out on his chance to be adopted by the Knights. Who would suffer the repercussions if she circumvented the red tape, only to have Joe Knight keel over from a bad heart? Ethan couldn't guarantee that his mother wouldn't see it as an opportunity to break free of domestic obligations. Think of the damage to Jeremy then. And it *could* happen. Ethan might believe that because Elaine was a devoted mother, that she would never put her freedom first. Regan knew better. Victoria, her own mother, had done exactly that.

Though more men than women opted out of parenting and simply walked away, Regan had handled caseloads that dealt with both. When it came to ensuring that kids didn't get the raw end of the deal, no set of rules was too involved or too tedious, in her estimation. That cop could sneer all he liked; Regan had unwritten promises to uphold. Promises she'd made long ago on behalf of kids who had no other advocate.

ETHAN HAD BEEN so irritated with Regan Grant when he left her office, he'd completely forgotten the reason he'd dropped by in the first place. He didn't recall until he'd put Taz in his patrol car and driven off. As he braked for the first stoplight, the crinkle of the recipe card in his pocket reminded him he hadn't delivered it.

He'd parted from Odella in the hallway. He'd been so hot under the collar because of Regan that he'd flirted shamelessly with Nicole when he stopped to collect Taz at the reception desk. Though he found her immature, he'd actually let her wiggle out of him the date of the next Schutzhund competition. Ethan's initial plan had been to invite Regan Grant to attend. *Well, forget that!*

It was beyond Ethan how a woman he barely knew could alternately stir his pulse and push so many of his buttons. Before they parted, Odella had casually mentioned that Regan jogged every morning at 6 a.m. She even dropped the name of the high school where Regan used the track. Perhaps he ought to try to connect with her on some level other than work. It was obvious they were miles apart on that.

Jogging was good.

Healthy. Fresh air worked up a sweat and an appetite—for a lot of things. Ethan abandoned himself to a vision of what it would be like to take the cool CHC supervisor back to his house after a sweaty run, where they'd add to the sheen of sweat by tumbling across the sheets. He practically drooled on the steering wheel picturing the steam they could create if the lady wrapped her long legs around his naked hips. He sizzled thinking about it.

Taz barked in his ear, and Ethan realized he'd been sitting at a light well after it had turned green. People around him, heeding his marked car, hesitated nervously, as if expecting some calamity to unfold in the vicinity. Gritting his teeth, he looked neither right nor left, gunned the engine and took off.

"Sheesh, Taz, I'm some kind of cop. Here I am daydreaming about Regan Grant like some high-schooler." He had been so busy categorizing the lady's attributes, he'd have missed a bank robbery if it'd been going down on that very corner.

The dog placed a paw on Ethan's shoulder and licked his cheek. While Ethan dipped his head to the side and rubbed his chin across the soft fur, Taz uttered a throaty whine of sympathy.

"Yeah, pal, not only do I strike sparks off her, she's not too crazy about you, either. I think it's plain fright, even if she tries to gloss over it."

Ethan pulled up behind the courthouse at a site where he'd arranged to meet Mitch. "Maybe I should give her up as a lost cause, Taz." He and Taz came as a pair. "Yeah," he said, ruffling the dog's fur. "It's a case of love me, love my dog."

Mitch opened the passenger door in time to hear the last of Ethan's comment. "What, or maybe I should say who, has you talking to yourself, buddy?"

"Nobody." Ethan fought a flush. "You know I always talk to Taz."

"Right. Except this time you sounded like a lovesick moose. 'Love me, love my dog,'" Mitch chirped in falsetto.

"Buckle up and shut up," Ethan growled. "Since I know you won't quit until you worm it out of me, I'm thinking about setting up an accidental meeting with Supervisor Grant tomorrow morning." Ethan proceeded to tell his friend how, on a couple of occasions, Regan Grant had reacted oddly to Taz.

Mitch whistled. "If you want my advice—which you never take but which I'll give you, anyway—write her off. She sounds phobic. You have about as much chance of a zebra losing its stripes as you do of unscrambling someone's phobia."

"You may be right," Ethan mumbled. But he knew there was something about Regan that made him want to try.

CHAPTER FOUR

IN THE QUIET following Ethan's departure, Regan sorted out the files of clients she planned to visit that afternoon. She couldn't shake Jeremy's case from her mind. Experience had taught her that no matter how inadequate—or destructive—a child's biological parents, they often exerted enduring ties broke only by death. Sometimes not then. Frequently the guilt attached to hating what a parent was or did followed children into adulthood.

Deciding Odella'd had time to return to her office, Regan picked up the phone. "Odella, it's Regan. After you left, I started to wonder who in the agency will inform Jeremy Smith of his mother's arrest." Regan listened to Odella explain that the boy's regular counselor was on vacation. Since Jeremy had a good relationship with the Knights, she went on to say, perhaps the chore should fall to them.

"It's our responsibility," Regan argued. "He's under our jurisdiction. How he accepts the news may have a bearing on whether we should proceed with adoption or name-change requests."

"I doubt it," Odella said. "If you're concerned, I don't mind asking Ethan to tell Jeremy about Shontelle. Ethan has a way with kids, and Jeremy idolizes him."

Regan rubbed at a furrow that had apparently taken up permanent residence between her eyebrows since Ethan Knight had burst into her life. "I ought to run this by Nathaniel. If he's in favor of contacting Shontelle's attorney, I'll visit Jeremy at school. We've met, and he's aware that I planned to look into his petition for a name change. Adoption, though, is so final. He needs to know it'll likely end any further association with his birth mother. I'll call you. Do you have a cell phone?''

Jotting down the number, Regan signed off. She collected Jeremy's file and walked slowly toward their director's office, rehearsing what she'd say as she went.

Piggot was alone, just shrugging into his suit jacket. It was evident from the bulging briefcase and car keys lying on his desk that he was heading out.

"I only need a moment," Regan said. "Something's come up with one of our kids, and it needs immediate attention before we can progress."

Piggot beckoned her past his administrative assistant's empty desk. "I'm on my way to Phoenix to a state budget meeting. If your question involves money, the answer is no. I warned you about the staff here, did I not? With them, everything's an emergency."

Regan quickly explained what she'd learned from Odella about Jeremy Smith's mother.

"Odella Price is always pushy." Pacing the room, Nathaniel tugged at his lower lip. "However, pushy or not, she's been instrumental in reducing our welfare rolls. The governor's finance team likes to see dwindling numbers. So I'm glad the Smith woman, or whatever her name is now, has become Utah's financial burden. If Odella can get the kid adopted so we can quit shelling out bucks to foster him, I say go for it." Hefting his briefcase, the director herded Regan into his reception area. "Otherwise, how are you doing?" he asked as they proceeded down the hall together. "My assistant tells me you're probing into Anna M.'s shortcuts. I'm pleased. My predecessor appointed Anna, you know. She was too well entrenched in the civil-service grade system to get rid of by the time I took over. Believe me, I wanted to fire her."

Regan frowned. "Her methods may be questionable, but so far the foster homes she set up—the ones I've visited, anyway—are excellent. Far above average."

"I don't doubt it. Under Anna, our welfare rolls exploded. She and that damned cop, the one our esteemed commissioner calls the Baby Cop, set about placing every kid who showed even minor neglect into foster care. That overran our budget, and I don't mind telling you my tenure's under scrutiny because of it. I trust you'll reverse the damage they've done."

"I...I'll do my best." Regan paused a few steps from the staff lounge. She wasn't prepared to have this conversation. Up to now, in the case histories she'd read and the homes she'd visited, there'd been no sign of any children being placed who weren't clearly in need of help.

Nathaniel patted her shoulder with a fleshy hand. "I'm counting on you to whip this department into shape, Regan. I'm sorry to rush off. One day soon, after I get the budget done, we'll have lunch, and I'll lay out my cost-cutting ideas. By the way, have you fired Danielle Hargreaves? I'd like to be able to tell the boys in Phoenix that we've eliminated one salary."

"I...um, no. Dani's carrying a big caseload. All our caseworkers are over the limit already. She's at the low end of the pay scale. We couldn't replace her for less."

"Don't replace her. I'm trying to cut costs. Are you saying every caseworker we employ is working the maximum number of cases?"

"All of them are over the recommended limit."

"Find out how many cases are legitimate and how many aren't. By Monday's meeting, Regan, I want a count of the number we serve who are in Desert City illegally. Our federal program director said it's causing some state rolls to triple."

"Can we even get a count? The illegal population in Phoenix had an underground system rivaling none. Hungry kids just showed up at homes that already had caseworkers assigned, and of course, we added them in."

"Well, I won't tolerate that in Desert City. We have the federal government's backing. I will not increase our budget to feed nonresidents. Period!" Nathaniel was practically frothing at the mouth, the subject apparently made him so livid.

Regan found his stand unconscionable. "Are you saying we should let kids starve on our streets because an adult smuggled them across the border?"

"I'm saying we're not responsible for feeding or clothing anyone who hasn't come to Desert City through proper channels. I don't condone breaking immigration rules any more than I approve the methods by which Anna and her pet cop foisted ragtag kids onto our system. I expect you to support me in this, Regan."

"Aren't you comparing apples and oranges? It's one thing to disagree with placement methods. It's another to refuse basic services to hungry destitute families."

Piggot's jowls shook in time with the pudgy finger he wagged in Regan's face. "I didn't bring you into the department to question my edicts. I moved your application ahead of others because I believed you had the balls for the job. If not, I can easily replace you. One way or another, this city's welfare numbers will be reduced."

He stomped off, leaving Regan staring after him in

shock. By the time she managed to control her own burst of temper, she was surrounded by staff who'd been on break in the lounge and overheard her heated exchange with Nathaniel.

"Piggot's a bastard!" Terry Mickelson exclaimed. "He's blowing smoke. You've passed the probationary period. He can't terminate you without cause. With your years in the system and your record, he'd have to document three or more offenses before he could remove you from the post. Even then, you'd have a right to a hearing."

Dani Hargreaves stepped forward. "Nikki heard you stand up for me, Ms. Grant. I'm sorry for the way I've acted. I thought *you* were the one trying to have me fired. I should've known it was Piggot. All he ever thinks about is dollars and cents. Never about staff workloads or client services."

"Yeah," said a soft-spoken male caseworker Regan had only seen at the monthly meetings. Jeff Perez, she thought his name was. "Piggot expects us to run the third-largest welfare department in the state on a shoe-string. But if you examine the last four yearly budgets, you'll see he wangled himself a substantial raise."

Regan had hoped, with time and hard work, to gain the respect and trust of her co-workers. She felt uncomfortable doing it at the expense of the man who'd hired her. "Look, the conversation some of you overheard should have been conducted in private. I regret that it wasn't. I think it's obvious there are some things beyond our control. Our primary mission is to pull together for the good of the families we serve. Now if you'll excuse me, please, I believe we all have work waiting." Regan hurried off, feeling numerous pairs of eyes follow her until she entered her office and shut the door.

Nathaniel's verbal attack had caught her off guard. She was more shaken than anyone back there realized. Regan knew it was due in part to old tapes playing in her head. Her mother, before she'd finally left Regan and her dad, had been extremely critical. So had Jack after she'd moved in with him. Darn, she thought she'd come out of all that unscathed.

She made her way to the washroom. Grasping the rim of the sink with both hands, Regan stared at herself in the mirror. Except for the faint white scars, she looked like any one of a million other thirty-one-year-old professional women. The scars were noticeable, but they were only skin deep. *Only skin deep.*

Leaving the room, Regan swiftly bundled up the files she needed. She turned off the overhead light, locked the door and exited the building. When she reached her five-year-old Honda Accord, she'd rid herself of the effect of Nathaniel's threat. Still, after she slid into the driver's seat, she leaned her forehead on the steering wheel for a moment. Just to subdue any lingering lapse of control. She'd worked too hard over the years to conquer her insecurities; she refused to fall into the trap again. It wasn't only the years of therapy she'd undergone after the dog's attack. She'd studied psychology to learn what really made people tick. Especially what made *her* tick.

She'd succeeded, too, until her poor judgment with regard to Jack Diamond. Their public fight, followed by an abrupt move and the added pressure of a new job, had probably sapped her reserves. To say nothing of the unexpected run-in with Ethan Knight and his scary dog. Today's altercation with her boss was sort of a last straw.

But she'd survived last straws before, and Regan vowed to do it again. She was not the person she'd been twenty years ago, when a neighbor stood up in court and announced to a jury that Regan Grant was a weird kid with her light eyes. The man her family thought was a friend urged people to shun them. Which the whole town did.

Even her own mother had taken off.

Regan had begged her father not to sue the dog's owner. Other kids had mercilessly teased the poodle. Not her, but others who walked the same route to school.

To her dad, how people viewed her didn't matter. With him, it was about winning. The court ruled in her favor and had the dog destroyed. Neighbors were incensed. Ultimately her father had to use the settlement to send her out of state to boarding school or risk something worse than a dog attack. His business suffered, and he had to sell out. He said he didn't blame her, but Regan was never fully certain.

Lifting her head, she gripped the wheel, sat back and turned the ignition key. That was all behind her. No one in Desert City, Arizona, knew that kid from Ohio. Mostly Regan managed to keep those old feelings buried deep.

Everything, including the incident with Piggot, was relegated to the back of her mind when Regan parked in the visitors' lot at Roadrunner High School. Regan was the picture of professionalism when she presented her credentials to a secretary.

"I'll have to check with the principal before I call Jeremy out of class. Is he in trouble?" the woman asked.

Regan smiled. "No. The agency has received some news that may affect his future. I'll be happy to speak with the principal first."

The principal, Carla Rodriguez, invited Regan into her office. "This is Jeremy's first year with us," she said. "And he's already our star J.V. basketball forward. I hope your urgent business isn't going to move him out of our school."

"I shouldn't think so. You do need to be aware of the situation, though. Sometimes matters of this nature cause youths to act out inappropriately." Regan recapped the plight of Jeremy's birth mother. She also mentioned the prospect of his being adopted by the Knights. "That isn't a sure thing," Regan added.

"It would be wonderful if Elaine and Joe did adopt him." The principal smiled warmly. "I attended high school and college with Amy Knight. Her parents had a revolving door for troubled kids. They've worked miracles with quite a few boys and girls, Jeremy included."

"Then you don't see Joe Knight's heart condition as a complication of concern to Jeremy's future?"

"You mean if another heart attack should prove fatal?"

"Yes, although I hate to even suggest anything so terrible."

The principal leaned forward, clasping her hands together. "Obviously you're new to Desert City. The Knights are something of an institution when it comes to law enforcement and community good works. Their family is tight-knit. If anything did happen to Joe, he has three sons and five sons-in-law, any of whom would happily step in to serve as surrogate father to Jeremy."

Regan glanced up from jotting notes in the boy's file. "Well, then, I guess how we handle the next step is up to Jeremy."

"Do you mind if I sit in on your visit with him?" the principal asked Regan.

"Not at all. In fact, I'd welcome your attendance," Regan said after Carla dispatched an aide to locate Jeremy.

Some ten minutes later, he entered the principal's office hesitantly. His large dark eyes rested warily on Regan a moment before flashing to Mrs. Rodriguez. "Is something wrong at ho…home?" His words jerked. "Da…Dad, it's not his heart again, is it?"

"No," Regan hastened to assure him. "Have a seat, please, Jeremy. I'm afraid this visit has to do with your birth mother. The agency received a fax—"

The boy exploded from his seat. "You ain't gonna send me back to live with her? I won't go! I don't gotta, do I, Mrs. R.?"

"Let me finish, Jeremy." Regan pushed him gently back into his chair. "Your mother is in a Utah jail."

"I…but I don't have enough money for bail. I only got what Ethan gave me yesterday to buy new running shoes." The boy's smooth brow pleated. "I guess Ethan or Dad will know how to contact the people holding her in Utah."

"This isn't about bail, Jeremy. Your mom's accused of fatally stabbing the man she'd been living with. The evidence against her is strong. I'm here because Odella Price, one of our caseworkers, thinks Shontelle's lawyer might be able to work a deal with her to release you for adoption if you're still interested. Although time is short, you don't have to answer right this minute. I'd like you to discuss it thoroughly with your foster parents. I have several calls to make this afternoon, and I'll drop by your house when I'm through, around five o'clock. I'll need your decision by then, Jeremy. Do you have any questions I might answer?"

Eyes that had been dull sparkled suddenly with tears and a darker emotion. "I tried to help my mom, and I couldn't." He blinked rapidly. "Can I call my dad or Ethan to come and get me? They'll know what to do.

Just 'cause I don't want to live with Mama don't mean I don't feel nothin' for her.''

"I know, Jeremy." Regan curved a hand over his bowed shoulders. She cast a worried look at Carla Rodriguez. The decision to release Jeremy from school early was hers to make.

The principal, having pulled Jeremy's student record card, reached for the phone. She punched in a series of numbers and after a brief conversation, hung up again.

"Central dispatching said Joe Knight is out on a call. Ethan's at his desk. I asked them to send him. He shouldn't be long.''

Jeremy nodded. He slumped lower in his seat and blotted wet eyes with the sleeve of his sweatshirt. "Man, if she's charged with murder, she could get life or... Does Utah have the death penalty?''

Regan felt her stomach go into a spin. "I don't know, Jeremy. She's only just started the process, I think. Here, take this packet of tissues.'' Duty decreed she stay with the distraught boy until someone close to him arrived. And yet she knew that wherever Ethan went, his dog probably followed. Regan really, really wanted to make herself scarce.

Of course she was right about the dog tagging after him. Although this time, when Ethan burst through the door, he left his pet outside in the waiting area. Going down on one knee beside Jeremy, Ethan gripped the shaking shoulders. "Did you break something playing ball? Hey, kid, I know tryouts for varsity are next week, but Dad will talk to the coach, or I will. You've got a month before he'll make a final roster. What's important, is to get you to a doc.''

Rising, Ethan seemed to notice Regan for the first time. He pulled up short. "What the hell are you doing here? Or is that one of the new rules? You have to sign off on whether or not a foster kid can go in for X rays?''

"Stop it, Detective. Jeremy's not injured. I came to deliver the news about his mother. Jeremy needs to go home where he'll have a chance to fully digest what I told him. As his foster father was unavailable to come for him, Jeremy requested you drive him home. If you're otherwise committed, I'll take him.''

Ethan took a closer look at Jeremy's tear-streaked face. Then with one hand, he grasped Regan's upper arm, lifting her bodily from her chair. Ignoring her squeaking protest, he propelled her out the door and around the corner, where he lowered his voice. "This is some damned insensitive way to notify a kid his mother's up on a murder rap. But then so was calling me to his school through urgent dispatch. I thought he'd been hurt!''

"I'm sorry you were needlessly worried. That wasn't my intent. It's our job at Family Assistance to deliver any bad news. His caseworker's on vacation, and it's my duty to fill in for absent staff members.''

"Anna would have phoned my mom first. She *is* the kid's acting guardian. He doesn't know you from Adam.''

Regan couldn't explain why that struck her as funny. "Wouldn't it be more appropriate to say he doesn't know me from Eve?'' Her smile softened her stiff features.

"Touché.'' Ethan sighed, unable to keep from running an admiring eye the length of her very feminine form. "So what did you hear from Shontelle's lawyer? Will she go for adoption, or did she renege on even letting him take our name?''

Technically Regan didn't owe Ethan any explanation. But because she knew Jeremy would relay everything, anyway, and in his emotional state might leave out something pertinent, she relented. "Our director favors the adoption. However, before we call the attorney, we need a signed authorization from your parents. And, of course, Jeremy has to want to go forward."

Ethan whistled through his teeth. When he did, Taz cleared the counter that separated visitor seating from the staff work area. The secretaries thought Taz's leap was hilarious, until Regan let out a bloodcurdling scream. She practically tore the door to Carla Rodriguez's office from its hinges in an effort to escape the dog, who'd stopped dutifully at Ethan's side.

Ethan scratched his head. Everyone here knew Taz was a pussycat and could vouch for that to Regan Grant. If she'd listen. For whatever reason, Taz terrified her. Ethan wondered again if Regan's fear was confined to Alsatians or all dogs. He intended to find out. But not right now. Jeremy was his top priority. The boy had a lot hanging over his head, and Ethan's first order of business was to look after his family.

Grabbing hold of Taz's collar, Ethan cracked Carla's door ajar. "Hey, Jeremy, buddy. Will you take Taz to my patrol car while I sign you out on the books? Is there anything you need to grab from your locker?"

"My math book. Taz can come, too. Can't he, Mrs. R.?"

The principal, who continued to eye Regan with skepticism, nodded absently to the boy. "Ethan, go with them. The freshmen lockers are closer to where you're parked. I'll sign Jeremy out."

"Thanks, Carla. So long, Supervisor." Ethan's eyes

sought Regan's. She'd retreated to the side of the room farthest from the door, her back against the wall.

As if she realized how silly she must look, Regan shoved herself away. "Tell Elaine I...I'm sorry for the short notice, but I need Jeremy's decision regarding adoption, by five today. I have several visits this afternoon. The last one should wind down by four or four-thirty. I'll stop by your parents' home then."

"I heard one of your appointments is with Jessica Talbot. I hope you don't charge in there like a rampaging bull. Mike and Kimi Hammond haven't been with Jess very long. They're still panicky around strangers."

"I'm aware of how long they've been in the Talbot home. They're two of the three children you took the liberty of improperly placing after I came to work for the department. The transcripts of Mr. Hammond's arraignment mention he has a brother living near here. Did you consider him as a possible guardian, I wonder?"

Ethan shook his head; he knew Hammond's brother. Dean's rap sheet wasn't as long as Bruce's, but according to Mitch, Dean's live-in girlfriend had two child-neglect charges filed against her. "Don't punish those kids because of problems between us. They're still sleeping poorly at night. Kimi misses her mom. Mike suffers screaming nightmares. If you read my report, then you know Mike saw his dad beat their mom to death."

"I read it." Regan spoke from between clenched teeth. "You're quite descriptive. Eloquent with words. Your reports tend to read like crime stories."

"They are crime stories. True crime. I just have a penchant for happy endings."

"So do I, Detective."

"Ethan. We agreed to use first names."

Before Regan could offer a suitable comeback, someone else used his first name. Jeremy tapped Ethan on the shoulder and urged him to hurry. "From the way Taz is pacing, Ethan, I think he's gotta go outside. If you know what I mean."

"Okay. Better dash. Carla thanks again. Regan, I'll see you later. In fact, I may drop by Jessica's while you're there."

"There's no need…" Regan began. She found herself speaking to the wall. "Darn that man." After rubbing her temples, she clenched her fists and pounded softly on the door.

Behind her, Carla Rodriguez coughed discreetly.

"Oh. Sorry." Regan felt abashed. "I'm afraid the detective had a very different relationship with the previous CHC supervisor. He and I are more like two cats fighting to establish our individual territories."

"Hmm. It's not like Ethan to tread on anyone's toes."

Regan mustered a wry smile. "Well, tread he does. And as you see, he has much bigger feet."

"From what I hear, your predecessor did, too—she left large footsteps to follow," Carla said as she rounded her desk and walked to the front entrance with Regan. "Will you or Elaine let me know what Jeremy decides? I like to keep abreast of student concerns."

"I'll ask Elaine to phone you tomorrow. But I have a hunch nothing's going to change."

"Oh. You think not? It's common knowledge how badly Jeremy wants to be a Knight."

"I could be wrong. Either way, I think Jeremy's on the brink of losing his boyhood. If Elaine and Joe have helped as many troubled kids become productive adults as you say, I believe they'll support Jeremy's decision not to abandon his birth mom. He'll be torn, but his roots and his heritage lie with Shontelle. The woman has precious little. If Jeremy ever becomes a star basketball player, for instance, his name on that uniform could be the woman's one bright spot. The Knights have a string of grandchildren who'll make them proud. And they'll continue to be in Jeremy's corner, since they'll be the ones available to attend his games and cheer him on. So really, what's in a name?''

Carla hit the center bar to open the double doors leading outside. ''There really are two sides to every situation. Before I listened to you, I was a hundred percent in favor of adoption for that kid. Now I'm hoping he's secure enough in the Knights' love to make the manly choice. If he does, I'll stand you to a glass of wine next week at the neighborhood pub. I only go there when I have something worth celebrating. If I stopped there each time I left here in a blue funk…well, suffice if to say, I don't.''

''I'm not much of a drinker, but I do enjoy some wine now and then. Call me—you have my card. If I'm wrong about this, I'll bring chocolate to your house. We'll pig out together.''

Grinning, Carla Rodriguez stood at the entrance until Regan guided her compact car out of the parking lot. The two women exchanged a last wave before the principal turned and went inside again.

Regan drove to the home of a foster family who, according to the file, had three school-age boys, biological children, and a four-year-old foster daughter. A handicapped child. Little Wendy had suffered a spinal injury when thrown down two flights of stairs by her stepdad.

The foster mother, a pretty redhead named Caroline, welcomed Regan hesitantly. Ushering her inside, the woman called softly to a pixie-faced child peering around curtains clipped back on either side of an archway. "Wendy, sweetie. Come say hello to Ms. Grant. She's replaced Anna. Remember, Anna went to live with God?"

The child eased out from behind the curtain and moved slowly toward them, pushing a silver walker propelled by two sturdy little arms and a good left leg. Her right leg hung useless. Regan felt something squeeze her heart. No matter how many years she worked in this business, whenever she saw a suffering child, she felt a visceral urge to inflict real damage on the cruel or thoughtless adults responsible. But in her position, she had to hide her true feelings.

"Hi, Wendy." Regan opened her briefcase and took out a small stuffed kitten. His fur was white, his eyes big and green. "A little bird told me you have a kitty collection. Is there space in your bedroom for this guy?"

"Mom?" Big gray eyes lit up as her foster mom nodded her approval.

"Anna's an angel, not a bird," Wendy announced when she got close enough to Regan to take the toy.

"Wendy?" Caroline appeared puzzled.

Regan understood at once. "In a way, Wendy, Anna did tell me about your kitty collection. She wrote about it in your file. Would you show me? I'd like to see them."

Wendy proudly led the way to a pretty, pink-and-white room. "Nice," Regan murmured.

"Aaron and I always wanted a girl. Ethan knew that. He and Aaron served on the same squad for a while. Now Aaron's working vice. We'd love to adopt Wendy, but her paternal grandmother objects. She isn't in a position to care for Wendy. She claims, though that one day her son will come to his senses. We love her as though she was our own child, Ms. Grant."

Regan picked up a framed family photo. Until she looked at the whole family, she hadn't realized how much Wendy resembled her foster mom and one of her foster brothers.

"Uncanny, isn't it? I've been sick with worry since you phoned. You aren't going to move her, are you?" Caroline asked in a voice so soft only Regan could hear.

"No. Certainly not." Regan set the photo down. She admired every cat in Wendy's collection before the adults finally left her to play with the new addition while they adjourned to the living room to talk.

"Aaron and I found a surgeon in California who's perfected an operation we think will allow Wendy to walk normally. Terry, our caseworker, said Family Assistance can't cover the cost involved. Aaron and I aren't rich, but we're willing to get a second mortgage on our home to give Wendy this chance. Terry said the director refused to ask the court for consent. I'm sure he thinks the surgery is risky, but…the procedure has a high rate of success. Why wouldn't he just ask the court, if it's our money?"

Regan shook her head. "I have no idea. I didn't see any notation in the file. It may be the fact that we have no reciprocal agreement for medical care with California, and it wouldn't be right to let you go out on a limb. It's also possible that the birth father's the stumbling block. I'll look into it. In any event, could you get me more details about the operation? I'm fairly new to Desert City, but in Phoenix, there were service organizations that helped out in similar situations. It would be better, of course, if the surgeon came here."

Caroline covered her trembling lips. "Could that happen? Maybe you're more like Anna than anyone has thought," she said softly. "I feel bad. Lexie, Jessica and

I have been on a three-way call all morning, trying to decide what kind of ogre you'd be. Lexie heard you'd chewed Ethan out for getting us to participate in the foster-parent program. Frankly, I'll admit I expected you to breathe fire and have two heads.''

"I did chew him out. He didn't follow our rules bringing any of you in. He's made decisions a qualified team of professional social workers usually makes." Regan couldn't hide her exasperation.

"Don't you like Uncle Ethan?" Wendy queried in a tiny voice. The women whirled around. Neither had heard the child enter the kitchen.

"She does like him, sweetheart," Caroline exclaimed, hauling the girl onto her lap. "Everyone loves Uncle Ethan, you know that."

"Yep." Wendy nodded sagely. "Daddy says Uncle Ethan's like Mother Hubbard and Santa Claus rolled into one." She squinted at Regan and propped a finger against one temple. "That's funny, 'cause men can't be mothers. They're only daddies."

Regan laughed, and then decided to leave before Wendy or her mother tried to turn Ethan Knight into some kind of saint.

Six blocks away, at Lexie Knight's home, Regan encountered the same ideal conditions she'd viewed in the other homes. And Lexie, too, had nothing but glowing words of praise for her brother-in-law.

It was after three o'clock, and Regan considered skipping the visit to Jessica Talbot. However, she'd assigned herself the task of looking into every last one of Ethan's special cases. And the Talbots fit the bill twice over. Regan had read the file on a pair of sisters who'd been in their care for ten months before a judge turned them over to relatives. The girls weren't gone a week when

Ethan placed two other kids with his cousin. Between friends and relatives, the man had more contacts for safe houses than the Secret Service, judging by the number of files Records had pulled for Regan.

She started toward the door but heard childish laughter coming from the backyard and made a detour. On tiptoes Regan peeked over the gate. Ethan Knight, sans uniform, clad in a black bathing suit and an all-over tan, stood in the shallow end of a swimming pool, looking like a statue of a Greek god. He did nothing to counteract the head-to-toe splashing a pint-size girl was enthusiastically delivering. A beautiful blonde floated in the deeper end on a bright orange inflatable lounge. A boy of six or seven sat on steps leading into the water. He wore a mixed expression. Partly wistful, as though he wanted to join in the splashing but considered himself too mature for such childish activity.

What struck Regan was how natural the scene looked. It was like gazing on a tableau of the perfect family vacation.

Regan waged a tug of war with envy, which surprised her. Shocked her, really. She'd never allowed herself to regret not being able to have children. Her empty shaking hand spread across a stomach that would be forever barren. Rare tears sprang to her eyes, but she did nothing to wipe them away.

She backed up a step, struggling against a need to flee. It was obvious what she'd find in interviewing Jessica Talbot. A repeat of the excellent foster homes she'd discovered throughout her previous visits. Regan would have left if Ethan hadn't noticed her and directed the boy in a loud voice to open the gate. Regan continued to back away, as if in slow motion.

"Regan. Ms. Grant. Come on in. Quit worrying," Ethan called. "I left Taz with Jeremy."

By then, the boy—Mike Hammond, Regan assumed—had opened the gate. With huge solemn eyes, he invited her into the yard.

Five more steps would get her to the car. Regan wished she'd followed her earlier instincts to run. The beautiful blonde had floated to the steps. She'd climbed out to stand beside Ethan, who now held a shivering Kimi Hammond.

Jessica Talbot wrapped the chilled girl in a fleecy towel. "I'll take Kimi and get her dressed. Mike, you're driest. Would you please run into the kitchen and fix Ms. Grant a glass of lemonade? I'm guessing that's who you are," she said to Regan, "since Ethan was galloping around screaming your name like a demented banshee."

He looked affronted. "I merely called out to stop her. It seemed as if she was about to leave. I thought maybe she hadn't seen us."

"I saw you," Regan said, glancing at the sky, then the pool and finally her feet. Anywhere to keep from gazing at that tanned expanse of male flesh. Muscular flesh that left her feeling overheated and overdressed.

"I told you we should wait in the house," Jessica hissed. "Now she probably thinks I'm far too casual for someone who agreed to this meeting."

Ethan tilted one dark eyebrow. "I'll bet Regan's dying to get into the pool. You two are about the same size, Jess. Don't you have an extra suit she can borrow? Kimi and I will get the beach ball and play catch while you hunt one up. Casual visits are best, don't you agree, Regan?"

His voice ensnared her. Regan's blouse stuck to her skin under her fitted suit jacket. Her throat felt like sand-

paper. The pool with its sky-blue water was tempting—
yet all she could think about were the ugly scars that
still marred her stomach, right hip and thigh. The plastic
surgeon in Phoenix hadn't begun to repair those. She'd
already decided to use her first vacation to go back and
let him finish the work he'd started. Even then he could
only repair her outer scars. No one could give her back
her uterus. That portion of the original surgery was ir-
reversible.

"No, I don't want to go in the pool." Her tone was
harsh. Too harsh. "I don't swim," she said, hoping to
wipe away the tense look that had settled over Jessica
Talbot's face. It wasn't anyone's fault that Jack had
made Regan utterly self-conscious about her scars. She
thought she'd gotten over worrying what other people
thought, until her fiancé made such a big deal over them,
insisting she wear longer shorts on their morning runs.

Regan could well imagine what Ethan Knight would
have to say about her imperfections, flawless specimen
of manhood that he was.

"You're all having such a good time. I can reched-
ule. I'm, ah, running late as it is." A glance at her watch
told Regan *that,* at least, was the truth. She turned again,
not caring at this point that Jessica Talbot might find her
behavior bizarre.

"Wait." Ethan thrust Kimi, towel and all, back into
Jessica's arms. He grabbed a pair of jeans tossed over a
nearby lawn chair and pulled them on. "Dad dropped
me off. I thought I'd catch a ride back to the folks' house
with you, Regan. I promised Mom I'd prepare you for
Jeremy's decision." Ethan snatched up his shirt and
shoes, kissed Kimi on the cheek, grabbed Regan's arm
and steered her toward the gate. "Bye, Jess. Bye, Kimi.

Tell Mike I'll pick him up after school tomorrow to take him to Jeremy's game.''

Ethan obviously didn't care that he left abruptly, or that he'd caused Jessica to gape after him in astonishment.

Regan felt the coolness of his pool-damp body through the unlined linen of her suit. His nearness and his partial state of undress contributed to making her stumble. He was close enough to notice the white scar on her neck...if he cared to look. Regan ducked her chin and dug in her handbag for her car keys.

"I'll drive," Ethan said, plucking them from her hand.

She opened her mouth to protest, then realized if he drove there'd be less chance he'd notice the scar.

"You surprise me, Regan. I expected you to lambaste me with every girl-power slogan on the books. It's not that I think men are better drivers than women. I just know the backstreets around here better than you probably do."

Regan glanced up from buckling her seat belt. She tried but failed to quell a spontaneous laugh. "For the record, Knight, I don't fit any of your little square pigeonholes."

A slow smile spread across Ethan's face as he popped her small car into gear. "Pigeonholes are round, Grant. And, let's see, so far you've fit three out of three."

His tone dared her to ask what they were. And she wanted to do exactly that. Instead, refusing to let him distract her, she calmly opened her briefcase and exchanged the Talbot file for Jeremy's. "So, prepare me for Jeremy's decision."

The glance Ethan aimed her direction was one of admiration.

Regan battled a flutter of awareness that began in her stomach and traveled upward to knock down a few of the barricades she'd erected around her heart after Jack Diamond had finished with her.

CHAPTER FIVE

ETHAN GLANCED at Regan, then stepped on the gas pedal; she didn't bat an eyelash. "How long since this car had new shocks?"

"Not since it rolled off the line, smart mouth. Quit trying to change the subject and fill me in on Jeremy. Or shall I make a citizen's arrest? You've got a lead foot, Detective. These may be backstreets, but they're residential."

Ethan slowed, still dancing the fingers of one hand along the rim of the steering wheel. "Where to start?" he said, growing suddenly moody. "The kid has begged Mom and Dad to adopt him for years." A streetlight turned yellow and Ethan stopped.

"But now Jeremy's having second thoughts?" Regan hauled in a deep breath. "I figured that would be the case."

He scrutinized Regan. "Why? It makes no damned sense. This may be his last chance to be free of a woman who's done nothing but make his life hell. He's gotta know we love him like he's family."

"That's where most people err. They've been taught that love is the strongest motivator. In reality, guilt sets deeper hooks in a person's heart and soul."

"Guilt?" Ethan snorted in disgust. "A kid who's been treated the way Jeremy has doesn't have a thing to feel guilty about."

Regan stared out the side window. One finger plucked idly at the tab on Jeremy's folder. "He's experienced the fear of abandonment," she said in a distant voice. "Because he's a sensitive kid, he can't bring himself to walk away from the woman who gave him life. There's no tie more binding than that of child to mother. So…yes, he feels guilt at the idea of abandoning her— even though she abandoned him first." Regan remembered pining for her own mother, how keenly she still felt the loss. She'd spoken to Blair last night. Her half sister went on and on about all the shopping she and her mom were doing over spring break. Stuff like that still rankled. She couldn't be angry at Blair, though. Nor Dee Dee, for that matter.

"So that's what they taught you in all those advanced psychology classes, huh?"

"No. It's what I learned during five years in the trenches as a social worker. Isn't that how you claimed to come by *your* vast experience?"

He considered that for a moment. "I've been a cop three times longer than you've been a social worker. What I hate most is watching people like you send kids back and back and back into homes where there are parents like Shontelle, or worse. I guess I'll have to differ with your opinion. I believe love can conquer guilt or hate or…fear," he ventured boldly. "Jeremy can't help Shontelle. It's too late to try."

"I refuse to think it's ever too late. Say they give her life with parole or reduce the charge to second-degree murder. She may get counseling in prison that will turn her life around."

Ethan laughed bitterly. "Families are in the mess they're in because the majority of counselors don't live in the real world. That's what I liked about Anna Murphy. She saw a spade and called it one. Have you ever really taken a good hard look at the statistics on rehabilitation? Nine out of every ten rehab efforts fail.''

"I'm not going to debate the issue with you. Our programs were tested and implemented by social workers with far more experience than I could ever hope to have. I've read the follow-up studies. They work.''

"Not much works with the dregs of society.''

Regan pursed her lips. If he was determined to have the last word, then fine with her.

Ethan might not have let it go so easily, except that he rounded the corner near his house and saw his partner, Mitch, knocking on his front door. Ethan braked quickly, pulled to the curb and honked the horn.

Regan braced a hand on the dash. "What are you doing? This isn't your parents' place.''

"It's mine. That's my partner. He's off this afternoon. He's also a gentleman rancher, so normally he has better things to do with his free time than show up at my door. I wonder what's up.'' He honked again.

Regan paid scant attention to the man in hat and boots who bounded energetically down the walkway. Ethan's house drew her interest. Sprawled among a row of well-kept homes, it was built in a style known as Territorial, typical of early southwestern homes. Flat-roof, burnt-adobe brick walls. Ethan's roof was bisected by a double chimney. Regan imagined it vented smoke from two fireplaces. Territorial homes generally had open beamed ceilings and real saltillo-tiled floors. None of the phony stuff contractors laid in today's tract homes. Regan loved the place on sight and envied Ethan.

A pair of narrow, jean-covered thighs suddenly cut off her view of the house. The jeans were replaced by a face in need of a shave as Ethan's partner bent to see who was in the small car.

When Ethan nudged her shoulder, Regan hurriedly rolled down the passenger window.

Eyes so dark a brown they looked like Turkish coffee assessed Regan by degrees. The man behind the eyes gave a heartfelt wolf whistle, clasped both hands over his heart and said softly, "mio bellino amore."

Regan felt the soft brush of curls on her cheek as the man outside swept off a cowboy hat, stuck his head in her window and kissed her soundly on the lips.

"Down, boy," Ethan ordered, reaching a muscular arm across Regan. His grip on Mitch's shoulder brought his buddy to his knees.

Mitch only continued his wicked laughter.

Regan remained stiff and unmoving in her seat.

Ethan scowled at Mitch. "Cut the theatrics, Valetti. This is Regan Grant, CHC supervisor. Regan, this jerk is Mitch Valetti." He lowered his voice. "Can't you see she's dressed for business, you meathead?" Ethan nodded at the open briefcase on Regan's lap. One look at Ethan's stormy eyes, and any fool would back off. It was all too clear to Ethan that his partner was loving the heck out of his displeasure.

Ethan slammed out of the car, rounded the hood and clamped hold of Mitch's arm. Ethan propelled his partner down the walkway to a beautifully restored 1968 baby-blue Corvette. It was Mitch Valetti's pride and joy. "What in hell did you think you were doing, kissing Regan on the mouth like that?" Ethan hissed.

Mitch peeled Ethan's fingers from around his brawny biceps. "How in hell was I supposed to know that was the battle-ax?" He kissed the tips of his fingers. "Those jokers at the station oughtta have their heads examined.

The lady tastes like peppermint candy and looks like a model for Victoria's Secret.'' Spreading his fingers, Mitch rocked his wrist back and forth, indicating Regan was just too hot. "Hey, since you aren't interested, I guess you won't mind if I go and ask her out to dinner."

"Who said I wasn't interested?"

Mitch planted his boot heels apart and crossed his arms. "*Didn't* you say that? Well, maybe not in so many words." He thumbed a lip. "Hmm. What about her dog phobia? Come to think about it, where is ol' Taz? If you shuffled him off to please the lady, you must have it bad. So if you've already staked your claim, why not admit it?"

Ethan glared. "Taz is at my folks' house with Jeremy. Which is where Regan and I are headed. And don't be yanking my chain. You know how much Taz means to me. Quit clowning around and tell me why you were banging on my front door."

"Oh, yeah. Jorge Jiminez and Ron Glendenning caught me on the radio before I clocked out. They found a kid. A girl. Around seven or eight, they think. No shoes. Torn clothes. One eye swollen shut. Red welts on her cheek and a deep cut. Jorge said it looked like she'd been backhanded hard. She's refusing to talk. They thought you might try bringing her out of her shell and maybe find someplace safe to take her."

Ethan swiped a hand over his mouth and chin. His gaze wandered to Regan, still sitting in her car. "They'll have to call CHC on this one. My hands are tied as a result of the rules and regs they're sticking to down at Family Assistance."

Valetti rammed his hands in his back pockets. "This is one for the books—Knight playing by the rules. Hell, man, you've got the head honcho from CHC eating out of your hand. Surely she'll sign a waiver for her *amante*.'' Teasing dark eyes dared Ethan to argue.

"She's not my lover," Ethan muttered. "And you damn well know she's not the head honcho. She's second in command. So far Regan hasn't given me any reason to believe she'd sign a waiver even if I brought her a kid we found bleeding to death in the gutter. Well, she'd do *something*. She's not heartless."

"So you're gonna ask her, right?"

Spinning on the heel of a boot more worn down than that of his partner, Ethan aimed a kick at the Corvette's back tire. He hadn't taken two steps when he called back to Mitch, "I must have 'stupid' engraved across my forehead, but yeah, I'll ask her. In fact, I'll do more than that. I'm going to deliver this kid into her hands and see how she handles it."

Whistling jauntily, the Italian Cowboy dug out his car keys and sank into the front seat of the Corvette. As he left, dust kicked up from the wide wheels.

"If you've got trouble at work," Regan said when a grim-faced Ethan returned, "I'm more than capable of finding my way to your parents' house alone."

"A couple of guys from my squad found a kid wandering the streets. Sounds like a case for CHC. If you don't mind delaying your visit to Jeremy, I'll contact the uniforms and have them meet us somewhere." He had his cell phone at his ear before Regan could formulate a reply.

"Jorge, it's Knight. Mitch said you picked up a battered kid." Ethan squinted at the street signs and gave the man at the other end of the phone his coordinates. "You think her face needs stitches? Sure, I'm about five minutes from Desert City Hospital. I'll meet you in the ER."

"Ethan," Regan gasped after he'd clicked off. "You can't authorize treatment for a child! What if her parents or legal guardian objects?"

"You think a stranger stole her shoes and knocked her around?"

"She's barefoot?" Regan swallowed what she'd been about to say. "Did…did those officers ask her any pertinent questions?"

"Of course. Do you take us for idiots? She's mute. If not from a disability, from trauma or fear. You'd know about that, I guess."

Regan shut her eyes to ward off a bout of light-headedness.

Still irritated with Mitch, Ethan snapped, "Maybe I'll swing by Mom and Dad's and pick up Taz. Kids generally warm up around him." Ethan slowed the car at the next intersection.

Regan thrashed her head from side to side. "Let me out here! I'll walk to your mom's and call Intake from there. Then I'll call you at the hospital and tell you what they say. That's provided our agency needs to get involved."

"*Needs* to? Are you suggesting we dump the girl back with the jerk who knocked her around?"

"No." Regan willed away the panic that struck at the mere idea of coming face-to-face with Ethan's dog. "You're jumping to conclusions that a parent beat her. Once you have the facts, that's the time to notify CHC. *If* we're needed. Maybe the child fell in the park or something."

If Ethan had doubted her panic before, he had no reservations now. His mention of Taz had made her a basket case. "We're closer to the hospital than to my folks'," he said gently. "I need to stop at the gift shop

to buy a stuffed toy for the kid. You don't have an aversion to stuffed animals, do you?''

"I...what do you mean?'' Regan sucked hard on her
bottom lip. She felt sweat pool in the palms of her hands
and hoped he was too involved in his driving to notice
how unsteady they were.

"Nothing. This isn't about you or me. It's about a
little girl who needs our help.'' He stabbed a finger toward a row of parked cars. "There's Glendenning's patrol car. Come on,'' he said, parking behind them.
"They've gone inside.''

Regan barely had time to grab her briefcase, in case
she needed to fill out forms on the child. Ethan Knight
moved quickly for a man his size. He'd shut off the
engine, pocketed the keys and all but snatched her out
of the car before Regan had a chance to assess the building. Visiting the trauma unit had been on her list of
things to do. This hospital treated most of the city's in-
digent-care cases. Therefore, Regan wanted to forge a
good relationship with the staff. "You seem to be under
the impression that I don't want speedy treatment for
our clients. That simply isn't true,'' she told Ethan, running to keep up. She caught him at the cash register in
the gift shop, where he peeled money from a silver clip
to pay for a stuffed brown bear, a bear with a bright red
bow around its neck. "It's just...there are policies in
place. For all we know, the girl may already be one of
ours. If so, we can bypass Intake.''

Ignoring Regan, Ethan strode down the hall to the ER.
He got his first look at the tattered child with the bloody
face and dead eyes. "Consider them bypassed,'' he said.
Glancing neither left nor right and giving no response to
a nurse who tried to waylay him, Ethan walked straight

to the child, sank to his knees and set the bear in her lap. "I brought a friend for you, Joey."

The child touched the bear's nose and eyes without acknowledging Ethan's presence in any other way.

"You know her?" Regan asked in the same hushed tones he'd used.

Standing, Ethan pulled Regan aside. "Yeah. Her name is Joey Hawkins."

Two police officers who stood to one side deep in conversation with a wiry woman of indeterminate age bearing a clipboard suddenly spotted Ethan. The relief they felt at seeing him showed in the smiles that wreathed their faces. The swarthier of the two loped over to Ethan's side. "Glendenning and I have to get back out on patrol, Ethan. You're a welcome sight, I've gotta say. Uh...Juanita has a copy of our initial write-up. She's needing somebody to fill out treatment forms." Peering over his shoulder, he gave his partner a high sign. As fast as butter melting into hot bread, the two escaped, leaving Ethan holding the bag, Regan noted.

The woman with the clipboard descended on him. "Detective Knight. Am I to assume this is another of your rescued waifs?"

He canted his head toward where Regan stood gripping her briefcase. "You've got previous files on Joey. She's been here three times that I know of. Once she fell off a chair at home and broke her arm. Another time she got burned pretty bad—apparently playing with matches. Last time she had several bones in her left foot crushed. Looked to me like a boot heel might have landed on her, but her mother said they were taking groceries into the house and a five-pound can of pork 'n beans fell off the counter." His clipped tone told Regan something she already knew—how rarely agencies disputed a mother's version of events—and that he thought the mom's reports were a pack of lies.

Juanita jotted down the name. The look she sent the child was a mixture of sympathy and pity. "That cut needs sutures. I'll let you see what information you can wrest out of her before I place a call to her sweetheart of a mother."

Ethan sighed. "She's not talking, Juanita. According to what Jorge told my partner, she's refusing to say a word this time. In the past the kid's corroborated her mother's accounts of the accidents. The school nurse, Joey's teacher and CHC have all questioned her. Even the neighbors in the surrounding duplexes clammed up."

"Do you mind if I try?" Regan came closer, studied the silent child. "If I had to make an educated guess, I'd say those welts on her face match a man's handprint. If she so much as hints at abuse, I can petition a judge to order temporary respite. It's not much, but if we take her out of the home even briefly, it might convince a neighbor to come clean."

Ethan's gaze settled on Regan with new warmth. "That's not going to compromise your precious policy, is it?"

"I won't dignify that with a response." Regan didn't know what had made her volunteer to intervene or for that matter, why Ethan's approving blue eyes lifted her spirits. Her stomach still knotted. Probably because any intervention on her part went against standard operating procedure. But who in this business wouldn't do the same once they'd laid eyes on that poor child?

Without further comment, Regan helped herself to the empty chair next to the girl. "Nice bear," she said lightly after the child's thin shoulders sagged a bit. They'd tensed noticeably when Regan sat down. She mentioned school but got no reply. So she tried another tack.

"I had a bear that looked like him once, when I was about your age. I called him Cocoa. What do you think you'll name this guy?"

The girl straightened the red bow for such a long time Regan thought she wasn't going to answer. When she did, Regan's stomach spasmed again. "I could call him 'Little Shit.' That's what Chip called me when I axdently spilled soup on him today. Chip calls me that all the time. It's not nice, is it?" She hugged the bear and gazed at Regan with huge eyes. "If Mama lets me keep him, I'll call him Teddy. She won't, though," the girl said in abject resignation. "'Cause Chip don't like toys underfoot."

"Who's Chip?" Regan asked in a conversational tone. "Your older brother?"

"Mama's boyfriend. I don't have no sister or brother." The girl shook her head, and matted brown curls stuck to a pixie face. "Oooh!" she cried, dropping the bear to clutch her bleeding cheek.

Discreetly opening her briefcase, Regan turned on the small tape recorder she'd put in to record Jeremy. Bending over to retrieve the fallen toy, she pulled Joey's hand away from her cheek and wrapped it around the bear. "I guess Chip wears a pretty big ring," she said mildly. "That's some hole. He must've really been mad about that spilled soup."

"Yeah," the child said. "But I got away this time before he could give it to me good. I wish I didn't have to go back today. I do, though, huh? Mama's real sick. That's why Chip kept me home from school. Why I was fixin' his soup."

"Is your mother sick often?"

Joey blinked and scrambled to the far corner of her chair. Wide dilated eyes cast furtive glances between Regan and the door. "No. Mama's got a cold is all. And I was clumsy to spill the soup. It's wasteful. Money don't grow on trees."

"Honey, spilling soup can happen to anyone. I've been known to knock things over, too. That doesn't give anyone the right to hit me. It was wrong for Chip to hit you. What if I said you didn't have to go back home today?"

"Mama would worry."

"I'll let her know you're safe."

"And you won't let Chip hurt her?"

"Does he do that sometimes, Joey?"

The girl nodded, but grimaced, as moving obviously hurt.

Regan clicked off the recorder. "Will you be okay for another minute? I need to talk to Detective Knight. He's going to help me find a nice place for you to sleep tonight. And have a hot meal. You're probably hungry."

"Yeah. We didn't have any cereal, and Chip threw the soup pot across the room. Where's the policeman's dog? At school, he had a nice dog."

Trying not to shudder at the mention of Taz, Regan explained that Ethan's dog was at home.

Seeing her rise, Ethan started toward her, but she motioned for him to wait. "You got her to talk. That's good. What next?"

"I have enough on tape to request a judge to let us remove her from the home until we can investigate." She flipped out the cassette and gave it to Ethan. "I don't know if it's enough for you to send someone to pick up that creep Chip. I hope so."

"I'll have your court order here in fifteen minutes.

Will you stay with Joey while the doctor checks her over?''

"Ethan, I can't authorize medical care. She'll have to be processed first."

"Did you look at the hole in her face? It needs stitches. If we let it go, there's a greater risk of infection—they might not be able to sew it up. And it could leave a scar." He drew out his wallet and handed Regan a credit card. "Go on, take it," he said when she pulled back. "Use it. If I get reimbursed, fine. If not, okay."

She cast a worried glance at Joey. It was the mention of possible scarring that had Regan brushing aside her better judgment. "Okay, just this once we'll do it your way. Because the wound is on her face. When you get back with the court decree, I'll telephone my office and see who's next on the list offering temporary care. But I'll pay this time," she said, returning his card.

Ethan had accepted the card with obvious reluctance and started to leave, then stopped and retraced his steps. "I know the perfect place. Dani Hargreaves's sister-in-law has been licensed for care. They have a girl about Joey's age. That way, getting Joey outfitted in pajamas and shoes and such shouldn't be too difficult."

"No. I let protocol fly out the window on treatment. We'll go by the rules on selecting a caregiver. We're taking the next available on the list, and that's final."

His shrug said he didn't like it, but they'd do it her way. Until he disappeared through the ER doors, Regan hadn't realized she'd been holding her breath, expecting him to argue. She was awfully glad he hadn't.

Things moved quickly once Regan filled out the forms on the clipboard and handed them back to the clerk. They were whisked into an examining room.

"That's a nasty cut," the doctor said after the nurse

had cleaned all the dried blood. "L-shaped. To minimize scarring, I'll use four small dissolvable sutures. You and that bear are going to have to be really brave," he told Joey.

She didn't cry, but she reached for Regan's hand and clasped it tight. Regan's throat closed when she glanced at the tray filled with syringes and needles.

"Are you okay?" Joey asked in a high thin voice. If nothing else, her question acted like a swift kick in the pants for Regan.

"Yes, honey. You lie still as a mouse and don't worry about me."

Ethan found them before the minor procedure was over. "I'll keep Joey company while you go make your call," he murmured to Regan.

"Is it all right with you, sweetie, if I go and Detective Knight stays?" She smiled at the girl and smoothed her limp brown hair. Joey couldn't nod, but she indicated her acceptance by transferring her hand to Ethan's.

On the way to the bank of phones in the hall outside ER, Regan marveled at Joey's ability to so easily place her trust in virtual strangers. From the sound of the life that poor kid led, one might think she'd be brimming over with fear. Regan thought about the fact that Joey wasn't fearful.

The doctor finished sewing up Joey's wound at the same time Regan completed her round of calls. "You'll be pleased to know," she told Ethan dryly, "that Dani's sister-in-law was next on the list. If you're driving us, here's her address."

"I know where Maddy lives."

Maddy, was it? The name Intake had given Regan was Madeleine. But she didn't say anything.

"There you go again with that look. Any families I

recommend to take in kids have been thoroughly checked out by me before they ever go to your agency for investigation.''

Joey's presence saved Regan from having to get into a discussion on a subject she felt was better left alone. She knew agency screenings sometimes allowed people who shouldn't foster kids to slip through the cracks. An occasional screwup was inevitable, considering the sheer number of applicants screened. Ethan Knight was to be commended. So far, the homes she'd visited that had received his stamp of approval were excellent. His concern and his active involvement made him different from other cops she'd known. Which, she guessed, narrowed down to Jack and his pals. Their only interests were sports, body building, fast cars and women. Not necessarily in that order. Ethan seemed cut from a different cloth. But Regan couldn't really say why she felt off-kilter dwelling on the attributes that made him stand out.

She listened to him chat with Joey. He had an easy way with the girl. He didn't talk down to her and he answered her questions about the family she'd be staying with honestly. ''I've known Maddy and Greg a long time. He dated my youngest sister until Maddy moved here from Texas, and Greg fell in love with her at first sight. Their daughter, Sorrel, is seven.'' He smiled at the child in the back seat as he casually mentioned the school Sorrel attended.

''I'm almost eight,'' Joey boasted. ''I *love* school.''

''What do you like best?'' Ethan asked.

Joey pondered only a moment. ''My teacher. And… hot breakfast and lunch. At home…well, I don't cook so good.''

Regan and Ethan exchanged glances. Regan made a mental note to dig deeper into Joey's home life. An almost-eight-year-old shouldn't be expected to cook. Although Regan had once imagined how she'd teach her daughter to make holiday cookies... A very old dream that started the Christmas after her mom walked out on the family. The whimsy of an abandoned child. Of course it could never happen. Not now.

"Here we are." Ethan pulled Regan's car into a sloped driveway in a subdivision where every fourth house looked alike. All had neat front yards landscaped with colored rock and desert plants. In the fading afternoon light, Regan saw that the stucco had all been painted shades of beige. Only the trim around the doors set one home apart from another. The Hargreaves place had been trimmed in dark teal.

Joey didn't rush to unbuckle her seat belt. When Ethan helped her out, she shifted from one dirty bare foot to the other and hugged her bear for all she was worth. Regan slipped an arm around the girl's bony shoulders.

Maddy opened the door and came out. She was an attractive woman with long black hair and a ready smile. "Hello, Joey. My husband, Greg, is on his way home from work. That gives us plenty of time to settle you into your room, let you shower and try on the jeans and shirt my daughter Sorrel wants you to have."

Joey moved closer to Regan, a look of concern pinching her lips. "Ha...have I missed dinner?" As if to punctuate her hunger, her stomach gave a loud growl.

Maddy's smile faded. "No. We generally don't eat until seven o'clock, but I'll give you a glass of milk and a couple of oatmeal cookies right now. I'd planned beef tacos and a fruit salad for dinner. If you don't like tacos, I'll fix something else."

Joey immediately perked up. "I love tacos. Can I have two?"

"You certainly may. Three if you'd like. No one leaves our table hungry."

Joey skipped up the walk. Halfway to Maddy, she stopped, realizing Regan and Ethan hadn't followed her. "Do you gotta go?" she asked anxiously.

"Yes, Joey, we do." Regan answered. "I have a boy I still have to visit today. And I want to see if maybe I can get your mother some medicine."

"Tell her I won't forget her," Joey said in a small voice. "She's sick, you know."

Bobbing her head, Regan didn't trust her own voice.

"Her mom's sick from drinking a pint of rotgut whiskey," Ethan said, stabbing the key viciously into the ignition after they'd climbed back into the car.

"And you don't think drunks can be rehabilitated, either?" Regan challenged.

"I didn't say that. Why are you so ready to think the worst of me?"

Regan supposed she could answer him in two words—Jack Diamond. Instead, she pulled a yellow legal pad out of her briefcase and started writing.

"How would you like to stop for a cup of coffee before we go to talk with Jeremy?" Ethan asked.

"Oh. I, uh, don't think so." Regan felt hot, then cold and then hot again at the thought of sitting knee to knee with Ethan at a table.

"Come on," he wheedled. "One cup. Cops run on caffeine."

So did social workers. Regan did, in fact, feel a little low on fuel. What could it hurt to have a cup of coffee with him in a public place? "All right. You twisted my arm. But no refills. I have a lot left to do, and Odella is waiting to hear about Jeremy."

"I told you his decision. I'm surprised you didn't call her from the hospital."

"He's fifteen. He's probably changed his mind that many times since you told him goodbye," she said as Ethan swung into a parking space in front of Flo's Café.

As they went inside, it was easy to tell this was a favorite place of Ethan's. The hostess greeted him by name, as did another waitress who passed them as they were being seated. In a booth. Regan groaned inwardly. Booths placed them in much closer quarters than a table would have.

Ethan studied Regan as the waitress, daughter of a precinct captain, poured steaming cups of rich black coffee. "This guy takes his coffee leaded and so thick it stands up and walks out of the cup," the girl told Regan. "So do the guys he usually tromps in here with. He's never brought a lady before. You must be someone special. How do you take your coffee, ma'am?"

"The same as his. But with sugar." Leaning back, Regan smiled into the curious green eyes. "We're here for a quick *business* meeting." It did Regan's heart good to see the tips of Ethan's ears turn crimson. But the waitress left, clearly satisfied.

"She has a major crush on you, Detective." Regan spooned three teaspoons of sugar into the coffee. She rarely took hers black.

"Tracy is the daughter of a friend. A nosy kid. Why did you say we were here to discuss business?"

"Well, aren't we?" Shrugging, Regan raised the cup to her lips. "And surely you don't want your friend's daughter starting the rumor that I'm someone special to you."

"On a different subject," he began, "I can't help but noticing how nervous you get around my dog. Next weekend he's entered…well, he and I are entered in a search-and-rescue competition. Most events are viewed from bleachers that were built so people like you can watch service dogs in action."

"People like me?" Regan set her cup down fast.

"Yes. People who aren't really familiar with dogs or think they're only family pets. Taz saves lives. He's been trained to search disaster sites for hidden victims. His speciality is finding lost campers and hikers. If they're hurt, he locates me. If they're merely lost, he leads them to safety. Taz has personally made over a dozen rescues in the last three years."

"I'm sure he excels in his field." Regan realized the hand reaching for her coffee shook. She hastily returned the cup to its saucer. "Look, people have differing interests. I don't happen to share yours in dogs. Not even heroic dogs."

Ethan toyed with his spoon. "That's too bad. Taz is a big part of my life. I'd like to think a woman I'm interested in can accept him fully."

Regan realized she'd spilled her coffee—she'd knocked over the cup when she sprang from the booth. Seeing a stream of coffee threatening to run over the edge of the table, Regan grabbed frantically for napkins from an adjacent booth. She sopped up the coffee automatically. Her brain had gone numb.

Ethan threw down money to cover the coffee and a tip. As customers were beginning to eye them oddly, he took Regan's elbow and escorted her out.

Neither said anything until they were in the car and had traveled several blocks. Regan finally spoke. "Don't be interested in me, Ethan. We can't have more than a work-related relationship. It's simply not possible.''

''I think you're wrong,'' Ethan said clearly and succinctly, pulling over to let Regan's car idle at the curb outside the Knight home.

''It doesn't matter what you think,'' she insisted. ''I'm telling you how it has to be.''

Before Regan could unbuckle her seat belt, and before Ethan had turned off the engine and handed her the keys, he casually leaned across the seat and planted a solid kiss on her lips.

He stroked the sides of her face and softened the pressure until Regan sighed and allowed his tongue to delve between her damp lips. He took his time, wanting to make his kiss unforgettable. Ethan didn't ease up until he felt her fingers slide up his chest to touch the bare skin at the base of his throat.

Moving away slowly, Ethan smiled and ran his thumbs over her swollen bottom lip. He looked her straight in the eye. ''I'll go make sure Jeremy has Taz closed in the backyard. You look as if you need a moment to reflect on whether or not there's potential for more than a working relationship here.''

Regan's pulse danced a jig in her throat as Ethan pressed the cool keys into her sweating palm. Her nerves shattered like glass when he stepped out of the car and slammed his door, rocking the whole frame. *No.* He didn't understand the depth of her fear. Her fear of dogs, even little ones, was embedded in her bones. Any kind of personal relationship between her and a dog owner wasn't just a foolish notion, it was impossible. Not to mention all the other reasons she couldn't get involved with him—a man who obviously loved kids. A man who'd someday want a family of his own.

CHAPTER SIX

REGAN WAS TOO SHAKEN by Ethan's kiss to think about running a comb through her hair or restoring her lipstick. How she managed to find Jeremy's file and pull herself together enough to leave the car and enter the house mystified her. Yet it wasn't as if being kissed like that was an everyday occurrence. At that moment she couldn't even question why Ethan had kissed her, or why she'd allowed him to. He had, and she'd liked every second of it.

It helped that he wasn't around when she reached the house. Elaine answered Regan's knock and greeted her warmly. She immediately plied Regan with fresh-squeezed lemonade and warm shortbread cookies.

"Ethan barged through here a minute ago. He took Taz for a run," Elaine said. "He mentioned you'd be by shortly to talk with Jeremy. I believe he's in his room. Let me get him. Please, go easy on him. He's been in a quandary all afternoon."

Seated in the living room behind the coffee table, Regan felt a degree of control return. She took refuge in the normalcy of returning to business, spreading agency forms out around her; it made what had happened between her and Ethan recede into a foggy dreamlike place.

Regan rose when Jeremy clomped into the room and

threw himself onto one of the room's two recliners. "Man, I knew you'd come back before I was ready."

"I'm sorry, Jeremy. I explained that we needed to call your mother's attorney tonight. Ethan indicated you'd made up your mind."

"I had it all set in my head what I was going to do. Then I got scared and mad, and now I'm all confused." Luminous dark eyes beseeched her to bear with him.

Regan set the frosty glass of lemonade on a coaster. Picking up a pen, she rolled it between her palms. "I can try and answer any questions you might have, Jeremy. But I cannot influence your decision in any way. I'm truly sorry I can't give you more time."

"Nah. More time would only make it worse." Hunching forward, he clasped his hands between his knees. "Do you think my mom will get out before I'm twenty-one?"

Regan shrugged. "There's never any second-guessing a jury. At this point we don't know any of the circumstances surrounding the, uh, incident. If your mom acted in self-defense or if she didn't plan to, ah, fatally wound him, those are factors that affect the verdict and sentencing."

"I don't want to...you know, like, kick her when she's down." He twirled his thumbs, never raising his head. "Smith is her last name—her maiden name. She told my grandma she didn't know for sure who my dad was. That sucks, doesn't it?"

"Where's your grandmother?" Regan thumbed through the pages and found no mention of any living relative.

"She died when I was six. I have two aunts somewhere. Texas, maybe. They didn't show up for Grandma's funeral or for the hearing when the judge took me away from my mom.''

"How did you feel about that separation?" Regan probed skillfully but gently.

"I hated the people my ma hung out with. Her *friends.*" He spit the word. "They made me steal stuff. Even so, I wasn't real nice when Ethan hauled my mom off to the drunk tank and brought me here. Not the first time, anyway. In my old neighborhood, kids are real scared of cops. Especially white cops.''

Regan sipped her lemonade. She'd always found it best to let troubled kids talk through issues without interruption.

Jeremy squirmed in his chair. "At dinner Dad said he'd ask for some time off work. If I'd like to, he'll fly with me to Utah.''

"That's nice of him.'' Regan clicked her pen and jotted a note in the file. "So you think you'd like to go see your mom?"

"No. I puke every time I walk into a jail. I told Dad, if she can take calls, I'll phone and talk to her. I guess they'll have her sobered up.'' He sounded hopeful.

"I'm sure they will.'' Regan glanced discreetly at her watch. She not only needed to call Odella, it was imperative she be out of here before Ethan and his dog finished their run.

Jeremy saw her gesture. He sat up straighter and patted his knees. "You know, Mom and Dad—all my foster brothers and sisters, and Coach, too—they've tried to make me see it's what's inside a person that counts. A name by itself doesn't mean anything. It only reflects how good or bad the man who's wearing it acts. So that's my decision," he said when Regan continued to wait. "I want to leave things as they are. I'll show everybody there's some okay Smiths around," he said, lifting a shoulder partway to his ear in a modest shrug.

A smile slowly blossomed on Regan's face. "The Knights will be very proud of you, Jeremy. I certainly am. Your decision shows adult reasoning—and compassion. Do phone your mother. If you'd like," Regan said, gathering her belongings, "I'll have the court in Utah keep us up-to-date on Shontelle's case."

"I'd like that." Jeremy grinned, looking more like a fifteen-year-old again as he snagged a basketball from the corner and dribbled it to the door.

Elaine appeared behind Jeremy just as Regan was about to head down the walk. "Don't wait for a review of Jeremy's case to come back and see us again," she said. "Ethan tells me you're new in town. We have people your age drifting in and out of here every weekend. Sunday-evening meals are at six o'clock. We usually barbecue in the backyard. Feel free to show up anytime."

"Why...uh, thank you." Regan bumped her briefcase against her legs. "But work keeps me occupied, even on weekends. Anyway, I wouldn't want to intrude on family gatherings."

"Nonsense," Elaine chided.

"Let Ethan ask her," Regan heard Jeremy's exaggerated whisper. "Don't you know he's got the hots for her, Mom?"

"Jeremy!" Elaine shushed him. "Pay no attention to him," she said. "He's at the age where he's discovered girls. Now he thinks every member of the family who's single ought to be making cow eyes at the opposite sex."

"Well, Amy and Ethan need to speed things up," Jeremy proclaimed, giving his foster mom a grin. "Last night I heard you tell Dad you think Ethan likes Regan, uh, Ms. Grant.''

Not wanting to hear more, Regan forced a laugh. ''Concentrate on schoolwork and basketball, Jeremy. Forget girls and matchmaking. My job makes my life too complicated for the type of relationship you're imagining. Bye, now. Take care. Call if I can be of further service.''

When she got into her car, Regan discovered her hands were shaking. Silly. Ethan had killed any romantic chance for them by reaffirming the importance of his dog. Pursuing anything personal was futile. Digging out her cell phone, Regan deliberately put the Knight family out of her mind as she dialed Odella.

They talked business for a few minutes, and then Regan turned her attention to navigating the busy streets. It was well after dark by the time she swung past her office and wrote up a preliminary report on Joey Hawkins and a final follow-up on Jeremy Smith.

She checked with the precinct and found out that Joey's mother had indeed been drunk when they went out to pick up Chip. Too drunk to care that her daughter had been placed in foster care. The charges against Chip were based on Regan's taped interview with Joey. Of course, the tape was inadmissible in court, so holding him for long was out of the question. He'd been assigned a public defender who probably wouldn't get around to visiting him before morning. If they were lucky, Chip would spend a couple of days behind bars to reflect on his behavior before he made bail and went back to his abusive ways. And he would. Before that happened, could Regan remove Joey more permanently from harm?

Probably not. She dropped her chin and massaged throbbing temples. All these years in the business, and she still didn't see why judges felt it incumbent upon them to return kids to bad parents.

She sighed. Hers was not to reason why, but to render aid when possible. Shaking off her melancholy feelings, Regan shut down her computer. She was in no mood to visit Joey's mother tonight. Everything considered, seeing her tomorrow would probably be more beneficial.

It was ten o'clock by the time when Regan climbed the stairs to her apartment. Not surprisingly, she found herself too tired to think about preparing dinner. A hot bath appealed more than food.

She switched on her disk player and let a Celtic instrumental fill the room. She resisted pouring a glass of wine. Coming home late to an empty apartment after a trying day often triggered a deep sense of loneliness. If she'd learned anything from her job, it was that people who drank to lift their spirits had it all wrong. Alcohol exacerbated depression, it didn't relieve it. Warm baths, sweet tea and videos of some old 40s comedies were Regan's preferred methods for beating the blues. She didn't want to examine too closely her reasons for feeling blue—although she admitted that on this particular occasion, Ethan Knight had played a part.

REFRESHED AFTER A FULL NIGHT'S sleep, Regan rose early the next morning. She stepped out on her small balcony, an eye-opening cup of coffee in hand. The dark eastern sky was tinted with lavender and orange threads. A perfect morning for a five-mile run around the school track. Running always cleared her head for the trials of a busy workday.

Floodlights were still on at the track when she arrived. As Regan crawled out of the car and began her stretching exercise, she heard a dog bark. It didn't sound close.

She'd just never heard one here before. Frowning, she tugged at the headband she used to keep her hair subdued. There were no houses near the track, which sat between the main school building and the football field. Bleachers bisected the oval.

A stray dog could have wandered onto the campus. Regan shivered and paused in her stretches to rub away the gooseflesh on her arms. Strays were the most worrisome of all dogs. They were totally unpredictable.

An elderly woman dressed in navy sweats jogged slowly past the parked cars. She lifted a hand to acknowledge Regan and continued on to make another revolution around the track. Regan saw the woman almost every morning. She certainly hadn't acted as if the track held anything out of the ordinary.

Shrugging off her silly apprehension, Regan started slowly. Little by little she drifted into her normal stride. Approximately one mile into the two-mile circuit, she rounded the corner and saw the dark silhouette of a man running toward her. At his side loped a very large dog. Regan's steps faltered. Her chest heaved from exertion, but she stumbled and stopped, trying to catch her breath. Frantically she hunted for cover, but there was none. They would meet on a clear stretch of track.

The runner broke his own stride as he drew near Regan. He stopped adjacent to her. By then she was too frozen in fright to see what he looked like. Her eyes were trained on the animal trotting beside him.

"Regan?" The deep male voice slipped through a pulsing haze of fear.

Ethan had identified Regan the moment she came around the curve. He'd kept his eyes pealed for her. She was the sole reason he'd selected this particular track for his early-morning workout. Now, seeing her fright,

Ethan kicked himself. A word in Dutch sent Taz streaking back to the SUV. The dog would sit there forever unless Ethan gave him counter instructions.

The minute Taz was out of sight, Ethan walked up to Regan. He took her carefully by the upper arms and pulled her against him. Making soothing sounds in his throat, Ethan slid his hands to her back, then lightly massaged her shoulder blades until her teeth stopped chattering.

A man loped past, and then a woman doing a fast power walk. Both eyed the couple. The woman turned to glance back. She was apparently mollified by the police insignia on Ethan's T-shirt and shorts.

It was about then that Regan grew aware of her surroundings. The man's eyes remained on them, so she eased herself out of Ethan's arms, not wanting to attract further attention.

He didn't let her go completely. Instead, his hands slipped back to her elbows. From there he slid them down her arms. "God, Regan, I'm sorry for looming out of the dark like that. I tried phoning after you'd left the folks' house to ask if we could meet here this morning. When I didn't reach you, I got busy with other things. Suddenly it was midnight and too late to call. Odella mentioned that you jog here most days, so I took a chance and showed up, hoping I'd run into you. Now that I've thoroughly ruined our workout, how about we go someplace for coffee? I'd like to know why you shut down completely at the mere sight of Taz. I assure you he's harmless. He'd never hurt a hair on your head."

Regan made the separation complete. She'd only heard about half of what Ethan said. She wanted to laugh hysterically at his remark about Taz being harmless. He could have been a Chihuahua and her reaction would have been the same.

"At the police academy they taught us the only way to combat fear was to face and conquer whatever caused it."

She did laugh this time. Bitterly. "I'm not a child, Ethan. Do you think I haven't tried to overcome my fear of dogs? Nothing works. I can't even stand to look at a picture of one. Better psychoanalysts than you have failed to cure me—if cure is the right word. So forget it, Ethan. Forget me." She moved around him and started to jog away.

He clamped a hand around her wrist and for a moment kept pace. "That sounds a lot like a challenge, Regan. As my family or anyone on the force can tell you…the bigger the challenge, the more I dig in. We can start slow. What if you came to Taz's competition next weekend and just watched what he can do?" Ethan named a location on the outskirts of town. "Bring field glasses. You can see the dogs work from a distance. It's a first step," he said. "Watch as much or as little as you can handle. Take dogs in small doses. You can overcome anything if you try."

"Why do you persist?" She almost stamped her foot, the man exasperated her so.

Ethan drew the knuckles of his right hand slowly down her left cheek. "Darned if I can tell you." He really did appear stymied.

"Well, I don't want to be your *challenge,* detective. So buzz off." Kick starting herself, Regan left him staring after her as she pounded around the next bend.

Why *did* he persist? Ethan wondered, hooking his thumbs negligently into the pockets of his shorts. Then Regan breezed around the next curve and a newly risen sun made a halo of her streaming blond hair. Sun-kissed limbs, long and straight, pumped fluidly, reminding Ethan of a loping tigress. Or more like a frightened gazelle, fleeing a predator. Her beauty, her vulnerability, his sense of passions that lay beneath the surface—were these the reasons he pursued her when she'd made it quite clear she didn't want to be pursued? Ethan wasn't sure. He only knew that Regan Grant heated his blood as no woman had in years.

He liked women and had tried to get serious over one or two. Especially during the past five years. The more weddings he attended, the more acutely he felt odd man out at functions and parties. And he'd backed out of a few casual relationships when he'd realized he was being pushed toward the church by well-meaning family and friends.

Admittedly Ethan had known Regan Grant—what? A week? And yet he already lay awake at night picturing what she'd look like at sixty or seventy or eighty. Mostly though, he wondered if he could somehow erase the haunted look that filled her beautiful wary eyes. Why he felt a calling to do that was anybody's guess. Just now, as he jogged slowly back to the SUV and Taz, he doubted he'd ever succeed.

REGAN APPROACHED the parking lot with caution. She was familiar with Ethan Knight's dirty black vehicle. How had she missed it earlier? The answer was obvious. She hadn't been looking for it. She'd run this track three or four mornings a week for several weeks now and had never seen Ethan or his dog.

"Good," she mumbled half under her breath. It appeared he'd taken the hint and gone. She'd issued more than a hint, really. Regan felt a twinge of guilt over how

curt she'd acted. Ethan wasn't Jack Diamond. She had
to keep that in mind. Frankly, she couldn't envision Jack
or any of his cop buddies spending their own money on
a child like Joey. Oh, they'd do their job to the letter.
Jack would have taken Joey to the station, where he'd
assign an underling the task of calling Family Assistance. Jack would have written a neat short report. Regan
doubted very much—no, she *knew* Jack would never
have questioned the child himself. He'd have left it up
to someone else. If anyone chanced to break through to
the kid, it wouldn't have been Jack. He'd have been long
gone to another case. In terms of the number of cases
closed, Jack Diamond looked like a good cop—but he
was insensitive. He didn't care about the human cost of
crime and neglect. Ethan was his exact opposite, which
made it difficult for Regan to walk away and not think
about him afterward. She thought about him too much.

As she left the track and went home to shower and
dress for work, he was still on her mind. At least two of
her therapists had dispensed the same advice as Ethan.
To conquer fear, a person has to face it head on. Not
new information, by any means. It sounded different
coming from a man who wasn't being paid to analyze
her.

Regan turned off the shower and grabbed a towel. She
stepped out, naked, and in front of a full-length mirror.
The scars always looked their worst after a dip in hot
water. The ones below her breast, at her waist and upper
thigh, still in need of plastic surgery, stood out now, ropy
and ugly. Her throat ached as it always did when she
thought about the internal damage she'd suffered.

Regan whirled away from the damning exposure, and
with hands not entirely steady, smoothed cream over the
whole mess. Cream kept the scars supple. Otherwise

they hardened and itched, even after so many years. If she started thinking about the attack, it seemed like yesterday. An unwise and unproductive exercise.

Hurriedly she stepped into the silk-and-lace underwear she'd bought to help combat her dissatisfaction with the appearance of her body. After blow-drying her hair and pinning it into a twist, Regan dressed in one of her many suits. Today's was black, teamed with a royal-blue silk shell. She clipped on a wide gold herringbone necklace and gold knot earrings. Then she remembered her first appointment—Joey Hawkins's mother. Regan switched from the silk shell to a pale-pink cotton blouse with a collar. She felt that dressing less affluently was just more respectful toward families who had so little in the way of material goods.

On the drive to the neglected area of town where Mrs. Hawkins lived, Regan tried to decide what she'd say. Unfortunately her thoughts rambled backward to her meeting with Ethan earlier. What he'd said about watching working dogs at a safe distance intrigued her. Nagged her. The rational side of Regan's brain knew some dogs saved people. Some went into burning buildings and found victims. Others sniffed through earthquake rubble and rescued survivors. Still others were companions to the blind and disabled. Maybe if she focused on the good they did—she'd never approached her phobia from that angle before. She'd try anything. She hated living with this stupid debilitating fear.

Regan knew Jack thought she used her impairment as a crutch to get sympathy. He'd said so often enough after he'd moved into her apartment.

She shook her head to rid herself of the past. What Jack assumed to be true didn't matter. Ethan intuitively recognized that she needed to go through a step-by-step process.

Before she reached the Hawkins house, Regan had talked herself into attending the dog competition. Next weekend, Ethan had said. Having decided on a positive first step, Regan felt a mixture of pride and fright, even as she parked in front of a run-down duplex and checked in all directions, making sure no dogs were running loose in the neighborhood. She'd been greatly hampered in her work by this unnatural fear. The indigent seemed to have an abundance of children and pets and, frequently both lacked care.

There was no rule in the rule book that said she needed to visit Mrs. Hawkins in her home. Regan could have asked the woman to come to her office. It was her own preference to see a client's living conditions whenever possible.

Her knock at the sagging front door was slow in being answered. When finally a bleary-eyed woman yanked open the door, Regan saw that Joey's mom hadn't sobered up from yesterday. She already had a drink in her hand. At 9 a.m., Regan noted, holding her business card steady for the swaying woman to read.

"So you're the bitch who took my kid away and had my guy tossed in the slammer?" She wagged a glass half-filled with amber liquid under Regan's nose. Regan recoiled from the pungent smell.

"I'd throw this in your face, but there's no sense wasting good booze. I'm telling you now I want my kid back home today. You get her. You have no right to separate a ma from her daughter. Or from the man who puts food on their table."

"Mrs. Hawkins, you can call me all the names you like. I do have the right to keep Joey in custody. In this state, a child's right to a safe environment takes precedence over a familial relationship."

The woman erupted in sobs. "I don't understand,"

she whined. "You got all this fancy talk. What's it mean? I went through the pain of birthing that kid. That gives me rights. She owes me—she has to take care of me when I'm sick."

"And you *are* sick, Mrs. Hawkins. No one in Family Assistance will deny that. But Joey's too young to cope with taking care of you, plus the household duties and going to school," Regan said in a gentler voice.

The woman gripped the glass in both hands and began to shake. "When I was Joey's age, I took care of Pa and my two younger brothers. Then Pa was kilt in the mine. I quit school and raised those boys. For all the thanks I get. They wouldn't give me the time of day when Joey's dad run off. Me and Joey lived in a packing crate out behind a joint called the Watering Hole until one day Chip came out back to take a whiz and found us. Took us home for a good meal. He's not all bad. It's only since he got laid off that me and Joey've been gettin' on his nerves."

Regan stepped inside the three-room hovel. A wobbly kitchen table tilted under the weight of empty beer cans and liquor bottles. Three cartons of unopened cigarettes sat on the kitchen counter amid filthy dishes. "How does a man who isn't working afford beer, whiskey and cigarettes?" Regan knew, of course. Lucy Hawkins's family-assistance folder said she received aid for having a dependent child. Money meant to provide for Joey went to feed Lucy and Chip's addictions.

"Mrs. Hawkins, the state will care for Joey until you can clean up your act and get on your feet. We'll help you get sober and enroll you in a program designed to train you for a job. You have to want that enough to come into my office and ask for help. Our address is on my card. Come before the end of the week and I'll pay for your cab fare. Joey loves you," Regan said as she turned to leave. "By the way, does she know either of her uncles?"

"No. Leave Freddy and William outta this. Their bitchy wives think their kids are too good for my Joey." Mrs Hawkins clung to the door frame, too drunk, apparently, to stand on her own. She finally did pull herself up straight and looked Regan in the eye. "I got off booze once before, for a while. Reckon I'll try again for my kid. If you'll help me."

Regan smiled, went back and curved a hand around the woman's wrist. Her dry skin was a consequence of the constant drinking, which left her looking a decade older than twenty-nine, the age listed in her file. "You can count on me."

Regan left feeling better. She glanced at her watch. Joey should be in school by now. Regan wanted to pay her new teacher a visit, anyway. She'd tell Joey her mom was going to try to make things better. Regan had been in the business too long to make firm promises. Especially in cases where the outlook was as dim as it was in Lucy Hawkins's case.

As a backup measure, Regan popped a new tape in her recorder and left a voice note to herself to locate Fred and William Hawkins. One rule the state did have was to keep families together whenever possible. That meant involving aunts, uncles and grandparents if necessary.

The remainder of the week passed in a blur. Regan had spent two days searching for an organization willing to assist little Wendy Brewster with her out-of-state surgery—and she'd succeeded. Her foster parents had cried with joy.

Ethan phoned Thursday to tell Regan his co-workers had made a good case against Chip for possession and dealing drugs. The judge had sentenced him to an automatic five years.

"Ethan, that's wonderful news." Regan sat back in her office chair and wound the phone cord around her index finger. It was good hearing Ethan's deep voice and picturing how he looked, so big and solid. And he was genuinely interested in the fact that Joey's mother had promised to come into the agency, although she hadn't yet.

"Mitch and I are winding up an investigation of a crack house we closed down across from Desert City's largest high school. It's not far from where Mrs. Hawkins lives. I'll be glad to drop by on the pretext of informing her about old Chipper. Maybe I can get a feel for whether or not she's still thinking of getting help."

"Would you do that?" Regan bit her lip. "This isn't an official follow-up for me, Ethan. So don't give Lucy the impression we're working together."

"Okay. But what's wrong with exchanging information? Anna called on the cops to help her out all the time. Not just me, either."

"What's wrong is that our agencies technically have no connection. They provide different services. Your job is to put criminals away. Ours is to pick up the pieces for the families and victims they leave behind."

"So what doesn't connect? Seems to me they go hand in glove."

"I don't think your chief and my boss see it that way. But in this one instance only, I'd be glad to exchange information." She paused. "Mrs. Hawkins has a brother living in a neighboring town. I may have to pressure him into taking responsibility for Joey. She has another uncle, but he moved to Iowa. I'd prefer not to ship her out-of-state to strangers."

"Why would you have to? She's thriving at Maddy and Greg's."

"Our studies show it's better not to distance a child from an extended family. It appears that you and I may not agree on that philosophy. Ethan, I have to go. I've got a call coming in on another line. Can we talk later?"

"Sure. How about if I take you out to dinner tonight?"

"No. I, uh, can't tonight. We have a policy meeting scheduled with our part-time counselors."

"Damn. And I can't tomorrow night. I'll be getting my gear ready to camp out with Taz over the weekend."

He dangled the information like a carrot in front of a horse. Regan wanted to tell him she planned to attend the Sunday portion of the event, which she'd discovered was billed as a regional Schutzhund. But if in the end she broke down and decided not to go, she didn't want him to accuse her of chickening out. "I have to hang up. Goodbye," she said distinctly, then ended the call without waiting for his answering farewell.

All afternoon she imagined what it would be like to go out to dinner with Ethan. She wondered if he was a shake-and-burger man, or if when he asked a woman out, he used the meal as a setup for seduction. Picturing them seated in an intimate booth at a place known for candlelight and elegance sent shivers up her spine. And a hot flush to her cheeks—which Odella mentioned when she dropped by Regan's office to tell her that Shontelle Waters, Jeremy Smith's mother, was being charged with murder one. "Her attorney plans to plead self-defense."

"Did you ask if Jeremy could phone Shontelle?"

"I did," Odella replied, "and the answer is yes. I passed the information on to Elaine via Ethan. I hope that was all right."

Regan rubbed a pen between her palms. A habit she had when she felt her nerves drawing tight.

"It's not, I can tell. So flog me," Odella said, extending both bared arms.

"Odella, discretion isn't *my* rule. It's agency practice. We owe allegiance to our clients."

"I finally got a call-back from the Utah public defender at home this morning. On my way to work, I stopped at a convenience store for coffee and ran into Ethan and Mitch. He was picking up a gallon of milk for Elaine. It seemed to me I was saving time—and as a result, saving the agency money."

"I know the temptation to cut corners is great. We're all so busy. Swamped is more like it." She picked up a sheaf of papers from her desk and fanned them out like playing cards. "I got six memos from Nathaniel this week on keeping a lid on agency spending. And three on not letting other departments within the system send us clients. It's all part of a current state-wide push to cut welfare spending."

"Been there, done that," Odella quipped. "Nobody asked me," she said before sailing out the door, "but I say the machine would run smoother with more inter-agency cooperation, not less." She paused, half in, half out of Regan's door. "Are you interested in going on a hike in the Catalina foothills this weekend?"

Regan turned the idea over in her mind. Odella had just offered her the perfect excuse for skipping the competition of hated dogs. But somewhere inside her head hammered an insistent message—*coward, coward, coward.* "Another time, Odella." Regan smiled. "I already have plans. If you want to go the Saturday after this, I'm free." She hauled out her day planner and opened it to the third week in March.

"It's a date. I'll go through my book of day hikes and

phone you back with a time and place to meet, if that's all right. Are you up to a grade three or four climb?''

Laughing, Regan flexed her muscles. ''Like a mountain goat, lady.''

''Then let's do it.'' Odella closed the door on her delighted laughter.

Regan sat for a time doing nothing other than enjoying the fact that she seemed to be creating a niche for herself in the community. Odella had kept after her to do something she enjoyed. A nice man had asked her out—so what if she'd turned him down? His mother had invited her to come for a barbecue. Plus, she and Carla Rodriguez, Jeremy's principal, were meeting tomorrow night for that glass of wine.

Spinning circles in her chair, Regan hugged herself. Things in her life were definitely looking up. Sunday, at the Schutzhund, she might work up enough nerve to hang around and talk to Ethan. To tell him she'd decided to collect on her rain check for that dinner. Surely he wouldn't take his dog along on a date—would he?

MIDMORNING SUNDAY after Regan had left her hair loose and worn her best designer jeans and brightest red shirt to enhance her normally pale coloring—all to impress Ethan Knight—she got the surprise of her life. When she pulled into the parking lot, their agency receptionist, Nicole Mason, was the first person Regan saw. The girl had Ethan backed against his unwashed SUV. Her arms were twined around his neck. His hands were flat against Nicole's curvaceous butt. He seemed to be laughing uproariously at something the girl had said.

Regan thought *girl* because Nicole wasn't more than twenty-one if she was a day. And here Regan was, attending today's shindig at the man's request, in spite of her own screaming nerves. Now this!

Regan refastened her seat belt with one hand and reached for the Honda key with the other. She intended to slip away before either of the pair saw her. Nicole certainly wasn't paying attention to her surroundings. She only had eyes for Ethan. Unfortunately he glanced up, over Nicole's shapely back, and spotted her. Unwrapping himself from the young woman, he set her aside and literally ran across the lot. He jerked open Regan's car door.

"Well, hello," he said in a breathless husky voice. "This is a surprise. I must say you're the last person I expected to see." Deftly Ethan slid his arm across Regan's entrapped body and extracted the key from the ignition.

His words slapped life back into Regan. "No kidding," she said in a tone drier than the surrounding desert. She might have said more, but Nicole had followed her man and again had him in a possessive wrap. Her eyes dared Regan to lay any claim.

Regan, who reminded herself that she'd had her fill of cop Casanovas, would have dived off a cliff before she let on in front of a staff member that she was here for any reason other than to see the dogs—an activity that in itself might just force her over a cliff. From where she sat she could see five handlers lined up with five massive dogs.

It helped to remember Ethan's audacity in inviting two women. Nonetheless Regan had to concentrate hard to keep from upchucking her breakfast all over him and his companion.

CHAPTER SEVEN

ETHAN SKIMMED Regan's outfit with frank masculine approval. It was his spontaneous smile that eventually coaxed her from her car.

"Ms. Grant?" Nicole, who'd wiggled underneath one of Ethan's splayed arms, dashed a disbelieving glance between the two.

Regan threaded a loose curl behind her ear and mumbled, "Away from the office, please call me Regan."

"Really? Uh, Regan, then. What are you doing here?"

She started to say that was a good question when Ethan grabbed her hand. Sounding as possessive as the action implied, he said quite simply, "I invited her."

"Why?" Judging by her demeanor, Nicole was dumbfounded.

Regan's impulsive laughter sputtered.

Ethan didn't seem in the least flustered at having two dates. He refused to let Regan pull free of his grasp, only wrapped their fingers tighter and drew her against his side as he shut her car door. "Regan's here as my guest, Nikki."

"But...but you invited me." The purple-shadowed eyes clouded in confusion.

"I don't believe I did. Not in so many words. Schutzhunds are open to the public. And this time the *Desert City Daily* ran a schedule of events." He glanced at the rapidly filling bleachers. "It's great to see a good turn-out. Dogs are like kids—they like to show off in front of an audience."

Regan finally managed to escape Ethan. "I'd better go grab a seat. I want to sit in the top row. That way I'll, uh, have a view of the whole field."

Attuned to her sudden nervousness, Ethan knew Regan wanted to sit as far away from the animals as possible. It was equally evident that she wanted to hide her feelings from Nicole. "Regan, did you bring binoculars?" Ethan asked.

"No." She shrugged. "I forgot I might need them. Well, maybe I'll skip today's event and catch another one in the future." She tugged her car keys from Ethan's hand and reached around him to unlock her door.

Just as quickly, he slipped a hand over the lock. "Hold on. I have an extra set of field glasses in the Suzuki. Come with me and I'll get them for you." He'd already turned her in the direction of his vehicle.

"I need binoculars, too," Nicole said petulantly.

"Go ask Mitch for a pair. I see he's got both a long-and short-range set hanging around his neck." Ethan pointed. "He's over there jawing with Captain Broderick from the Coronado Police Dog Squad."

Nicole seemed to brighten visibly at the prospect of talking to the obscenely good-looking Detective Valetti. Fluttering her fingers, she set off.

"Go catch her," Regan urged Ethan. "I really don't know why I'm here. I'm sure it's a huge mistake."

"Not." He grinned, careful to open his back hatch with one hand and extract a pair of small beige binoculars the same way. "For the record, I didn't invite Nicky Mason to come today. I did ask her to one in the past. She makes a fuss over Taz whenever we visit Family Assistance. She and Anna spoiled him rotten with treats.''

Regan accepted the field glasses with a frown. ''Did I ask for an explanation?''

''No, but I saw how you looked at Nicky and me. Some women are demonstrative. Nicole's one of them.''

''Woman?'' Regan snorted. ''If she's old enough to drink, I'd be surprised.''

One of Ethan's dark eyebrows rose to meet a lock of hair that had fallen over his brow. ''Ask her and she'll tell you she's cursed with a perpetually young face. Actually, she graduated from college with my sister Amy. Poli-sci majors,'' he drawled. ''Amy's a police dispatcher and Nicole a receptionist for CHC. Anyway, they're both twenty-eight,'' he finished, expelling a puff of air.

''You're making that up.'' Narrowing her eyes, Regan watched the antics of the shapely redhead, who was now openly flirting with Ethan's partner.

''Swear to God.'' Ethan solemnly raised his hand. ''If you don't believe me, I'll take you over and introduce you to Amy. One of her girlfriends has a big Rottweiler named Rambo entered in competition today.''

Regan felt the blood drain from her head at the thought of a dog named Rambo. Again she questioned her sanity in coming to this event. ''I'll, uh, take your word for Nicole's age. I really wasn't looking at you and her with any…disapproval, Ethan. You're both free to date anyone you choose. It doesn't matter to me.''

Ethan found himself wishing it *did* matter to her. That *he* mattered. But of course it was too soon in the relationship to make any remark to that effect. She was skittish as a captured bird. The slightest comment could send her into flight. He thought it meant something that she'd shown up today; he'd take heart in that.

She started to speak, and Ethan held up a staying hand. "They're calling Taz's class. I guess the first-level dogs are headed into the second phase of their event. That's the search-and-rescue test. Out here in front of the bleachers you'll see the endurance tests. Stair climbs, drainpipe excursions, sniffing techniques, ability to fetch and a lot of other tasks demonstrating physical fitness. Oh, also how steady a dog remains under gunfire."

"The series of pops I heard earlier. Was that gunfire?"

"Yes. Go ahead and find a seat. Taz and I are both going to wear the number forty. That way you can pick us out in the field. From this distance, all Alsatians and handlers will look pretty much the same."

"Alsatian?"

"German shepherd is the more common name. The dogs bred and trained in Holland have better dispositions."

Regan didn't want to hear about any dog's disposition. Turning abruptly, she struck out for the bleachers, calling over her shoulder, "The announcer said that was the final call for dogs and handlers in Schutzhund II. You'd better go."

"Yeah." Ethan frowned after her. "The whole series of events takes two or more hours. Level III is after ours. Those are the older, more experienced trackers and protector animals. When they finish, the awards will be presented. I'm sure Taz will place again in level II, so…I'll see you after the trophies are handed out."

Waving backward at him, Regan continued toward the bleachers. She could feel the nerves in the back of her neck beginning to tighten. She already regretted her reckless decision to come today. Nicole's presence was the only thing keeping Regan from bolting right now. She wouldn't have the receptionist speculating on the reasons for her hasty departure. After the debacle with Jack, Regan had been on the receiving end of office talk in Phoenix. It had been most unpleasant. She didn't know precisely how—probably through Jack shooting off his mouth—but staff there had learned about her unreasonable fear of dogs. For weeks until she received the offer for the position in Desert City, co-workers had eyed her and whispered. Some assumed her phobia stretched to other areas. Areas that might affect her work. That was false, because her fears were confined to one thing—dogs. However, because she found it so difficult to talk about those fears, it made convincing others next to impossible.

Ethan kept Regan in sight as he wound his way through the crowd to get Taz out of his crate. True to her word, she climbed to the bleachers' top row and sat there all alone. Most spectators who came to Schutzhund competitions wanted to be closer to the dogs. Regan hadn't asked about Taz's whereabouts. But she was here, he kept reminding himself. That said a lot.

From the highest point in the stands, Regan surveyed the mix of people who'd given up a free day to come and watch demonstrations by dogs named Spike, Lobo, Goliath and even one called Homicide. Not everyone in the audience was dressed casually in jeans. There were several men in white shirts, ties and suits. An occasional woman in a dress. In general there were eighty percent more men than women. Regan lifted the binoculars to her eyes, gazing at the other spectators. Even while she tried not to notice the dogs, a gorgeously slender, dark-haired woman in her mid to late twenties, strode confi-

dently through the crowd, making a beeline for Ethan.
It wasn't until the two had hugged, exchanged an enthu-
siastic kiss and the woman wearing the to-die-for gray
silk pants suit was greeted no less effusively by Ethan's
partner Mitch, that Regan saw the woman resembled
Ethan. She was younger than the three of Ethan's siblings who served as foster parents.

Regan mentally sorted through the photos she'd
looked at on Elaine Knight's walls. The only two Knight
sisters Regan hadn't met were Katherine and Amy. Due
to the familiar way Mitch Valetti touched her while flirting outrageously with Nicole, Regan decided it had to
be Ethan's unmarried sister, Amy.

Regan already knew from Mitch's impulsive action in
grabbing and kissing *her,* a complete stranger, that he
was the audacious sort. Still, she doubted he'd be so free
with Ethan's married sisters. She wondered why it was
that some men, like Ethan and his partner, touched people so unselfconsciously. Others, her father, for instance,
had difficulty demonstrating any sort of affection. Regan
used to wonder how he'd managed to have babies with
two women. She didn't recall ever seeing him hug her
mother or her stepmom. Her half sister, Blair, had joked
about it once. She said she thought they'd found her in
a pumpkin patch.

Regan realized she was stalling—using an interest in
the crowd to avoid looking at the dogs. She deliberately
raised the binoculars to her eyes once again and sought
out Ethan and Taz. As the glasses brought the row of
salivating dogs practically into her lap, a wave of diz-
ziness and nausea gripped Regan so hard she thought for
a minute she'd tumble out of her seat. It was at that point
she discovered something stronger than the all-
encompassing fear of dogs—fear of disgracing herself in

front of a co-worker, and Ethan's family and friends. She almost laughed at the picture reeling inside her head and gave thanks to whatever bit of vanity allowed her to maintain her seat, however shakily.

Once she got past the initial shock and successfully wrestled her demons into submission, she derived some satisfaction in studying the field of hated dogs, knowing she was well out of their reach.

Taz had a thick pretty coat of fur, and a *happy* face. Regan didn't know how else to describe him, as opposed to the more brutal-looking Rottweiler. Next to Taz sat a gold-colored dog with a wide head and sleek fur. A yellow Lab she heard someone below her say. The animal appeared calm except for a slight wag of its tail. Regan decided to focus on Taz, the Lab and their handlers.

If her binoculars lingered too long on Ethan, she didn't think anyone could blame her; certainly no woman would. Ethan Knight looked about as good in jeans, boots and a lumberjack shirt as any man had a right to look. The way his dark hair glinted in the sunlight practically begged a woman to run her fingers through it, particularly the back section he wore a little too long for regulation police cuts. Regan found his hands appealing, too. They were broad and tanned and masculine. Strong and capable, yet not rough against her skin. Gentle and soothing, too, when he picked up Joey and consoled her.

Moving the glasses back up to Ethan's face, Regan noticed a small scar in the laugh lines curving around his mouth. A devilishly seductive mouth. He'd probably learned how to use it to his advantage about the time he learned to walk. A fatal result when combined with thick-lashed eyes so deep a blue a woman could lose herself in them.

Surprisingly Regan felt the slow-climbing heat of womanly interest blanket the fear that had shaken her only moments before. Wryly she tried to figure out which reaction was worse. Being scared of dogs or falling for another cop, especially a cop who owned a dog. A really stupid thing to do.

Facing up to the truth—that her heart skipped into a mating dance whenever Ethan Knight came into view or into her mind—Regan did some serious thinking while sitting alone atop those bleachers.

The tests starting on the soccer-sized field below distracted her briefly. Handlers made the dogs sit and heel on and off a lead rope. The animals retrieved and carried heavy dumbbells over one-meter jumps and six-foot walls. They worked without voice instruction. At the conclusion of the obedience section, the announcer said that protection tests and then tracking would follow.

The first pair to perform in the protection phase was a huge Rottweiler and his female handler. The handler looked so small Regan wasn't sure she could watch.

It ought to have occurred to her to leave the minute a helper placed a row of realistic-looking dummies in the center of the field. When the handler's slight hand twitch sent the dog off to attack the dummy, Regan swallowed a panicked scream and dropped Ethan's field glasses. A man standing below her picked them up and handed them back. Her fingers shook so hard she had difficulty grasping them.

The man, stocky and gray-haired, shaded his eyes and gazed sympathetically at Regan. "This must be your first time at a Schutzhund event." When Regan all but toppled from her perch, the man climbed up and took a seat beside her. He steadied her, placing an impersonal hand on her shoulder.

"I'm a retired police-dog handler," he said in undertones. "Schutzhund protection tests are the most misunderstood by the general public. What's important out there—" he pointed, and in spite of bile clawing at her throat, Regan followed the line of his finger "—is the relationship of dog to handler. Not only are Schutzhund dogs trained to attack criminals swiftly on command, they must stop without hesitation at a single command issued by the handler. Only Schutzhund-trained dogs are under the absolute control of their owner. It takes complete trust between dog and man, or in this case woman." He laughed.

The words registered with Regan; however, some part of her couldn't get past her shock at the initial attack. She felt each shake the Rottweiler gave the dummy. Fear churned in her stomach and she fought screams begging to erupt.

"Hey, you're as white as a mountain blizzard."

The man's voice came to Regan from a distance, through a massive ringing in her ears. She'd been stupid, stupid, stupid to think she could deal with something like this. Like she was stupid to dream anything more could develop between her and Ethan Knight.

She tried to stand, but her legs responded like Play-Doh.

"Let me help you," the retired police officer said kindly. "Over the years I owned three different Schutzhund-trained dogs. My wife quit coming to these events because she never got used to this part of the test. You'll feel better if you get down and walk around. Come back to watch the tracking. The dogs have to find people stashed in ravines or deep in the trees. The dogs are only allowed a single sniff of an article of clothing. Tracking can be the most satisfying part of the test," he murmured. "We all like to hear about lost kids being found alive, or strayed hunters and campers."

"Thank you," Regan finally managed to blurt out after the stranger guided her to the ground. She didn't tell him that she wasn't planning to return for the tracking event. She felt she'd accomplished a major feat, just standing erect and walking to her car through a crush of people, as if she were out for a simple stroll.

She didn't feel safe again until she was seated at her kitchen counter, hands wrapped around a cup of hot tea. It was only when she slid the cup toward her and felt it clink against metal that she realized she'd walked off with Ethan's binoculars. The man who'd retrieved them from the ground, the retired policeman, must have looped the strap around her neck. The fact that she'd driven all the way home and made tea without noticing they hung around her neck showed how terrified she'd been.

"Well, it's over now," she muttered, wrenching the strap over her head. She'd take them to work with her on Monday and ask Nicole to get them back to Ethan, certain that the younger woman would be glad of the excuse to see him.

The sweet herb tea worked its magic. It warmed the cold pit in Regan's stomach and settled her nausea. But she'd been left with a vague restless energy, which she put to use doing domestic chores she often avoided until they could be avoided no more.

First she cleaned her refrigerator. Then she went shopping to fill it. Grocery shopping was never high on her list, especially when she got home late from work. Food rarely appealed when she was so tired.

Once she'd stored her purchases, she tackled her least favorite chore, cleaning the bathroom. Even after that she couldn't sit still. She vacuumed, then washed her windows until they gleamed. By then the sun was little more than shreds of orange and pink clinging to the mountaintops visible from her balcony.

Regan paused in her frenzy of cleaning to watch the color fade away. It was the time of day she liked best. Sunset. Some people claimed sunrises in the desert were more beautiful. Regan preferred the hot colors at day's end. Besides, she was always too busy in the mornings. Even on the track during her workout, her mind was racing ahead toward work.

She lingered at the sliding glass door until the sun was little more than a faint glow on the horizon. Deciding she'd depleted her energy, she put away her cleaning supplies and ran a steamy bubble bath. As she sank into the water, it occurred to her that this was one of life's pleasures she'd given up during her sojourn with Jack. He'd been perpetually restless. Never liked staying home. Jack made plans to be on the go every minute they weren't working. Hiking, boating, bar-hopping, eating out. The only thing he liked to do at home—other than sleep—happened in bed. Now that she'd analyzed how she'd let Jack change her habits—form her into the woman he wanted, not the woman she was—Regan vowed never to let that happen again. She knew there were things about herself that needed fixing. But she wouldn't correct them to please a man.

Sinking deeper into the aromatic water, she wondered if that was why she'd gone to Ethan's competition today. To please him. After thorough deliberation, she decided no, she had needed to see if she was ready for that next step. Which obviously she wasn't.

The water had begun to cool by the time she stopped thinking about the day. She supposed that, she'd sat and looked fear in the eye for a good hour and a half. And she'd come out unscathed.

Regan had no more than dried off and slipped into her underwear when she heard her front doorbell chime. *Was* it hers? She knew so few people in Desert City.

Snatching a peach-colored satin robe from the closet, she sashed it tight. With her heart pounding, she hurried to the door. And realized her door had no safety chain, or peephole. The bell rang again, and this time there was no mistaking that it was hers. She unfastened the dead bolt and opened the door a crack.

Ethan Knight peered at her through the narrow opening. "Hi," he said, holding up a trio of brown sacks. "Call me presumptuous, but I brought dinner. I hope you like Chinese." Smiling his naughty-boy smile, he pushed the toe of his boot against the door and moved Regan a step or two so that she opened it wider. Gaining a closer look at her fresh-scrubbed face and the death grip she had on a very sexy satin robe, Ethan stopped and shifted the bags in his hands.

"I should have called, I guess. You're obviously getting ready to go out. I'll, uh, see if I can catch up with Mitch so this doesn't go to waste." He lifted the bags again.

The wonderful scent of Hunan spices wafted past Regan's nose. That one cup of tea was all she'd put in her stomach since the slice of toast she'd had for breakfast. At the moment she was so hungry she didn't bother to debate the wisdom of inviting Ethan inside. "I'm not going out. I spent the afternoon cleaning house. I, ah, you caught me just climbing out of a bath." She pointed toward the kitchen. "If you want to dish it up, I'll go throw on some clothes and be right back. I'd say grab a beer, but I didn't buy any today. Maybe a soft drink if you'd like one, or wine. I think I have an unopened bottle of chardonnay.''

"Soda is fine. I'm not big on alcohol. Comes from having seen too much of what it can do when people let it get out of hand,'' he said. "Hey, if you're comfortable in what you have on, don't bother to change on my account. I grew up with six sisters, don't forget. The food's hot now, and I'm no stranger to sitting at a table across from all manner of bathrobes. Believe me, yours is a heck of a lot more presentable than some of the ratty ones my sisters wore.'' He stepped fully into the apartment and shut the door.

Regan blushed and gathered the robe more tightly around her. "Well, I grew up in an all-girl boarding school. I'm not comfortable wearing this in front of…company. I'll go change. There's a microwave if we need to zap our plates.''

"Sure. No problem.'' Ethan digested the news about her having lived away from her parents. The tension between them seemed to be growing. He didn't want to have her change her mind and send him away before he had a chance to ask why she'd run off from the Schutz-hund without leaving him any word. "If you don't mind me rooting in your cupboards, I'll set the table.''

She relaxed minimally. "Be my guest. But I don't have a table yet. We'll have to eat at the bar or sitting on the floor at the coffee table.'' She waved a hand toward a nondescript low table that sat between two love seats. As if it dawned on her that she'd let go of the robe's lapels, she wound her fingers in them again.

Ethan took in the white-walled apartment. Its spartan decor surprised him. He thought all women wallowed in wall hangings and knickknacks. Regan's place held only the bare essentials. He assumed she'd been in Desert

City long enough to have unpacked all of her belongings. But maybe not. "Eating at the bar's okay by me. Ever since I took a bullet in the hip, sitting on floors hasn't had much appeal."

"A bullet?" Regan's eyes widened. "Sorry. Did it scar you badly?"

"I didn't tell you that to look for sympathy. It happened when I was still a rookie. I never think about the injury unless it rains. Go on," he said gently. "Change."

Fingers working nervously at the collar of her robe, Regan hurried down the short hall. She fumbled as she took off her robe and tugged on a velour sweatsuit. During the early-spring months, the desert temperatures dropped appreciably at night. Regan still hadn't bought any logs for the fireplace. She was trying to save money to buy more furniture. One way was to layer her clothing and leave the thermostat on low. She'd seen Ethan studying her meager furnishings. What had gone through his mind? Maybe if she told him about Jack, he'd better understand her reluctance to allow another man into her life.

Or maybe it would only make him more determined. Ethan didn't seem bothered by the fact that she kept turning him down or running out on him as she'd done today.

"I would have warmed this place up," he said when she returned to the kitchen. "But I couldn't find your firewood." He didn't question why half her cupboards were bare, nor did he mention finding only a set of four plates, bowls, mugs and glasses. It wasn't that he'd been nosy, but if she owned more than a starter set of dishes, Ethan didn't know where she stored them. He hadn't been privy to exactly how much Anna earned, but from remarks she'd let slip, he assumed she made decent money. He couldn't begin to imagine what Regan Grant did with her salary—unless this was only an interim stop for her.

"Are you cold?" Regan asked as Ethan began to unpack the second bag, arranging cartons on the bar.

"I guess not. Most of the time in it's too hot to use a fireplace down here, so I have mine blazing every chance I have. It's the one advantage you get with those cold nights."

"In Phoenix I didn't have a fireplace. Next year I'll buy wood."

"So you're planning to stick around?" He opened a carton and stuck a spoon into the mixture.

Regan stopped unloading the third sack. "Do you know something about my job that I don't?" A smile played on her lips, but her eyes were puzzled.

"Nope," he muttered, then sighed mightily and gestured around the room. "It's none of my business, mind you. But your place has the feel of someone who plans to be moving on soon."

Retrieving two cans of ginger ale from her refrigerator, Regan climbed onto the stool opposite Ethan. She filled her plate and, in fits and starts, explained what had happened with Jack.

"What a jerk! I can't believe a judge ruled in his favor. God, I'm sorry. How do you suppose a guy like that lives with himself? That sort of behavior goes contrary to all police codes of ethics. Did you talk to his commander?"

She glanced up, but Ethan knew her eyes were looking into the past. "After the embarrassment of losing in civil court, I just wanted it behind me. It is. Chalked up to a lesson learned. Now I'm wondering if I've blundered again in telling you. It's not something that's easily lived down at a workplace like mine.''

He handed her a carton and urged her to help herself to spicy garlic shrimp. ''It really points up the cracks in our court system. An imbalance in the law. You see it all the time—women and kids getting the short end of the stick.'' He didn't conceal his anger.

If Ethan Knight wasn't for real, Regan thought as she chewed a piece of Szechuan chicken and blamed it for her watery eyes, he made a darn fine show of it. For someone working in a tough-guy field, he had a sensitivity she wouldn't have expected.

''On a different topic…I suppose you really came by to find out why I left so abruptly today.''

''I came to see if you're all right. Paul Heglund said you had trouble with the protection part of the competition.''

''Paul Heg— Oh, is he a retired cop?'' When Ethan nodded, Regan continued. ''He's a nice man. He tried to explain why the dogs are trained to…to…'' Giving up, Regan slid off her stool and crossed the room to stare out the balcony door. Stars studded the evening sky and a quarter moon was on the rise. A perfect night for unburdening the soul. Except that Regan knew from experience it didn't heal and it didn't help—not her and not the unfortunate listener. Two out of three hurriedly changed the subject, and the third cut his losses and took a hike.

Closing her eyes, she rubbed the telltale scar on her neck. The honest thing to do would be to ask Ethan nicely to leave. Whirling, she ran smack into him.

He caught her elbows and lowered his chin to gaze directly into her eyes. Regan wished he hadn't crept up on her. Hadn't touched her. She didn't want his pity. He had no idea—few people did—how far she'd come. She attempted to brush his hands away, but he held her too tightly.

"Help me understand this fear of yours, Regan." His warm hands and spicy breath blocked the coolness she felt wafting from the glass door. The living-room lamp, a tall one on a timer, turned on automatically, flooding them with light. She knew it revealed the scar running from under her chin to her collarbone, disappearing beneath the neck of her velour top.

It wasn't pity she saw in Ethan's eyes as he clamped her chin and angled her jaw for a better look. Anger simmered in the navy-blue irises. "A dog did this to you?" It was only half-questioning. Ethan already knew the answer. "How, Regan? When? That first day in your office, after I put Taz out of the room, why didn't you explain?"

"To what end, Ethan? You and he are inseparable. You said so yourself." This time Regan succeeded in wrenching her chin away. Ethan slid his hand to the back of her neck, where he exerted enough pressure to bring her body fully against his, and her forehead to his lips. He laid a trail of feverish kisses down her face—and along the path of the scar.

Regan felt her heart lurch into high gear while her body sagged and fit into his.

"I'll tell you to what end," he said fiercely. "For subsequent meetings I would've made other arrangements for Taz. And I sure as hell wouldn't have pressured you into attending the Schutzhund."

Regan didn't lift her head until the rumble of his voice died away. Then she leaned backward and frowned up at him. "What did you think about my going to pieces every time I saw your dog? Did you think I was faking? Or just that I was a nutcase?''

"Neither." He scraped aside her heavy hair, noticing then how a second, thicker scar curved behind her ear. Ethan followed it with a fingertip. Deep in her hair the scar branched into three welts. His heart filled with pain for all she must have suffered. "I thought you'd probably been bitten at one time. Pups get overzealous." The leaden tone of his voice said he now knew it was worse, much worse.

"Not a pup. A full-grown standard poodle. Please, Ethan, I don't enjoy talking about it. Do you imagine I *like* cowering in my shoes?'' Again she tried unsuccessfully to break away.

"Of course not," he murmured, leading her carefully to one of the love seats, where he sat and pulled her onto his lap. "But, Regan, running from this enemy of yours hasn't helped you conquer your fear.''

"You said in the police academy they told you it was best to face what made you afraid. I've tried," she said bitterly. "For over twenty years.''

"So you were what when it happened? Eleven or twelve?'' He wrinkled his forehead, letting out a low whistle.

"Ten. I was ten." She sighed and settled her head comfortably on his broad shoulder. "If I give you the whole sordid tale, will you go home and leave me alone?''

Ethan didn't say one way or the other. He steadily rubbed her back.

"It was a neighbor's dog," she said haltingly. "I was a skinny little kid. Jo Jo was bigger than me. He was always tied to a tree in the front yard. There were some older boys who teased the dog when they walked to and from school. Then they'd run off and I'd be alone when the neighbor came out to see why Jo Jo was barking. Mr. Banks yelled at me as if *I'd* been the one bothering his dog. One day the boys went from teasing to being mean. Poking the dog with sticks and pelting him with rocks. I ran up and ordered them to stop, the bravest thing I'd ever done. About that time Jo Jo's rope broke. The boys scattered. I was the only one left. He…he attacked me.'' Regan shut her eyes tight and curled closer to the heat emanating from Ethan's body. ''He tossed me around like a rag doll. The pain…was horrid. I thought I was going to die. I almost did.'' She shuddered and Ethan lay her back on the pillows, hushing her, trying to quiet her sobs with kisses.

''Shh. It's okay. I shouldn't have probed. Regan, do you have any medicine you take for these bouts of anxiety?''

''No. No. All the medication's addictive. I can ride it out. Remembering just brings it all back so vividly—it's not your fault. Go home, Ethan. I need to sleep,'' she whispered, her teeth chattering.

''Where's your bedroom?'' he demanded, rising and lifting her as if she weighed no more than a child. Not waiting for her answer, he strode down the short hallway in the direction she'd gone to change clothes. He placed her on the bed and watched her curl into the pillows. Biting off a curse, Ethan began yanking out drawers until he found a comfy-looking flannel nightgown. He shoved the gown into her hands and told her to put it on. ''I'll step into the hall,'' he said.

The shaking seemed to worsen the longer she lay there, the wadded-up gown held against her stomach. He turned the bedside lamp on low and sat down beside her. ''Regan, listen to me. Forget the gown. You need to cover up and get warm—it's how we treat shock victims. But get used to the fact that I'm not going anywhere until this passes.''

Regan seemed not to hear his words. She grabbed the hem of her velour top and dragged it over her head. As she tried to pull on the gown, still wearing her bra, light spilled over her torso and side. Ethan's stomach clenched at the sight of a network of scars mapping her soft flesh. They disappeared below the waist band of her pink pants. The scars were a mass of dark red welts. It made his heart bleed. He realized suddenly that she'd gotten tangled in the nightgown but was trying desperately to hide the scars from him. Failing, she lunged for the lightswitch.

''Don't,'' Ethan commanded. ''You think those matter?'' With steady hands he removed her bra, then lifted her arms and guided them through the sleeves. And with equal care, he drew the soft gown over her head. ''Off with the sweatpants,'' he said, kneeling at her bedside to ease them down over her bare feet.

''They matter,'' she whispered, curling into a ball after the pants had fallen onto his knees.

''Like hell.'' Ethan noticed she'd begun to shiver again. He peeled the covers back, moved her gently and cocooned them around her. Then he took off his boots, turned off the lamp and lay down beside her, spooning his body around against hers.

Minutes ticked by without either of them uttering a word. When at last Regan's breathing evened out and she relaxed enough to drift off to sleep, Ethan felt as if they'd crossed a major hurdle. He certainly understood the depth of her fear. He didn't have the faintest idea why he wanted—no, needed—to be the one to lead her out of the darkness. It didn't make a lick of sense. Taz was his companion. His buddy. Only a full-blown fool would hold out hope that this woman, who felt so right in his arms, could ever heal enough to accept Taz.

As the night wore on and Ethan lay beside Regan, at times nuzzling the soft skin below her ear, he came to understand that he'd embarked on a fool's crusade. Long before he slept, he knew that his course was set.

CHAPTER EIGHT

REGAN STIRRED, tried to roll over, but was stopped by a wall. Her sleepy brain couldn't make sense of it. Her bed sat in the center of the room. A room that was still pitch-black. No surprise—according to the bedside clock it was only five past three.

The wall at her back moved, groaned and spoke in a deep groggy voice. "What is it, Regan? Are you all right? Shall I get the light?"

At first Regan thought she must be dreaming about living with Jack. But he'd never budged at night, not even when she suffered a nightmare.

An arm reached over her and turned the lamp on low. *Ethan.* The previous evening came flooding back. Now he knew practically everything there was to know about her. *Why had he stayed?* It was the last thing Regan expected.

He had one arm braced on either side of her and hovered above her, bleary-eyed and in need of a shave. Regan couldn't think of anything to say. What was the appropriate remark when you awakened to find a strange man in your bed? Well, not really strange. Regan wished he *was* a total stranger, rather than a man she'd had a few nighttime fantasies about.

The circumstances that had brought them together in her bed weren't funny, so why did she feel laughter bubbling up? Maybe because laughing was smarter than what she longed to do, given the heat suddenly building between them.

Ethan felt it, too, and he experienced none of the reservations he saw in Regan's pale-blue eyes. Leaning higher on one arm, he freed the other and stroked her face with the back of his hand. "It's inevitable, you know."

Regan wasn't sure when or how she'd pulled the blankets up to her chin, but she clung to them with both hands. "I was engaged to Jack," she murmured. "I don't make a habit of sleeping with men. He's the only one—are you sure?"

"Yes. I have to ask, Regan. Your injuries…does making love cause you pain?" After he asked, he kissed all her visible scars. As his tongue traced damp circles over an exposed collarbone, Regan placed a hand on his lips.

"Not physical pain, no." Regan wondered if she ought to tell him about losing some of her organs. Like her spleen and her uterus. But it was so terribly personal, and Ethan Knight wasn't offering a long-term commitment here.

"I expect you'll want to turn off the lamp so you won't have to…to look at me." She shifted toward the lamp.

Ethan stopped her. "You're beautiful, Regan. All of you."

Turning back, she made a face. "You haven't seen all of me, Ethan. I'm sure you'll change your mind when you do. Jack couldn't…well, uh, perform if it wasn't dark in the room. He wanted me to have more cosmetic surgery on my body, like he insisted I get on my face and neck," she said in a strained voice. "He never understood how hard it was to go through. I do plan on doing it, but… In all, I've had nineteen surgeries. I…to voluntarily go under the knife again…'' Her voice broke.

Ethan lowered his chest, slowly letting her take his weight. He kissed her on the mouth, letting his tongue penetrate deeply. When he finally lifted his head, his eyes were black and shadowed. ''I'm not Jack, okay? I'm nothing like him. Starting now, we're going to erase him from your memory, Regan.''

A tiny growl, more like a purr, vibrated in her throat. ''Consider him erased.'' Her fingers unbuttoned Ethan's shirt from bottom to top. When she'd finished, she swept it over his shoulders and down his arms. Then she tumbled him sideways, leaving his arms shackled by the still-buttoned sleeves. She launched an onslaught of kisses like those he'd given her.

At first Ethan struggled against the helpless feeling. But as he slowly lost his senses to the thrill of her ministrations, he lay still and let the passion grow. He watched with interest as she shed her flannel nightgown. He squirmed when her soft breasts gently scraped the hair growing fan-shaped across his chest. ''Have a heart, woman,'' he muttered in strangled tones.

''Hmm.'' Regan nipped her way along his lips, down his neck and one arm until she reached his imprisoned wrist. She tarried there so long Ethan bolted upright, his jeans having gone so tight he thought he'd explode out of them.

Laughing, Regan released one set of sleeve buttons. The others popped off and flew across the room as Ethan tore his shirt completely off and struggled to do the same with his jeans. He wasn't satisfied until they lay in a heap on the floor and Regan was beneath him. ''Ethan, I enjoyed just looking at you. You have an almost perfect body. You're a beautiful man, you know?''

He reared up, balanced on his forearms and gave her a look that said she was crazy.

Regan wrapped her legs around his thighs. Feeling her damp and ready for him drove Ethan half out of his mind. Seconds from burying himself inside her, the lights flashing in his skull screamed *protection*. He twisted, sat up and leaned his sweating forehead to hers. "Hand me my jeans," he begged with a great deal of effort. "I don't think you want me to go wading without rubbers."

Regan hesitated, a confession rushing to the tip of her tongue. Then she remembered that condoms protected against more than pregnancy. Her biggest worry then was that stretching out exposed her scars fully to Ethan's view. One quick glance at his face and she realized that his eyes were glazed in the heat of the moment. He wasn't looking at her body, except maybe at her breasts—with a lust that threatened to impair her ability to move. It took two tries, but between stopping for kisses, she managed to hook his jeans with one finger.

Once Ethan had retrieved a well-smashed packet from his wallet and let her handle covering him, Regan didn't waste time thinking about scars, missing organs or anything else. She rode the waves that swelled higher and higher until she reached a crescendo of pleasure.

Breathing hard, they remained locked in an embrace and waited silently for the air around them to cool. Ethan combed the fingers of one hand through her tangled blond hair. The other stroked her arm but kept her carefully welded to his side.

Regan sighed softly as she nestled her lips into his chest. One hand smoothed his thigh. Stroking fingers recognized the puckered flesh as the scar left by the bullet he'd mentioned. Her fingers stilled.

Ethan lifted his head a few inches off the pillow and tried to see the expression on her face. "I hope all you're thinking here is that nobody's perfect."

"It's such a big hole."

"When you're a cop, risk comes with the territory, Regan."

She stirred against him. "I keep telling myself that life is full of risk. I wish I could shrug off my misfortune and go on like you obviously have. How did you? Your clothes must have been soaked with blood. You might have died."

One corner of his mouth quirked up. "I didn't, Angel Eyes. I decided it meant God wasn't through with me on earth. That's when I began trying to make a difference for those who are less fortunate. For defenseless kids."

She settled a hand on his stomach and her chin on the back of her hand. "Why did you call me Angel Eyes?"

Ethan dragged her up his body and took possession of her lips again. After thoroughly kissing her, he smiled complacently. "I've never seen anyone with eyes like yours. They fascinated me the first time I saw you. Since you just transported me on a trip to heaven, calling you Angel Eyes seems appropriate, don't you think?"

Regan scoffed. The movement of her body against his caused Ethan to want her again.

Just as she wanted him. But Ethan had no more protective packets in his wallet. Nor had Regan planned on ever needing any. She fully expected him to roll out of bed, dress and make his farewell. Instead, he snuggled beside her and initiated talk of his family and his job.

"A detective responsible for youth and family—what exactly does that mean?" she asked.

He gave a brief explanation. "You probably wonder

why I haven't tried to climb the professional ladder faster. A lot of guys with my years on the force have made lieutenant and a few are captains now.'' He fell silent a moment. "I like what I do. Trying to help kids go straight. Ease the transition when they get caught up in things beyond their control. Giving seminars at the schools. Working with young people in general. Little kids, too. Paperwork isn't my strength. I'm not a big disciplinarian, either. So heading a unit would be torture.''

"I'm not finding that part of supervising easy, either.'' Regan blew whorls in his chest hair and tickled him when he tweaked her nose. "Hey, truce,'' she squealed, burrowing into him again when he attempted to tickle her in retaliation. "I'm sure if you asked kids like Jeremy Smith and Joey Hawkins,'' she said, turning serious, "they'd give you five gold stars. You know the real trouble with government jobs, Ethan? They promote the best workers out of jobs they do well into management, where they're mediocre because they hate the work.''

"Then you don't think it's wrong to stay at one level?''

"Not if you're happy. Did someone say you should move on...move up?''

"Some of my friends. Both of my brothers. They're making a lot more money than I am.''

"What difference does that make?''

Cynically he told her his brothers said he didn't make enough to support a wife and kids.

"Oh.'' Regan rolled away from him and plumped a pillow. "I thought cops were masters at avoiding marriage.''

"Where'd you go?'' Ethan faced her and studied the way she'd subtly wrapped the sheet more tightly around her. "I'm not in a huge rush to tie the knot," he said, hoping to avert the tension he sensed in her. "My grandfather gave me that four-bedroom house," he went on. "Taz and I rattle around in it most of the time. As I said, I'm not in any rush, but I do see myself with a houseful of kids down the line."

Regan appeared even more uncomfortable. *Tell him,* said a little voice. But she didn't; she let the moment pass.

Ethan had been thrilled by their lovemaking, but he also took pleasure in lying beside her. He was reluctant to have their relationship end as a one-night stand, and yet he felt her pulling away. To lessen the distance growing between them, he stroked her shoulder and ran his hand to her elbow and back up again. "Don't tell me you plan to grow old alone, Regan. I thought when women hit thirty, they were the ones with the fast-ticking biological clocks."

"Ethan, I probably gave you the wrong impression. Isn't it too soon to be having this conversation?"

"Depends. Is it the subject of marriage and babies that's making you uncomfortable? Or is your problem seeing me in the role of husband, dad, provider?"

Anguish began to squeeze Regan's throat. "It's Taz," she blurted, knowing his dog was only part of the problem. "I said in the beginning that you and I shouldn't get involved. We can't, Ethan. There's...well, we just can't."

He stopped touching her and tucked an arm under his head, gazing at her steadily until he felt her begin to shift farther away. "Regan, honey, aren't we already involved? I don't usually pressure women to talk about performance. But I thought we were pretty terrific together. You'd better tell me now if you didn't feel anything."

"Of course I did. It was wonderful. You were…the best, believe me." Her words trailing off, she gnawed her bottom lip and looked distressed.

Moving slowly, Ethan pulled her, pillow and all, close to him again. His muscles bunched as he cradled her under his arm. "The thought of having Taz around used to bother my sister Amy, too. Today she asked to take him home with her for the night. She'd invited a guy she's only dated a few times to her house for dinner. She wanted Taz there for insurance."

Regan formed a picture in her mind of how Ethan saw his future. He and his wife entering their home, trailed by stair-step kids. Four or five—and Taz. Even as Regan accepted Ethan's warmth, she felt a chill start at her feet and slide up to imprison her. "I…I…can't promise you I'll ever be the woman you need. I *want* to be, Ethan. But I can't, for so many reasons."

"Shh, it's okay," he said, untangling her hair with his fingers. "Let's get some sleep. We're both facing long workdays tomorrow. I'm scheduled to be on shift until ten tomorrow night. I fix a pretty mean midnight supper. I'll go home and feed Taz, run past an all-night grocer and be here by eleven-thirty. What do you say?"

She didn't have to think long or hard. The idea appealed immensely. "I say that sounds good." Lifting her head, she strained to kiss him on the lips. When the pair of them came up breathless, it was evident the kiss had resulted in another erection. Regan stretched over him to turn off the lamp. Her voice held remnants of a smile. "I hope you have something other than food on your grocery list, big guy."

Ethan's chuckle was husky and erotic. "At the top of

my list, Angel Eyes. At the very top, because you're so special to me.''

Regan closed her eyes and snuggled close, lighter of heart than she'd been in many weeks. The prospect of sleeping next to Ethan left a lingering sense of well-being. Not once during the four months she'd lived with Jack had she felt *special*. Tomorrow night, she vowed, she'd tell Ethan about her other problem.

THE AROMA OF COFFEE woke Regan. She sat up, realizing she'd been huddled in an area of warmth left by Ethan's body. She'd been concerned about the morning after. Had thought it might be awkward, considering the intimacies they'd shared following their incredible love-making. She was grateful for his sensitivity, his considerateness, if that was what it was. Maybe it hadn't occurred to him that she'd prefer to get up alone, or that she might worry about his seeing her many scars in the harsher light of day. Perhaps he was simply an early riser. Whether accidental or by design, Regan welcomed the opportunity to shower, dress and brush her teeth before facing the man who'd shared her bed.

When she stepped out of the shower to dry off, she saw that he'd slipped in and set a steaming mug of her favorite morning tea on the counter. How had he known she often liked it better than coffee?

As she dressed between sips of tea, Regan began to hope against hope that they'd find a way to overcome all her problems. Not just her fear of his dog. The other ones, too.

When Ethan greeted her first appearance in the kitchen with a big kiss and a growl low in his throat, Regan knew the stakes had gone up for her. She had to try as never before to lay all her cards on the table tonight.

"That perfume you wear drives me crazy," Ethan murmured. "If you only knew how tempted I was to run out to the grocery store this morning."

A tremor went through her. Not in happy anticipation of morning sex but in dread. Shrugging out of his arms, she pulled open the fridge door and took out a carton of yogurt. "I'd offer to share my breakfast, but you probably meet Mitch and your other pals at some greasy spoon diner for breakfast."

"Flo's a respectable café, but that's not the issue here." Ethan propped a hip against her breakfast counter and crossed his arms. "Talk to me, Regan."

She glanced up. "I just did."

He pushed off from the counter and grabbed her arm before she could turn completely away. "Tell me what's bothering you," Ethan said urgently. "If you'd rather not have sex so frequently, that's fine. I do understand *no* when a woman says it."

She hesitated momentarily, then whirled to face him. "Seeing my scars in daylight just once would change your mind about morning sex, Ethan. I can barely stand to look at them in the mirror after a shower. And I've had time to adjust."

Anger flared in his dark eyes as he spun her around. "Sex isn't about pleasing me, Regan. It's mutual. It can be slow and sweet between already rumpled morning sheets. Or fast and earth-shaking under a hot shower. Satisfying to both partners, and not predicated on how either person looks."

"Ha! Like you ever look less than perfect."

"Yeah? Ask any of my sisters," he said around a little

laugh. "They'll tell you I look pretty scary in the morning."

Regan clutched the carton of yogurt and stared boldly and openly at his unshaven face and the uncombed hair falling into his eyes. "Oh, Ethan. You couldn't look bad if you tried. There's an innate kindness about you that…that just is. I can't explain it any better, but I think it comes from the inside out. One of the therapists I saw said trauma like mine corrupts the psyche. What if mine's too corrupted to change? That attack really damaged me." *Tell him. No, not this way.* She couldn't blurt out something so horrendous. Not without warning. Not to a man who wanted kids.

Ethan took his time running his thumbs lightly over her eyebrows and closed eyelids, her nose, her cheeks and lips. He waited until she opened her eyes, and then he kissed her, putting into his kiss all the caring he could muster. And he didn't stop kissing her until he felt her go pliant in his arms. He moved her gently away. "Angel Eyes, maybe part of your problem is you've never had anyone who believes in you strongly enough to help you beat that old devil fear."

"I hope you're not deluding yourself, Ethan." Rising on tiptoe, Regan kissed him back. All her hopes and dreams for a future with him went into that kiss.

"Wow!" Ethan gave a soft whistle when the kiss ended. "I can tell you right now, if I'd had a chance to buy that top item on my shopping list, we'd break some new ground. And we'd both be late for work," he lamented. "We will, anyway, if I don't get outta here and let you eat that yogurt you just popped the lid off and spilled down my back."

Her horrified gaze flew to the carton, disbelieving at first. Her expression changed to chagrin when she realized the back of his shirt was sticky. Yogurt had dripped on the floor, as well. "Why didn't you say something sooner?"

"And miss the best kiss of my life? No way." He winked and unrolled a wad of paper towels from the holder next to her stove.

"Give me that." She snatched it from him. "Neither of us has time for me to launder your shirt. Grab a bath towel from under the sink in the bathroom. At least it'll save your car's upholstery."

"Yeah." He danced from one foot to the other as she knelt and scrubbed at the floor. It was obvious that he felt reluctant to leave. But after checking his watch twice, he did go get the towel. "See you tonight," he said, heading for her front door. "Damn, I hate to go." He loped back, gave her another resounding kiss, then sighed and actually went out, closing the door with a bang.

The sound jolted Regan into the here and now. She sucked in a gulp of air and released it suddenly. The man had swept into her life like a whirlwind. Was it any wonder she felt shaky and off-kilter?

It was a normal workday, and she had no time to dwell on how quickly her personal life had changed. Feeling happy and giddy and even cherished, Regan tried not to question the wisdom of getting physically involved with Ethan Knight. Their relationship would have to play itself out however fate decreed.

What Regan noticed driving to work was the number of times she broke into a smile and hummed along with her radio. Ethan had said not to compare him to Jack Diamond. Every time she did—like right now—Ethan came out far ahead.

The phone on her desk was ringing when Regan unlocked her office door. She had voice mail, but she hurried inside and snatched up the receiver, singing out a hearty "Hello, Supervisor Grant speaking."

"This is Detective Knight. Just calling to see if you miss me."

"Ethan, you nut." Her voice softened. "We only just parted. Where are you?"

"At home. I had to change clothes before heading to Amy's to collect Taz. You're still uppermost in my mind, Angel Eyes."

"Stop." Regan shoved her purse into the bottom desk drawer while doing her best to combat a flush of heat rushing from her toes to her head. "Ethan, you can't call me at work and say those outrageous things. What if I was with a client or one of my staff?"

"What if you were? Are you planning to hide our relationship?"

Regan swiped her tongue over suddenly dry lips. "Yes, Ethan, I am. For the time being. Until we determine we *have* a relationship."

"We do from my perspective," he grumbled. "But if you still need time, I'll pretend we have nothing but work between us when I visit CHC. Desert City isn't so big, though, that someone won't notice my vehicle parked outside your apartment every night."

"Every night?" Her voice quavered. "You're willing to spend time at my place without Taz?"

"Regan, didn't anything I said last night or this morning get through to you? I said we'd find a way to overcome your fear of dogs. I won't force you to interact with Taz now that I know the full extent of your problem. If you can't come to accept him, well…we'll cross that bridge when we come to it."

"Thank you for understanding, Ethan. You're a terrific man, you know?'' Her heart contracted. He *didn't* understand her full problem. There was much more.

''I'm glad you think I'm terrific. If you ask me, we make a pretty good team, both privately and professionally.''

''Oh, there goes my other line, and I haven't even hung up my jacket. I'll see you later. I'm looking forward to tonight,'' she said, sounding breathless. She would tell him the total truth then.

''Me, too, Angel Eyes. Bye.''

Regan clicked to her other line immediately and launched into her normal phone greeting.

''Good, you're in the office.'' Piggot's secretary's cool voice gave nothing away. ''Director Piggot would like to see you at once, Supervisor Grant. With regard to Joelyn Hawkins.''

''Joelyn? Oh, you mean Joey? I have a handwritten report I can bring. I've dictated initial notes and the follow-up. They're still being transcribed.''

''Bring whatever you have without delay.'' The director's secretary hung up abruptly.

Puzzled by the odd request, Regan nevertheless sorted out Joey's folder. She scanned her notes briefly to ensure that she'd covered all the bases, then went out, locking her door behind her. Directors rarely, if ever, involved themselves in matters relating to clients. The Hawkins case was pretty routine.

The first person Regan saw on being shown into Nathaniel's office was Joey's mother. ''Mrs. Hawkins?'' Regan extended her hand. ''So you've come to us for help. I'm sure Joey will be delighted. I believe Lucy's here at my request, sir,'' she told Piggot. ''If you'll follow me...'' Regan smiled, expecting Lucy to rise and follow her out.

Nathaniel cleared his throat noisily. "Before you take a seat, Supervisor Grant, I'd like you to meet Ben Tucker. He's the attorney for a local parent-activist group."

The smile frozen on her lips, Regan turned and shook the soft hand of the man seated behind her in the room. "Mr. Tucker. I'm pleased to meet you."

"I doubt that you will be," the man snapped. He sat again and drew his chair into the circle of chairs ringing Nathaniel's desk. Pulling out a folder, the lawyer flopped it open on his briefcase.

Still confused about what was going on, Regan sat gingerly on the edge of another chair. "I know how busy you are, Director," Regan murmured. "Would you rather I conducted this interview in my office?"

"Not at all." Nathaniel's small close-set eyes narrowed perceptibly. "Mr. Tucker has come to me with a serious charge. He claims you and Detective Knight joined forces to wrongfully take this woman's child from her home and place her in foster care."

Regan darted a fast glance at Mrs. Hawkins. Why hadn't she realized when she first walked in here that the woman no longer even remotely resembled the drunk she'd been at their only visit? Keenly aware that Tucker had his pen poised to record her every admission, Regan opened her folder and pushed it across the desk to her boss.

"Mrs. Hawkins, we have a police report completed by Officers Glendenning and Jiminez. They found your daughter wandering the streets barefoot and injured."

"Joelyn ran away," Mr. Tucker injected smoothly. "The officers didn't return the child to her house or try to consult with her family."

"Because Joey's face needed sutures. And at the time,

she was too frightened to tell anyone what had happened.''

''Was she frightened by her injuries or because she was accosted by two burly men she didn't know? The police in this town can be intimidating.''

''The officers have a copy of my taped conversation with Joey, once I finally got her to talk. I'm sure the precinct will provide you with a copy of the tape, Mr. Tucker.''

''Why don't you just fill me in on what the child said, Ms. Grant?''

''Basically, Joey said her mother's boyfriend, Chip, struck her in the face because she spilled a pan of soup. Soup she'd been expected to prepare. Did you know she's not even eight years old?''

''I represent Joelyn's mother. She was ill the day this happened. And the man who struck Joelyn is in police custody. You have no call to retain the girl in foster care.''

''Lucy Hawkins was drunk when I went to her home the following morning for my interview after placing Joey in temporary care. This was not Lucy's first encounter with our agency, nor with Joey receiving medical assistance for injuries inflicted by an adult living in the home. I offered Mrs. Hawkins help with her alcohol problem. And I left Joey in her foster home, because I deemed it in her best interests to do so.''

Nathaniel rapped on his desk, drawing all eyes. ''My concern, of course, Supervisor Grant, is how you came to process this case. Mr. Tucker asked to review our intake records so he could contact the child's current school and set up a time to see Joey. Intake has no Joelyn Hawkins listed.''

Thrown off balance, Regan didn't answer immediately.

"I see there's a mention of Detective Knight in your report. If he bulldozed this through to you without following proper procedures, Supervisor Grant, I assume you've notified or intend to notify Knight's commander? It's what I told you to do."

Regan cleared her throat. "How I got involved, sir, is this. I happened to be visiting a foster boy residing with Detective Knight's parents when he received a call concerning this child. And there should be a record of the case at Intake, because I phoned and left all pertinent details. The Intake officer gave me the name of the next foster family on our list." Regan was surprised to find her voice rising. From the gleam in Nathaniel's eye, she feared that defending Ethan had been a mistake. Lacing her fingers in her lap, she wound down her explanation with a shrug.

"The fact remains that this case did not follow procedure. As a result, I want the child returned to her mother. To protect the privacy of the foster parents, Ms. Grant, you'll pick Joey up after school and deliver her home. Meanwhile, I'm taking the liberty of drafting a formal reprimand on your behalf regarding Detective Knight. Naturally I'll sign as the head of this agency, and have it delivered to the precinct chief by courier. I trust this is satisfactory to your client, Mr. Tucker?"

"Mrs. Hawkins might like an apology from Family Assistance. On the other hand, if you strike this unfortunate incident from my client's record with your agency, I'm sure that will suffice as an apology."

The woman seated stiffly in her chair made no comment. It was evident to Regan, who'd worked with many alcoholic clients, that Lucy Hawkins badly needed a drink and was holding on by only the merest thread.

"Mr. Tucker, as Joey's advocate, I strongly object to removing this incident from our records. Regardless of how I came to enter into the case, the fact remains that various CHC reports, including mine, show your client has an ongoing problem with alcohol. This is also documented by her daughter's school, the emergency room and police files. Before I strike this charge, I'd like some assurance that Lucy will enter a rehab program at once."

The lawyer pursed his lips. Nathaniel broke the silence. "I'm striking the charge, Regan. If you'd stay a moment please, I believe our business with the counselor and Mrs. Hawkins has been satisfactorily concluded."

To Regan's dismay, the man and woman rose on cue and marched through the door without so much as a word of goodbye.

She felt her stomach start to burn. "Surely, sir, you saw that Lucy hasn't been dry eight hours. Four, tops. What kind of shape do you think I'll find her in when I deliver Joey after school?"

Nathaniel sliced a hand through the air, cutting off anything else Regan might say. "You disappoint me, Regan. The very day you let Knight pull this stunt, I expressly told you to reduce our rolls. What I see is a biological mom with enough on the ball to contact a parent-activist group. Which you might have seen, too, if you hadn't let Detective Knight rush you into making a hasty review of the case."

"Ethan was doing his job. With all due respect, you weren't at the Emergency Room. You did not see this badly frightened, injured child."

"Ethan, is it?" Nathaniel said with a sneer. "Let me say this once and once only. The detective and your predecessor were thorns in my regime far too many years. Supervisor Murphy is gone. This is my chance to nail that Knight bastard's hide to his precinct door. His job, Ms. Grant, is to rid our streets of criminals, not meddle in affairs under my jurisdiction. I haven't got time to question his motives for making himself the Pied Piper of Desert City. Perhaps you ought to. Anna refused to consider the possibility that he might have pedophile tendencies.''

''That's absurd!'' Regan burst out. ''I want to see the letter going to Ethan's commander.''

Her boss looked stern. ''After noting your thorough work on that project we did last year, I gave you credit for seeing through Knight's veneer. Ask yourself why an unmarried officer doesn't hate being called the Baby Cop. Why does he buy stuffed toys, which he uses to ingratiate himself with abused kids? Why does a single man volunteer to be Officer Friendly at every elementary school in town? How well do you *really* know Ethan Knight?''

Regan flinched each time Nathaniel made a point and poked his pudgy finger at her.

''You're new here, Supervisor. That's why I'm confining my adjudgment of the Hawkins matter to Detective Knight's involvement. I have no doubt that after his chief calls him on the carpet, Knight will try to contact you. Don't take his call. There's no sense in giving him a forum to rail at us.'' The director shook his head, jowls quivering. ''It's no secret that he hates me. He'd love to start something—and I'm sure you know a fight between our agency and the local police force would spread through the media like wildfire. We certainly don't need a departmental investigation at budget time. I want—no, I'm ordering you—to sever further contact with Knight.

I'll tell Nicole Mason he's persona non grata. From now on we simply won't deal with him.''

''You can't place that kind of restriction on a member of the police force.''

''I beg to differ.'' Piggot picked up the phone and in less than a minute had given their receptionist the edict. ''I believe our business is concluded. First thing Tuesday morning I'll expect a report on my desk formally closing the Hawkins case. Oh, and outside of taking her home, please limit your work to administrative duties.''

Regan was shaken by the verbal slap Piggot had given both her and Ethan. She'd thought her boss was bluffing. Especially when it came to blocking Ethan from the agency offices. Was Piggot unbalanced? Her temper barely leashed, she rose with as much dignity as she could, gathered her folder on Joey and left.

More frustrating even than Nathaniel's edict were her many unsuccessful attempts to contact Ethan throughout the day.

Eventually the worry about how she'd explain things to Ethan without jeopardizing either of their jobs took a back seat to the sick way she felt at having to return Joey to the hovel where Piggot and the lawyer had consigned her. Regan gave the girl over to a mother with more than a little liquor on her breath. A totally unacceptable situation. Perhaps Ethan would have a better idea on how to work around Nathaniel's mandate.

All the way home from the Hawkins house, Regan looked forward to her promised night with Ethan. He'd certainly understand how her hands were tied. And he'd commiserate, if nothing else.

HE WOULD, if he'd bothered to show up.

By midnight Regan gave up trying to reach him by

phone. At one she threw the dead bolt on her door, shut off the lights and slid into a cold lonely bed.

Ethan hadn't even called to request her side of the story. Maybe he wasn't the man she'd thought.

CHAPTER NINE

ETHAN AND MITCH returned to the station with Taz partway through a particularly trying shift filled with domestic disputes. Two years ago Mitch had been knifed in the stomach while intervening in a spousal fight. Now he and Ethan treated every case as potentially violent. Ethan thought three in one afternoon might be some kind of record. They still had several hours before their shift ended, and Ethan's mind kept wandering to his upcoming date with Regan. He wanted to get out on time, if not early.

"Hey, Knight," the sergeant on the desk called as Ethan and Mitch sauntered past on their way to check messages. "The chief wants to see you."

Mitch stopped. "Just Ethan or me, too?"

The sergeant shrugged. "Only Ethan, so far as I know. He's called out here three times to find out whether or not Knight's checked in."

"Maybe another undercover operation," Mitch muttered.

"Without you? Not likely." Ethan paused near the corridor that led to Chief Wellington's office. He dug in his pocket and pulled out some change. "I'll go see what he wants. Will you get me a snack out of the machine, Mitch? And a cola if the coffee looks too muddy. Oh, and would you fill Taz's water bowl? I'll open a new bag of kibble after I finish with the chief."

"Sure I shouldn't go with you? In case you need someone to hold your hand when the chief reams you out?" Mitch guffawed and slapped Ethan on the back.

"Very funny. He's got nothing to yell at me for. I'm even caught up on writing my reports. Well, outside of today's calls." Ethan quickly thought back over the day's docket. While there had been three calls of a domestic nature, all were more or less routine. At least, none had ended in death. The chief got edgy when the force couldn't keep a lid on crimes the media loved sinking their teeth into—like the Hammond debacle.

After Ethan and Mitch went their separate ways, Ethan met the chief in the hall, locking up his office. "I heard you wanted to see me, Chief."

"Knight. Damn right I did." The big man flicked a shock of snow-white hair off his forehead. Gripping a large key ring, he sorted through the bunch until he found the one to open his office again.

The chief never got that stern look unless he was ticked off about something. Ethan and others who'd worked under Wellington for a number of years had found it wise to give him time to chew on a problem until he cooled down. "Guess I caught you at a bad time," Ethan said. "Sandra probably has your supper ready. Why don't I stop back in the morning?"

"No. We need to talk about this now." Wellington couldn't get the key to turn. He punched the door with the palm of his hand and cursed.

"Before you bust the door, why don't you just tell me right here?" Ethan suggested. Might as well get it over with.

His boss glanced at the open doors along the hallway. Officers were going in and out of the property and evidence rooms. A change of watch commanders created a lot of congestion in the hall. "This is better kept private for the time being. Though I have no doubt that the contents of the letter will soon be common knowledge. With computers and e-mail, there's no such thing as a confidential memo anymore."

Ethan had no idea what letter the chief was talking about. He wasn't thrilled with Wellington's tone, either.

"Shut the door." Wellington shed his jacket and flipped on the harsh overhead lights. They illuminated a room showing the ravages of time. Charging around his battered desk, he opened a locked file and pulled out a sheet of letterhead stationery. Tossing it across the desk at Ethan, the chief sank into his chair. "When you piss off a lady, Knight, you do it in a big way. I'll give you two minutes to explain your side of the story."

"Lady?" Ethan's eyebrows knitted in a frown. He lowered himself onto a straight-backed chair and took the letter Wellington had thrown on his desk. At first Ethan gave it a cursory glance. Then as the heat flared in his body, he began at the beginning and read the whole page, word by damning word, up to and including Regan's name typed above Piggot's. Superimposed over it, Ethan saw himself in Regan's bed, locked in what he'd thought was a mutually fantastic experience. One he'd had every indication they'd repeat tonight—until this letter disabused him of that belief.

"Well?" Wellington laced his hands over his ample belly. "Did you go outside normal procedure to house the Hawkins kid? Of course you did." The big man snorted. "Same complaint I get from Piggot every time I land within shouting distance of that weasel."

"A safe house for Joey Hawkins," Ethan said emphatically. He smacked the letter with his hand. "The mom was drunk on her butt. She let her boyfriend slap the kid around. You tell me whose rights were violated! This whole thing is a farce. Anna would never have agreed to ask for a reprimand for my part in the Hawkins case."

"Bless Anna. She always ran interference for you. Dammit, Ethan. Piggot's got himself a new barracuda. This Grant dame was handpicked. Nathaniel hates you and me both. Nothing would delight him more than to hang us out to dry. I don't care how bad it tastes, eat dirt if you have to, but get this asshole off my back. The town council and the state legislators are clamoring for budget cuts. It's not the time to invite an internal investigation into police practices Piggot claims are shady."

"I didn't do anything shady! Supervisor Grant handled the intake proceedings herself. She was to contact Lucy Hawkins. Lucy is Joey's mother." Baffled, Ethan shook his head. "Honestly, sir, this letter is as surprising to me as it is to you. If Piggot's aim is to stir up trouble, wouldn't an apology from me be the same as an admission of guilt?"

Wellington thumped his thumbs alternately on his desktop. "I suppose. But if I agree to let you off the hook, I damn well want reassurance that you'll stay out of the new supervisor's hair. No fraternization. Zilch, do you hear?" He closed a fist and slammed it on the accusing letter. "Hell, I don't know why I'm even contemplating this. Everybody in Desert City knows to call you when they find a battered kid. If I ignore Piggot and Grant, I want your word in blood that from this day forward you'll handle every kid case by the book. I want you following every friggin' Family Assistance rule." This time when the chief smacked a fist on the desk, all the items on it danced. A stack of files slid sideways.

Ethan straightened them automatically. "The minute

I leave here I'll phone Regan Grant and ask why in hell she went to Piggot with Joey's placement.''

"No!" roared the man seated opposite Ethan. "Maybe you need your hearing checked, Knight. Not *one* word to that battle-ax. This is a dicey budget year. The state budget committee, on which Piggot has one vote, has targeted a list of programs they think police departments should cut. Domestic and youth intervention heads that list. My guess is, they're hammering Piggot's agency, as well. The more family feuds our cops overlook, means fewer women leave breadwinning abusers to place themselves and their kids on welfare.''

"I suppose Piggot would prefer we left bloody carcases lying around the city unattended," Ethan said furiously.

Wellington scraped a hand over a stubbled jaw. "We both know bureaucrats come and go, Ethan. Nasty pricks like Piggot and salty old dogs like me eventually work their way to the top of the heap. Public-service jobs make for strange bedfellows. Whether or not the various department heads respect one another, they still owe it to the people they serve to try and work together. I'm the one ordering you to stay away from the Grant woman and from Family Assistance. Cowboy can do any legwork that needs doing at CHC. And you'd both better watch your *p*'s and *q*'s when you're dealing with Piggot's counselors. I mean it, Ethan.''

Ethan shifted sullenly in his chair until it dawned on him that he was acting more like Jeremy than a responsible officer sworn to uphold the law. "I don't like it, but I'll go along with it.''

"Good.'' The big man heaved his body out of the swivel chair. "In case you're tempted to stray, be advised, Knight—another letter and I'll have you on bike

patrol in Desert City's high-rent district. We'll see how
you and Taz like tracking lost poodles for the crème de
la crème.''

Although Ethan still smarted over Regan's betrayal,
he couldn't imagine anything he'd like less than catering
to the whims of the city's rich and famous. Some real
jerks and weirdos owned lavish homes in the city's foothills. As a young cop he'd worked that beat for a year.
A year better forgotten. As apparently was his brief association with Regan Grant.

On leaving the chief's office, Ethan suffered twinges
of disappointment, together with deeper feelings he was
reluctant to identify. With little effort, he fancied he
could smell Regan's perfume as it had clung to her soft
soft skin.

Dumb, he thought. He sure as hell wouldn't lose sleep
over any woman who'd thrown him to the wolves the
way Regan had done.

Mitch glanced up anxiously as Ethan stomped into the
office and batted his long legs off the desk.

''Whoa, there!'' Mitch bounded up the minute his
boots hit the floor. ''Don't take your mad at the chief
out on me, buddy.''

''Sorry.'' Ethan sucked in a mouthful of the stale air
that permeated the old precinct. The partners shared an
eight-by-eight space. Yet they were among the few who
could claim the luxury of a window. After ripping open
a new sack of kibble and filling Taz's bowl, Ethan strode
to that window and stared moodily out at streetlights
beginning to flick on in the growing darkness.

''Are you going to fill me in, or do I have to guess
what made you snarl like a junkyard dog?'' Mitch, who
owned a small ranch on the outskirts of the city and

spent most of his free time on a horse, crossed to his partner's side with the hip-rolling gait of a true cowboy.

"Next week I'll have fifteen years on the force, Mitch. In all that time, there hasn't been one complaint filed against me. Today I got two."

"Wow, you hit the jackpot. Wellington backed you, right?"

"He's holding off on writing me up."

"That's good, isn't it?" Mitch hesitated in the wake of his friend's scowl. "Not good, huh?"

"Damn skippy it's not. I've been ordered to cease all contact with CHC."

Mitch whistled. "Why? And how did I miss being involved?"

"Joey Hawkins. You were off duty. She's the kid staying with Greg and Maddy Hargreaves."

"I thought you said Regan worked with you on that placement."

Ethan's lips thinned. "She did. Joey's mom hooked up with a parent-activist lawyer and they stormed CHC, crying foul play. The big bad police officers treading on Lucy Hawkins's civil rights."

"So shouldn't Regan have straightened them out and sent them packing?"

"There's the rub, Cowboy. Regan's charged me with rushing her into making a hasty decision with regard to placing Joey. That's not all. The letter from CHC makes me seem derelict because I didn't follow up with a visit to the home. I was going to," Ethan said bitterly. "Regan said she'd handle it."

"If you ask me, something sounds fishy. Like some wires got crossed."

"You're right." Ethan turned. "Regan probably doesn't know Piggot would love to have my badge. It's just…she gave him the opening. Now Wellington's worried this will spark a wholesale departmental investigation by the state budget folks.''

"Regan complained? I guess I got *my* wires crossed, pal. I'd have sworn from the goofy smile you wore all day that you'd spent the night tearing up the sheets and steaming windows with her. And now you say she gave you the shaft.''

Ethan slumped against the wall. "That's the hell of it, Mitch. Regan and I did…connect last night. And I thought we'd agreed to a repeat performance tonight.''

Mitch dropped into his chair again. "I don't know what to say, partner.''

Ethan shoved away from the wall and lunged for the phone. "The hell with Wellington's orders. I'm going to get her on the horn and ask why she put a knife in my back.''

"You can't.'' Mitch ripped the phone out of his friend's hand. "If the chief said no contact with the CHC, he meant no way, no how.'' He slapped the phone back into its cradle, but Ethan snatched it out again.

"Who's going to tell him? You? Anyway, after Wellington sleeps on this cockamamy charge, he'll come to his senses and tell me to go ahead and kick agency ass. The chief's got his own history with Piggot.''

"Sounds like this goes beyond anything personal.'' Mitch maintained his tug-of-war with Ethan over the phone.

"Maybe it's not personal from where *you* sit. Thanks to Regan's letter, the chief's threatened me with exile to the foothills beat.''

"All right. If you're willing to take the chance that Wellington's not serious, go ahead. Call up Grant and give her hell.''

"Well, dammit." Ethan slammed down the phone himself, barely noticing that his actions caused Taz to lift his head and growl.

"I'm sorry, too, Ethan. It's the first time in two years you've found a woman who interests you enough that you want to take her home from the dance and stick around for breakfast. And she turns out to be a nut-cruncher. Life sucks sometimes."

Mitch's convoluted sympathizing forced Ethan to smile. "I didn't know you kept such close tabs on my love life, Valetti. I thought you were too busy cutting a swath through the eligible ladies in town to care how I spend my nights."

Mitch grabbed Ethan's ear, holding him still long enough to knuckle his head. "I'm getting tired of assuring the other guys in the department that you're not suffering from erectile dysfunction, Knight. Who'll believe me now, especially if this relationship goes kaput after one lousy night?"

Ducking, Ethan restored order to his hair. "Do me a big favor, Mitch. Keep this between us."

"She really left gaping wounds, huh?"

Ethan shrugged, then finally said, "Yeah."

Mitch had found a stack of messages and was leafing through them. "If it makes you feel any better, maybe guilt got to her. She phoned you at one, at three-ten and again at six o'clock."

Accepting the slips Mitch extended, Ethan wadded them up and chucked the lot into the wastebasket. "Tough."

"Hey, I just had a thought. The chief didn't tell *me* not to rattle her cage." Mitch reached for the phone, but Ethan stilled his hand.

"I'm over the need to yell at her. As far as I'm con-

cerned personally, Regan Grant is history. Professionally, I've worked too hard securing a safety net for kids
in this town who are being mistreated. The chief said
you should deal with CHC from now on. You won't be
very effective if you get on Regan's bad side because of
me. Thanks for the offer, though."

"It's your call," Mitch said. "But hey, I could cuss
her out in Italian."

"No," Ethan snapped. "It wasn't that great a night,"
he lied, knowing his good friend would never back off
otherwise.

"Huh?" Mitch grunted. "Whatever. But I'm still going to find it damned hard to cut her any slack." He
paused, shaking his head. "It's been a while since I
darkened the door at St. Maggie's except to play a little
football with parish kids. Think I'll drop by the chapel
tonight and light a couple of candles asking for a mor-
atorium on warring spouses."

"If all it takes is candles, light a hundred," Ethan said
caustically. "Or have you forgotten the number of domestic problems we handled today? Let's flip a coin to
see who stays here and types those reports."

"You're gonna owe me big-time, but I'm volunteer-
ing. Otherwise you'll be stuck answering phones, too. If
I stay and the Grant dame calls again, we won't be jeopardizing your career."

"Don't call her a dame."

Mitch simply stared at Ethan, until Ethan swore and
emptied his clipboard of all their day's call-outs. He
dumped the pages on Mitch's desk, snapping his fingers
at Taz. The two of them stalked out.

Ethan knew he'd left Mitch gazing after him in astonishment. But how could he attempt to explain his reluc-

tance to remain angry with Regan when he didn't fully understand it himself?

REGAN DIDN'T SLEEP WELL. As short as her time with Ethan had been, she missed feeling her cheek against his chest. She missed hearing the sound of his breathing as he curled around her. Tossing about on the bed, Regan grieved the loss of a budding relationship, in the lonely hours before dawn, she shed tears over it. Something she hadn't done when her engagement to Jack fell apart.

Early the next morning, standing listlessly under a steamy shower that had little to no chance of improving her day, Regan gave up hoping Ethan had simply gotten involved in a case—that he'd missed her phone messages.

Drying off, she let go of the last vestige of hope that his not calling had somehow been a department glitch or an oversight.

Too bad. She wrapped her wet head in a towel. Too bad for Ethan if, in those hours they'd shared, those intimacies, he hadn't developed any faith in her professional integrity. She wasn't without contacts in the system. Nathaniel had overstepped the bounds of his authority. He should not have ordered Joey back into an unsafe environment. And he had no right to make Regan his scapegoat in a private beef with Ethan Knight. It would have been nice to have Ethan in her corner when she launched a crusade against her boss, but it wasn't absolutely vital.

After styling her hair, Regan dressed in a cherry-red suit that always bolstered her spirits. Buttoning the last button, she was struck by a very uncomfortable thought. What if Ethan had lied about wanting more than a one-night stand? That sort of behavior was so typically Jack. What if she'd let herself be hoodwinked again?

Forgoing tea and toast at home for coffee and a bagel on the way to work, Regan grappled with the obvious. Ethan Knight was a jerk.

Charging out of the busy restaurant, she argued in Ethan's favor again. After all, she'd watched him deal with Jeremy and also Joey. A man in Ethan's line of work had to have a tough outer shell. Underneath his beat a tender heart. And didn't Regan know how vulnerable tender hearts were?

Technically this mess was Nathaniel's doing. He'd sent the letter to Ethan's commander. She hadn't seen a copy yet, and until she did, Regan wouldn't know how bad he'd made her look. Wasn't it still possible that Ethan had gotten tied up with a case? Maybe she was blowing his absence last night all out of proportion. Their midnight assignation wasn't something he'd want to cancel through a department dispatcher. Especially if the dispatcher on duty last night was his sister.

As she parked at the office, she decided to leave him one more message at the station. First, though, she had to oversee the monthly meeting of counselors. And put out a few fires, no doubt. Overworked staff hated rumors of budget cuts. Regan had been a rank-and-file grumbler long enough to know that staff never blamed legislators. It was easier to gripe at a department supervisor. Well, she'd simply refer them to Nathaniel. He served on the state budget committee. And yesterday it almost seemed as if he'd relish cutting services to this community.

An attitude of that nature took some figuring. Perhaps he'd been a director too long. Perhaps he'd lost touch with the sad state of affairs out on the streets. The agency served more homeless individuals these days.

More single-parent families who struggled to make ends meet. And fewer hospitals were willing to serve low-income and indigent clients. Restricting already inadequate funds would have a devastating effect.

What would it take to wake Piggot up? Regan wondered as she breezed through the reception area, her mind so engaged with this problem that she missed the counselors' lack of response to her greeting. The staff was huddled in the meeting room, waiting for her to begin their monthly session.

A copy of Nathaniel's letter to Ethan's chief sat in the center of Regan's desk. She took time to read it, knowing she'd be late starting the meeting. She groaned after the first paragraph and became more livid with each successive one. At the end she grabbed the analgesic bottle, shook out two pills and quickly downed them with water.

Nathaniel had been too clever with his words. He'd used "we" throughout, suggesting that he and Regan were in complete accord. And he'd managed to place total responsibility for demanding that Ethan be reprimanded on Regan's shoulders. On paper, she came off sounding like a vindictive shrew out to save her own neck, or at least her job.

No wonder Ethan hadn't returned her calls.

Regan folded the letter with shaking hands and shoved it into a folder of personal correspondence. The situation was far worse than she'd imagined. As well as alerting higher-ups about this, she might as well explore transfer options. This type of news always leaked out eventually. Once it did, none of the counselors here would trust her to back them on tough decisions. None, she thought again, after reading another terse memo from Nathaniel. This one informed her to stay completely out of Mavis

Shiller's cases. He noted one in particular—Serena Trejo, a single mother with four-week-old quadruplets.

Damn, damn, damn. Just when I'd made headway with Dani, too. Standing on shaky legs, Regan gathered her meeting handouts and tried to calculate how many days she had before her stock in this department went into a decline from which there'd probably be no recovery.

Zero days, she discovered as she faced a hostile crowd. The first question thrown at her came from a veteran counselor, Mavis Shiller. A close friend of Anna Murphy's, Mavis had reportedly lobbied to get Regan's job. Now Mavis let her disenchantment with Regan be known. "Before you shove outdated methods for processing clients down our throats, perhaps you wouldn't mind telling the staff why you usurped one of my longstanding clients. Anna assigned *me* Lucy Hawkins." Mavis thumped her scrawny chest. "In the twelve years I've been a counselor, I've never had a supervisor take a case out of my hands without at least the courtesy of a phone call. Apparently that's not how we can expect to be treated now."

At first Regan prayed that a hole would open in the floor so she could drop through. She was furious with Nathaniel for landing her in this predicament, for exploiting her in his own territorial battles. But, determined to hold her own, she stood tall behind the podium.

"Mavis, I'll be happy to sit down with you after the meeting and go over facts that prompted my intervention in the Hawkins case. As you've just returned from vacation, perhaps you'd like to read the copies of my reports first. My door is always open to staff, as I said at our first meeting. Today, however, our agenda involves an area our director deems of paramount importance. Mr.

Piggot believes we're currently deficient in the way we follow standard guidelines. These state criteria are designed to maintain integrity and consistency in our agency. While it'd be ideal to tailor rules for individual cities and towns, the rules set forth in our instruction manuals work well in New York, L.A., Chicago and Phoenix. In other words, Everycity, USA.''

Regan snapped on an overhead projector and laid her laminated sheets on the podium. Quickly and efficiently she walked through the flowchart from intake to placement.

Of course everybody in this audience had once practiced the rules. But when Regan finished and snapped off the projection light, it was easy to tell from their uncomfortable expressions which counselors had found shortcuts. Several people seated in the back rows folded their handouts and slipped quietly from the room.

Mavis Shiller crushed her packet and threw it in the wastebasket. "New York, L.A. and Phoenix are going down for the third time in a sea of time-consuming paperwork," she proclaimed loudly. "Anna's record in Desert City speaks for itself. I know I'm not the only one who can remember when it took weeks to process a battered wife or mistreated kids or victims of rape. I challenge anyone in this room to deny that the network set up by Anna and Ethan Knight—unorthodox though it might be—has saved families and *lives*."

The staff bunched at the door waited to see how Regan would respond. A few affirmed Mavis's charge. Almost all made it clear that they were ready to hold Regan responsible for a crack in their system.

Terry Mickelson led a more personal charge. "What Mavis is trying to say is, if it ain't broke, don't let a supervisor mess with it."

"I'm saying more than that," Mavis shouted over the ripple of laughter. "We all think it's crappy the way *she* sticks it to Ethan one day and stands up here the next spouting off about *integrity.*"

That remark hit a sore spot with Regan. But she remained calm and in command. "Nevertheless these are the rules I want everyone to follow until further notice. Are there questions?" In the heavy silence Regan closed her folder. She wove through the assembled staff, shoulders straight.

Once inside her office, however, Regan let her guard drop. She rifled through an old employee packet and removed a transfer-request form. In bold black ink, she filled out page one and had started on two when she hit a snag. For employees to be eligible for transfer, they were required to have spent a full year in their current positions.

Now what?

Regan threw down her pen, which rolled to the edge of her desk. As she massaged stinging eyes with the heels of both palms, her office door opened without warning. She half expected to see Mavis coming at her for round two. But Odella Price walked in and shut the door.

"Sorry I missed the meeting. Last night at dinner I lost a crown. I was so excited when the dentist's office said I could come by first thing this morning and get it repaired, I'm afraid today's meeting flew out of my head."

Trying to hide the ravages of yesterday's frustration capped by today's, Regan leaned forward to retrieve her pen. "Have a seat, Odella. Here's a copy of the handout." Regan separated one from the stack. "It's self-explanatory. This is all we covered today."

"I heard. In fact, from the time I walked into the mob hanging around Nicole Mason's switchboard, that's *all* I heard."

"Yes, well...if you've come to add to what Mavis said, you'll have to do it without an audience."

Odella folded the handout into a neat square and stuffed it in her cocoa-brown suit pocket. Idly she inspected fingernails painted the same shade of orange as her lipstick. "If you look closely at personnel records, Regan, you'll see Anna was on the verge of retiring Mavis."

Regan reset the clasp that was doing a poor job of holding her hair out of her eyes. At first she felt a surge of interest at the news. Then, sighing, she said, "Odella, I'm sorry, but I won't discuss one counselor with another."

"Okay, then I have another question," Odella said bluntly, "Why didn't you tell them Piggot put you in the hot seat and left you to burn?"

"Why...I..." Regan shook her head. "People believe what they want to believe."

"Too true. But it galls me when Nathaniel pulls these stunts and gets off scot-free. Bottom line is that you and Ethan know whose fingerprints are all over that letter."

A guilty light kindled in Regan's eyes. "Letter?" she struggled to say.

Odella flung an arm over the back of her chair. "Tell me you've got too much on the ball to play fall guy for Piggot." Odella traced Regan's guilt-ridden expression to the papers lying under her hand. The older woman ripped the form out from beneath Regan's restless fingers. Her eyes scanned the form only briefly before she tore it into pieces the size of confetti and let them flutter all over Regan's handouts. "Time for that mind-clearing

hike we discussed the other day, girl. Weather channel
predicts high sixties for Saturday and Sunday on Mount
Lemmon. Couldn't be better hiking weather. I'm available either day. If we go early, I know of a gorgeous
panoramic vista that would give us a spectacular view
of the entire valley. You'll feel like you're sitting on top
of the world.''

Regan started to refuse. Then she thought about how
badly she needed to get away and clear out the cobwebs
caused by Ethan, Nathaniel and her job. ''Sounds fab-
ulous, Odella. Just what the doctor ordered. Saturday's
okay with me. Where shall we meet? I don't mind driving.''

''Now that's a deal I won't refuse. My husband's car
is in the shop until next week and we're playing musical
vehicles at my house. Is eight too early to pick me up?''
Leaning over Regan's desk, Odella scribbled her address
on the back of a handout. ''In case you misplaced my
business card,'' she said. ''Anyway, we can confirm on
Friday.''

Regan put the note in her pocket. ''Are hiking boots
in order?''

''Advisable. The Butterfly Trail has a few switchbacks
and steep grades. But there's awesome scenery every
step of the way.''

''Great. What about food and water?''

''I guzzle water when I hike. Two bottles minimum.
Crackers, cheese, trail mix. Or power bars if you like
them.''

''Sweatshirt or jacket?'' Regan busily made notes to
herself.

''Let's see, this is the tail of March going out like a
lamb. The sun sets at approximately six-thirty, give or
take ten minutes. We'll be back at the car before dark.

At that elevation the temperature drops fast. Make it easy on yourself, Regan. A sweatshirt or windbreaker. Maybe not both or you'll end up lugging one.''

"Okay—you're on. Sweatshirt, water, food. See you Saturday.''

The women grinned at each other like a couple of kids.

After Odella left, Regan's day zipped by faster than she'd ever anticipated. Her only moment of backsliding into pessimism came after she got home and checked her answering machine, on the off chance Ethan had had a change of heart and telephoned there, instead of the office.

Nothing.

Twice throughout a busy evening of paperwork and staff reviews, she reached for the phone to call Ethan again, to try to square things. Both times she curled her fingernails into a tight fist and resisted the urge.

She'd be darned if she would give him the impression of pining over him. Anyway, maybe he'd break down and phone her later this week.

He didn't. But the week finally ended, and Regan had her hike to look forward to. A day without thoughts of work, she promised herself. And without memories of Ethan.

Pretty unlikely on *both* counts.

CHAPTER TEN

ODELLA'S HUSBAND, Roger, a burly man with military-cut gray hair, escorted his wife to Regan's car in a courtly manner. Though newly introduced to his wife's supervisor, he chatted easily with her about the drive and the proposed hike, as if they were already friends.

Regan liked the way Roger handed Odella into the car and then unselfconsciously bent to give her a goodbye kiss. Their fingers twined for a moment after the kiss ended. Before they broke the connection, he issued last-minute advice about watching the mountain roads for spring erosion. He even blew her a kiss after he shut the door.

Regan's sigh mingled with the turnover of the car's engine. "Odella, you and Roger just showed me the real reason the man I was engaged to is my *former* fiancé. Looking back, I realize Jack never cherished me. Roger so obviously cherishes you, and that's what I want in my own life. You two have something special," she added, eyes slightly misty. A thought struck Regan out of nowhere—that Ethan Knight would be that special kind of husband or lover.

"Believe it or not, the credit all goes to my mother-in-law," Odella said. "She raised five boys on Chicago's south side. All five are gentlemen. That's the key, you know, to stamping out abuse. Mothers must insist on respect from sons."

"So you're saying fathers can be loudmouthed aggressive jerks?"

"Of course not!" Odella stretched like a long sleek cat and settled into in the corner of the passenger seat. "Listen to us. I promised you we'd leave our jobs behind."

"That's okay." Regan flashed a quick grin. "My attempt to understand men isn't limited to my work in social services. Since I haven't found Mr. Ideal Partner yet, I'm really hoping you aren't going to tell me I have to find me a newborn and raise him."

Odella's silvery laughter filled the car. "Sorry, I can only vouch for my husband and sons, and they're taken."

"All the good ones are," Regan lamented on a rush of exhaled air.

It appeared Odella might make another comment, but she shrugged abstractedly and pointed to a turnoff leading to the Catalina Highway and their ultimate destination on Mount Lemmon.

Regan read her hesitation. "What? If you have a list of good guys stashed somewhere, I'll be forced to hurt you if you don't hand it over."

That prompted Odella to erupt in a further peal of laughter. "Hey, you don't want to go to the mat with an old street-fighter like me." Odella's laughter disappeared. "Look, Regan, I tell it like it is. Or at least the way I see it. If I'm interfering too much, just tell me."

Regan shook her head. "Speaking out for unpopular views is a trait I admire. I'm afraid I've spent a lifetime trying to placate everyone."

"Yeah? Who took on Nathaniel over feeding hungry kids regardless of their immigration status?"

"Who *didn't* hand in her resignation when he deliberately used her to take a swipe at Ethan Knight?"

"I knew you weren't behind that letter, in spite of what Mavis Shiller insinuated." Odella kept shaking her head. "Damn, Regan, why didn't you toss that hot potato right back in Piggot's lap? You let the counselors think you were after Ethan's badge," she said, one eye on the scenery as they climbed.

"There's no easy answer," Regan mused aloud. "We're supposed to look at all sides of an issue before rushing to divide a family." A grimace flickered. "Ethan can be very passionate and persuasive on behalf of a child. As a result, I didn't look at Lucy Hawkins objectively. I concentrated solely on Joey."

"B.S. That mom knows how to work the system. Ethan's call-outs to that house have probably been too numerous to count. We need someone like him who can remain staunchly in a kid's corner."

"Ye…es," Regan said. "But this network of foster homes he's built may be too convenient. Which isn't to say they aren't all super places to put needy kids. What escaped me when I visited the first group of foster families he recruited is that maybe they're *too* perfect."

Odella frowned. "What are you talking about?"

The road went into a series of S-curves and out again before Regan replied. "Statistics show we return three out of five kids to their former homes. Are we wrong to let them taste a life they might never have?"

"Serve in this business as long as I have, Regan and you'll come to accept that we aren't God. Ethan thinks all kids deserve to see there's a life worth reaching for beyond the day-to-day struggle to survive. I wish the world had a million more men like him."

"I know." And Regan did. She shrugged helplessly.

"I do agree with that. I'm just feeling so…discouraged. Nathaniel's completely tied my hands. He's even forbidden me to look in on one of Mavis's new cases. Quadruplets born to a twenty-one-year-old single mom. Has she mentioned them?"

"Briefly. The story was in the news, as well. Mavis asked my advice on a day-care facility. She found the mother a job. From what she said, I believe everything is okay."

"Good. I'll touch base with her sometime next week to make sure. She's avoided me since our run-in at the meeting. Maybe I can start by telling her you said she's doing a fine job on the quads case. That way, she won't go to Piggot and accuse me of looking over her shoulder."

"Sure, feel free to throw my name around." Odella chuckled.

The next fifteen or twenty minutes passed with neither woman speaking. Finally Regan asked, "Odella, how much trouble do you suppose that letter got Ethan into?"

"If you care, maybe you should go to the police chief and ask him."

"Won't he think I'm a flake? I didn't sign it, but my name's typed at the bottom. Nathaniel signed on my behalf," she added bitterly.

"The police chief is not naïve," Odella said. "He's had other dealings with Nathaniel."

"I'll think about it, okay? While we're hiking." Regan scanned the saguaro-studded hillside the car now climbed in a series of switchbacks. Each curve in the road took them higher above the desert floor. The vegetation thickened with the advent of pine trees. "This road must have been hard to build. Didn't I read somewhere the original highway was built by prison labor?"

"Yes, the entire six-thousand-foot climb. Ethan could tell you more. His grandfather, one of Desert City's best cops ever, carried water by pack mule to the laborers during his off-work hours. He objected to making prisoners do jobs no one else wanted. It was largely due to his efforts that the men were paid for their work. Ethan has old pictures of this area in its most rugged state. Among other things, his family are staunch environmentalists."

"You wouldn't be trying to shove Detective Knight's sterling qualities down my throat, would you, Odella?"

A flush of guilt splashed Odella's smooth cheeks. "Too obvious, huh? I'll give it a rest," she mumbled, seeming content to watch the road.

"No. Now you've piqued my interest. Why does a man who looks like Ethan—not to mention that he possesses all those great qualities—need the help of matchmakers? I only ask because his sisters have let a few comments slip to that effect."

"I shouldn't have to tell you about the pitfalls of dating these days."

"The rise of AIDS and STDs, you mean?"

Odella opened a pack of sugar-free gum and passed a stick to Regan. She chewed on her own piece a few minutes before answering. "That's part of it. But there are other factors, too. After I retired, before I rejoined the agency, I taught a few sociology classes at the college. There's tremendous pressure on our young men and women to succeed in their careers. Marriage and family are steadily being pushed aside while they climb their various work ladders. The emphasis is on earning a lot of money in order to retire at fifty. Suddenly all these guys and gals wake up and find themselves facing a future alone, and they settle for it because it's easier than reaching outside their comfort zones. As a result, family life's on the decline. That's how I see it, anyway."

"You're pretty upbeat about families, considering the debris we wade through every day. I hate to be cynical, but what if the family as it's been defined in the past is obsolete?"

"Honey, surely you don't really believe that. Love is the ultimate basis of family, and that's what's missing. All species need love to survive. We shouldn't let life fly by in such a whirlwind of goals and profits that we lose the number-one ingredient for true happiness."

"I guess I'm not that philosophical. Propagation equals survival of any species. Our work certainly proves that lust, not love, is all that's needed to propagate."

"Yikes, will you look at the time?" Odella raised her watch to Regan's eye level. "We've been arguing about this for more than an hour. Up ahead, just beyond the next bend, is the turnoff for Soldier Camp. We'll park there. Starting at that point allows us a choice as to whether we hike all the way to the ranger station and complete the loop, or turn back halfway. I like having options, especially on the first major hike of the year. I'm still in the process of losing those extra holiday pounds."

Regan made a face. "We should all have your problem with so few extra pounds when we hit sixty. By the way, I'd rather not call our discussion an argument. Since moving here, I haven't had this kind of brisk friendly exchange with a colleague. You know, sharing information and ideologies. Except with Ethan the other night." Her lips curved upward momentarily in memory. Then she caught herself and cleared her throat. "I will make an appointment to see his chief, Odella. While I may disagree with Ethan about rummaging around in our agency business, he shouldn't be punished for wanting to make a difference in his community.''

Odella's smile was slow to spread. While Regan parked, she effectively hid her expression—the look of a cat who'd just bagged a fat mouse.

Regan was too consumed by the stark beauty of the panorama around her to think about anything other than the anticipated joy of communing with nature.

''It's cooler up here than I imagined.'' She brushed a hand over her khaki shorts as she climbed from the car. ''I wonder if I'll be sorry I didn't wear sweatpants,'' she said as she shrugged into a lightweight long-sleeved sweatshirt.

''My recollection of this trail is there's a lot of up and down. It's a gradual climb, but we'll warm up as we walk. We have to go up another two thousand feet to reach the lookout I brought you here to see.''

''Oh. Not to worry then. By midpoint I'll probably be dripping with sweat. I did bring a down vest, but I'll leave it in the car.''

Odella donned her own sweatshirt. ''We'll be deep in ponderosa pine long before we reach the waterfall at the halfway mark. It may even be cooler along the rim, although a sweatshirt should be protection enough.'' She frowned briefly. ''The only thing is, tree branches will still be wet from last week's storm.''

Regan tossed her down vest into the back seat and shut and locked the doors. ''It stormed last week? Where was I?''

''The weatherman said it was over the Catalina and Rincons and dropped several inches of rain. Not a drop in the valley, though.''

"It was so nice in Phoenix, I got out of the habit of paying attention to weather predictions. If we're going to try and hike with any regularity, I'll have to tune in again." She opened the trunk and put two bottles of water into her backpack, along with a compact first-aid kit and several energy bars.

"If you don't have room for that package of trail mix," Odella said, "I'll carry it. It's the least I can do since you have the added weight of a first-aid kit."

Regan shifted the kit to make room for the trail mix. "You could call the kit my security blanket. A throwback to an accident I had as a child. Not a neighbor for two blocks around had more than Band-Aids in their medicine cabinets."

"Did you fall out of a tree or go through a plate-glass window trying to catch a baseball? My kids did both. Their escapades taught me to stock a veritable pharmacy at my house."

Regan's fingers flew to her neck, an action that drew Odella's gaze. Sunlight filtering through the patchy trees revealed what the low light in their office building never had. Regan's hand wasn't wide enough to hide the long white line.

"Holy cow. My son's clash with the living-room window was nowhere near that bad. Forget a first-aid kit. From the extent of that scar, I'd say you owe your life to 911."

Regan dropped her sunglasses over her eyes and tugged an Arizona Diamondbacks baseball cap to the side of her head, angling the bill down to shade her neck. She stepped out fast along a paved road toward a sign introducing the Butterfly Trail. Stopping there, Regan studied a wooden billboard showing major scenic attractions along the path, which circled back to the starting point. Odella barely caught up before Regan moved ahead to read an informational sign posted by local rangers.

"You don't have to spill your guts to me." Odella adjusted her pack. "Any fool knows a person would rather not relive an accident causing an injury of that magnitude." She jogged past Regan.

Reaching out a hand, Regan snagged the back of Odella's jacket. "I went ten rounds with a dog and I lost." As Odella turned and met Regan's eyes, she added, "Some people in my hometown might tell you I won. Animal control put the dog down." Her chin quivered. Despite everything, despite her own fear, it still bothered her to think about the poor tormented animal.

The older woman's murmur of sorrow got lost in Regan's next question. "Did you read this bulletin about bears? It says that last year a young camp counselor was mauled on the mountain. Several bears had to be trapped and relocated."

Odella buried the toe of one hiking boot in undergrowth creeping over the trail. "Regan, you poor girl. It's clear to me now why you freaked out at the sight of Ethan's dog that day at the office. Mercy, is Ethan aware...?"

"Considering the way he dashes in and out of my office with that animal and how he twice caught me cowering in my car at his mom's," Regan admitted, "I had to tell him. He...he said he understood, but I'm not sure anyone does. Or can." Sliding a nervous tongue over her lower lip, she stared up the trail. "Aren't you spooked by this notice?"

"No. Last year was unique. I've hiked these trails on and off for years and I've never seen a bear. At most I've surprised some small burrowing creatures like rabbits, ground squirrels or prairie dogs. And birds. Eagles and hawks are plentiful. Are you okay with them?''

"Yes." Regan snapped out of her trance and laughed. "I'm not a total wimp. Let's go. We've wasted enough time on my pathetic woes."

"Given the ordeal you appear to have had, I don't think I'd term you pathetic or anything of the kind," Odella said. "Whaddaya say we let it go at that?"

"Odella, you're a gem. First stop, Novio Spring." Punching a fist in the air, Regan forged ahead.

"Just past the spring, we'll rest and grab a snack. Then we'll have lunch at the vista I told you about. If we don't dally, we can get there in plenty of time to return by the same route or if we prefer, we can complete the loop."

"Doesn't it give you a delicious sense of freedom knowing we don't have to keep to a schedule today?"

"Uh-uh!" Odella wagged a finger. "Work is beginning to creep into our conversation again. None of that."

"Okay." Regan danced along the trail, her laughter startling a covey of quail.

For the first few miles they drifted into a compatible pace. One that allowed Regan time to snap pictures of new sights and gave Odella at thirty years Regan's senior, intervals to rest.

Their sporadic conversation throughout the next two hours was confined to brief exclamations of wonder and delight at the ever-increasing wildness of the landscape around them. Canopies of pines muffled the steady tread of their feet.

"Oh, look. A deer." Regan crouched in the middle of the trail. "Two, and a fawn," she whispered, checking Odella's forward motion with a hand. "There, near the falls," she said in more normal tones, trusting the gurgling water to cover her voice and the camera's click.

"Incredible." Odella's voice was awed. "Whenever I get out like this, I wonder what made me put off doing it for so long."

"Me, too. This is my idea of how to spend a leisurely Saturday. Hiking Squaw Peak was never like this. At times there was more traffic on those trails than you'd encounter at the busiest mall. Hey, are you game to do this once or twice a month?"

"It's a deal. Oh, something scared our mama deer. If we're quiet while we eat, Regan, maybe they'll circle back to drink again."

Though they kept a sharp eye out and did see two Harris hawks swoop down to drink from the pool at the base of the falls, the deer remained elusive.

"Much as I'd like to while away the afternoon at this spot," Odella finally said with a sigh, "we'd better keep moving."

Regan stood and dusted the moss from the back of her shorts. "I'm ready to push on. I'm completely refreshed. Isn't it marvelous what rest and a snack will do?"

"We'll see if you feel the same way in an hour. The climb is steep for the next three miles or so."

Both women felt the added exertion. Conversation stopped as they called on inner resources. Wet pine boughs, pungent with the smell of pitch, formed a heavy arch over the trail. Patches of fog drifted in silently, bringing an occasional whiff of wood smoke from a cabin perched on a ridge across a dizzying ravine.

The trail suddenly made a sharp left turn. For some reason, Odella plunged straight ahead. Regan witnessed the move a split second before she heard Odella cry out in pain. With her heart skipping and jumping like oil on a hot griddle, Regan dropped to her hands and knees and pawed through the still-quivering underbrush. "Thank heaven," she gasped, overjoyed to see her partner seated at the bottom of a gentle slope, not tumbling headfirst down a slick canyon.

"Save your thanks," Odella moaned. "I really did a number on my right ankle."

Regan slid to where she could give Odella a hand up. Then the older woman grabbed a broken tree branch to use as a walking stick. "Oh!" She sank to one knee. "I think it might be broken."

"Let's get you back to the falls where I can take a closer look." Regan helped Odella hobble ever so slowly back the way they'd come.

"Phew, a bad sprain is all," Odella said after they'd done a better examination. "See, I can wiggle my toes."

"All swollen as sausages," Regan pointed out before she worriedly bit her bottom lip. "What shall we do? You can't walk all the way out of here."

"Of course I can. I won't break any speed records, but I will get to the car under my own power."

"And risk causing greater damage to your ankle? No. Let me think. How far up ahead to the ranger station? A lot fewer miles than going back, right?"

"The ranger station's at the first bend after you start down."

Regan began to pace. "You wait here. I'll go get a ranger. They'll have splints and wraps. There's no ankle brace in my first-aid kit."

"If you guys complete the loop, we'll connect faster if I mosey on back to the car."

"No. If you're going to do that, we won't split up."

Regan remained adamant. "The whole point of my going on would be to keep you off that ankle."

"Nonsense. I'll take it easy. Even if I move at a snail's pace, we'll still rendezvous more quickly. The rangers will have a gel ice pack I can use on the drive home."

Regan gave up. "All right. I'll walk fast and you poke along. If we beat you, I'll send the rangers back up the trail for you."

"What if I reach the car first?" Odella teased. "You have the keys."

"You couldn't possibly," Regan scoffed. "But if by some miracle you do, I keep a spare key in a magnetic holder clipped under the driver's-side wheel well."

Odella limped a few steps, grimacing with each one. "So, okay. It was a fanciful thought. At this rate, I'll be walking all night."

"I really dislike letting you start out alone. Let's both go back the way we came."

"Don't be silly. Your plan makes more sense. Plus, it'll give me time to get over feeling like an idiot." Odella gathered Regan into her arms for a reassuring hug.

Once they'd released one another, Regan waited only long enough to divide their food and water equally. "See you before dark," she promised solemnly as they parted.

A LITTLE AFTER TEN that night, Ethan Knight took a call requesting his help in locating an overdue hiker. He was just climbing into bed after a long frustrating day. He and Mitch, with the help of a woman's relatives, had closed the net on her abusive husband, only to watch him walk out a free man two hours later on a stupid technicality. Ethan's first inclination was to refer the lost-hiker call to the next volunteer rescuer on the list.

But that wasn't his nature. He yanked on a pair of clean jeans. "Tell me again what we've got, Dave."

"One woman injured and another who went for help at one o'clock this afternoon, but still hasn't made contact with the ranger station?"

Ethan spoke thoughtfully. "Remember there's a point where the Butterfly Trail converges with the Alder Canyon Trail and they both fork? The Butterfly crosses Sycamore Reservoir. Alder Canyon joins East Fork Fire Road for a mile and loops back. Your hiker is probably wandering around in circles near where those Sabrejet pilots collided and went down a few years ago. I'll bring all my gear, and Taz and I will hop aboard the chopper. I'll just bet your stray turns up in that quadrant. Have the rangers check it out, will you?"

Ethan didn't learn the lost hiker was Regan Grant until after midnight. He attended a briefing the volunteer rescuers received after the chopper dropped them off at Palisades Camp. At first he couldn't believe his ears. And no wonder. Regan had been on his mind throughout the dark bumpy helicopter ride. His breathing was no longer steady.

Normally, whether or not he was acquainted with a victim made no difference to the way he conducted his portion of a search. Knowing it was Regan stumbling around out there in the dead of night forced Ethan to reevaluate his usual plan. Regan, who would panic if Taz found her... He needed to talk to her hiking partner. When he asked if he could do so, he was led toward a woman huddled by the campfire.

"Odella? Is that you?" he asked in shock.

"'Fraid so," she admitted.

Ethan barged his way past a small group of reporters, two of whom had ridden up the mountain in the chopper with him. "Excuse us," he said none too gently, waving them away.

"Oh, Ethan." Looking tired and disheveled, the social worker he'd known for years broke down just seeing him. In a tumble of words mixed with tears, she told Ethan how she and Regan had come to split up. Odella accepted blame for the two having separated.

"Regan doesn't have a jacket with her," Odella sobbed. "She left her down vest in the car. On *my* advice. And look at me sitting by the fire wrapped in two blankets."

"Ranger Murdock said you ought to let them fly you back to an emergency center in town. He said you were hurt and suffering from exposure yourself when you showed up at the station. He doesn't know how you managed to drive with that foot."

"I might go now that you're here, Ethan. To keep Roger from bugging the hell out of the rangers. If you promise you'll call my house the minute you and Taz find Regan."

Ethan stroked his unshaven jaw. "Here's the problem, Odella. Any other case, I'd give Taz a good sniff of that jacket and turn him loose. Maybe Regan didn't tell you, but she has a fear of dogs worse than any panic she might experience over being lost."

"She did tell me." Odella's grief-stricken gaze swept the black pine forest that towered over the clearing. "I think, though, if our roles were reversed, I'd be damned glad for any sign of rescue. She must be terrified about now."

"You may be right. I'd like to send Taz off to do his thing. He can search a lot more ground tonight than I can cover. We human volunteers are limited by our flashlights.''

"Wait here, I'll get you Regan's vest,'' Odella said, fumbling through her pockets to produce Regan's car key.

"Let me do it. You tell Murdock you're ready to board that helicopter. And don't worry,'' Ethan said, managing a flicker of a smile. "Taz and I have worked hundreds of similar rescues. This one is fairly routine.''

SOME SIXTEEN HOURS LATER, after teams had combed and recombed the area, the last shred of daylight faded into a second night of darkness. For the first time, a dirty fatigued Ethan acknowledged that their search for Regan Grant had gone beyond routine. Even then, he withheld the true extent of his worry as he crouched beside a wavering campfire gripping a mug of hot coffee and listening to Ranger Murdock.

"There's no sign of her,'' announced the head ranger. "Fifty men have combed this sector three times, Knight. Not including your sidekick, Taz. Vanzandt's volunteers can't commit for another eight-hour shift. Most have full-time jobs. Frankly, considering the way the woman's vanished, I'm inclined to wonder if we're looking at foul play.''

"Foul play?'' The notion stunned Ethan. "She was out with a girlfriend for a simple day hike, for God's sake!''

"She and her friends weren't the only hikers out today. All I'm saying is foul play could be a possibility.''

Ethan combed a hand through Taz's tangled coat. Bits of pine twig were caught in his identification collar. Turning his back on Murdock, Ethan attached a fresh bottle of water in a sling under Taz's clinking tags. "Good boy," Ethan said, tugging the dog's ears.

"You're sending him out again? Shouldn't you both rest?" Murdock heaved his bulk to his feet.

"Not yet." Ethan stared toward sawtooth peaks that bisected a bright moon. A full range of towering mountains circled the valley where Desert City sat. "I figure Regan's mind was on getting help for her hiking partner. She must've accidentally taken one of the intersecting paths and become hopelessly turned around. But I'm sure she's all right, and she's out there."

"Anything's possible," Murdock agreed. "Maybe she saw the observatory way up at Bear Wallow and mistook it for the ranger station. None of the teams went that far." The head ranger finished his coffee and handed the cup to a volunteer. "Okay, Knight. You wanna check that sector, I'll pledge our support through midday tomorrow. If the woman doesn't turn up by then, I'm afraid I'll have to file my report and call off the formal search."

"I understand," Ethan said. He walked Taz across the road from the start of the Butterfly Trail, gave him a whiff of the perfume still faintly clinging to Regan's down vest and begged his pet to "Find Regan."

REGAN KNEW SHE'D LOST her way when darkness enveloped her and she didn't see even the faintest glow from the city's lights off to the west. Where had she gone wrong? Was she even heading in a westerly direction? She looked up and tried to glimpse the sky, but it was fruitless. She was too deep in a thicket of giant pines.

Never having spent a night in the woods, Regan felt panic take hold, driving her to stumble from tree to tree.

After she twice felt the slap of something wet and scratchy across her bare arms, she forced herself to stop and pull on the sweatshirt she'd looped around her waist a couple of hours earlier. She tried to take realistic stock of her situation.

She had not one clue as to her present position. If she wasn't so scared, it might be laughable. She, who'd made such a big deal out of going off in search of help for Odella, was herself in need of rescue.

When she lived in Phoenix, Regan had attended two desert-survival classes offered by the community college. So she knew that, lost as she was, it'd be stupid to flounder around at night by herself. It might not be pleasant spending a night alone on the mountain, but Regan could think of worse things. Or rather, she tried terribly hard *not* to think of anything worse. She had half a bottle of water, two energy bars and a small amount of trail mix. Hunkering against the broadest tree trunk she could find, Regan convinced herself everything would look better in the morning. For one thing, Odella would surely have reached the car. Eventually she'd notify the rangers. Huddled in her sweatshirt, Regan shivered through the longest night of her life.

When morning arrived, her situation hadn't improved. She was cold, stiff and grumpy—all night she imagined she heard animals rustling in the forest. She'd hardly slept a wink. Her inclination was to sit and wait for rescue. But she kept telling herself it was wiser to forge on and meet them halfway. In the end, she had to guess at the direction and set out on what she thought was a path.

By 10 a.m. she was awfully afraid something had happened to Odella and she'd have to find her own way out of this mess, after all.

Regan climbed a tree, hoping to get her bearings. She glimpsed the flash of sunshine off metal. ''Yes! That must be an antenna at the ranger station.'' Thankful for the sign, however small, she noted the coordinates—or tried to. After eating a bite and drinking sparingly, she headed in the most direct route toward the glint in the distance. ''Man,'' she muttered. ''I really got turned around.''

Twice the path petered out. Fighting the underbrush sapped her flagging energy. The next time she sank to her knees to catch her breath, her watch said 4 p.m. She almost cried. Every muscle in her body ached. It almost seemed, that after hours of walking, she was no closer to the antenna. Dammit, she *had* to be. Six hours of tramping uphill and down, scrambling over boulders, fighting thorny bushes. And the sun was now dropping rapidly on yet another day.

Regan swallowed her despair to keep it from crowding the breath from her lungs. Her water was nearly gone and she'd long since eaten the last of the trail mix. She gazed longingly at her remaining energy bar. Though tempted to gobble the honey-oat confection, she stuffed it back in her pack.

Tonight the air seemed colder. Shaking and with panic edging in, she decided to use the last minutes of daylight to find a secure spot to bed down for the night.

Half an energy bar would go a long way toward comforting her, she thought, sinking to the ground against a sheltered tree. The other half ought to provide enough energy to help her reach the ranger station tomorrow.

Wait until she saw Odella again. Before agreeing to another hike, Regan swore she'd buy an accurate map—*and* recruit a few experienced hikers. Obviously Odella had forgotten how far the ranger station was from the waterfall.

Regan hadn't meant to nod off. She jerked awake with a start, battling a terrifying moment during which she heard sounds like a pig snorting. Seconds ticked by before Regan's sleep-fogged mind merged again with her body. At first she didn't know where she was. Then she remembered. A white moon overhead shone brightly on a rocky clearing off to her right.

She blinked rapidly, then stifled a scream when a huge beast appeared in the moonlight. *A bear.*

Through chattering teeth, Regan tried to convince herself that the lumbering animal was a figment of her imagination. Until he turned, lifted his head and sniffed the air, seeming to covet Regan with his beady eyes.

Regan forced her stiff muscles into action. Her fumbling fingers dropped the backpack she had been snuggling against as she clawed her way up layers of rocks to the next line of trees. *Did the books say you should run or not? Climb a tree or not?*

Grasping the lowest branch of one, she swung aloft with arms that threatened to let her fall. It wasn't until she'd almost knocked herself senseless on a lumpy tree burl that she dared look down.

The bear, a dark blob of black or maybe brown, seemed content for the time being to shred her pack. *Damn.* The brute was eating her energy bar, wrapper and all. She watched him sit back and lick his paws.

While she stared in fear and growing fascination, another, rangier animal streaked into the moonlight from a far stand of pines. Snarls and growls rose to her ears as the new intruder sprang at the bear. The sounds were unholy. Regan didn't realize until the two furry objects separated that the assailant was a dog. A big one.

Sweat popped out on her forehead and poured into her eyes. She tasted the salt of fear on her lips. The small amount of water she'd drunk earlier rose to gag her.

Then the bear roared, and she did throw up as he turned his back on his assailant and came straight toward Regan's hideout.

Suddenly, without warning, he stood on hind legs and slapped at her tree. Something deep inside Regan shifted. Wrapping her arms tight around the swaying branch, holding on for all she was worth, she began a litany of prayers to aid the dog.

A still-functional portion of her brain said where there was a dog, there must be humans nearby. She started to shout. Bellow was more like it, hoping to guide anyone out in these woods to her rescue. "Help! Where are you? Help! Please, someone help me!"

The bear whirled in tight circles. Screaming like an injured woman, he took another wild swipe at the dog, who'd darted close. Blood splattered the rocks. At least from the dog's high-pitched yelp, Regan assumed the dark spray was blood.

"Don't...don't charge the bear again," she begged the dog, ending on a sob when he sailed through the air and landed in a limp heap in a narrow crevice in the rock. Regan shook so hard she was afraid she'd fall from her perch.

Emitting a huge growl, the bear left the base of Regan's tree. The crazed animal uprooted saplings with trunks as thick as her upper arm trying to get at the dog that lay still between the rocks. On the verge of hysteria, Regan swallowed heaving wails of distress. She thought surely the dog was dead, all the while praying he wasn't. Afraid though she was of dogs, he was all that remained between her and certain death.

Time stood still. Regan didn't know how long the angry bear tore up the landscape before finally, after a final snarl, ambled off. She might have stayed up in the tree until morning had not a series of pathetic whimpers reached her ears. Sounds she judged to be coming from the fallen dog.

Over the course of moments, the sounds of pain edged past the bone-melting terror that had kept Regan on her wobbly roost. The Samaritan in her responded to the poor wretched animal who had defended her so valiantly. Without his timely intervention, who knew if she might not be the one lying in a pool of blood? She felt a profound responsibility to help the dog, or at least make his last hours as comfortable as possible. Regan knew what it was like to be injured and alone.

Inch by inch she slid down the rough bark. Still shaking, she hunted for and found what was left of her tattered backpack. She retrieved her half-full bottle of water easily enough, since it had rolled to one side. Regan chanted a weak thanks for the steady glow of the moon. Its light allowed her to identify gauze packs, sterile bandages and tubes of antibiotic ointment that were mercifully intact.

It wasn't until she extracted a flashlight and crawled into the narrow crevice on quaking hands and knees that she saw the water sling around the dog's neck. A sling and tags stating that his name was "Tasmanian Devil." "Oh, oh," she moaned. "You're Ethan's dog." Tears tracked down her cheeks.

And yet it must mean that Ethan was among those searching for her. She simply could not repay his generosity by letting his pet die.

Touching the dog's fur seemed foreign. It was perhaps the hardest task Regan had faced at any time during this entire unbelievable ordeal. Consciously dismissing her own plight, she used the last of her water to cleanse a jagged gash running six or more inches along Taz's soft underbelly. There was a second cut on his chest.

Exhibiting as much care as she would in ministering to a child, Regan dressed the dog's wounds as best she could. The thought kept hammering through her head that they needed to leave this spot, since the bear might return. Though Taz was a dead weight, Regan struggled to lift him. Half-crouched and sobbing, she stumbled through black undergrowth that grabbed at her clothing until she could walk no more. Her muscles spent, she fell with the dog at the base of a huge tree.

In the dead of night, when Regan could no longer keep her eyes open to guard against unseen evil, she eased the dog's head onto her lap. Figuring he needed a drink as badly as she did, she removed the bottle from his sling and poured water into her cupped hands. She almost jumped, spilling most of it, when he started to lap at the water. She went through the process again, more carefully this time.

After he drank, he weakly licked her hand. Regan mustered the courage to speak to him as if he were human. "We're in this together, for better or worse." She yawned and awkwardly patted between his ears.

With that last gesture, her weighted eyelids closed and Regan slumped in exhaustion next to the very creature she most feared.

CHAPTER ELEVEN

REGAN STIRRED and noticed the foggy daylight filtering through a canopy of branches. She sat up and saw the furry animal at her side and instinctively recoiled. Scrambling away from his warmth, she clung to a tree trunk while her world spun drunkenly. She recognized the early throes of hyperventilation and had already begun to combat years of conditioned responses when Taz opened his eyes—eyes brimming with trust, but dulled by agony. Regan sank down next to the poor creature, connected to him through his misery.

"Oh, you poor thing. You need a doctor. A vet. Ethan will be worried sick about you by now. We've got to try and find him."

Regan wasn't at all sure how they were going to accomplish that. In the first place, she didn't know if Taz was fit to travel. From the way her arms still ached after carrying him to this point, she doubted she could do it again. Both of his wounds had closed, but the deeper one on his belly could reopen at any time.

Unfurling her last roll of gauze, Regan carefully bound fresh medicated pads in place. Taz shrank away and whined during her ministrations. But when it was over, he got to his feet, licked her hand and took a few wobbly steps. Head hanging, he picked his way among the trees. At a point where he would have disappeared, he stopped and gazed back at Regan, all but begging her to follow.

She grabbed what remained of their water and stuffed it and the leftover medical supplies into a nearly destroyed backpack. The bear had chewed through one strap, so she looped the good one over her shoulder and set out after an animal she had to force herself to trust. Mistrusting canines of all sizes, shapes and colors had become ingrained. With every step, Regan told herself this dog had saved her life. It soon became a mantra that drove her to plod behind him hour after hour.

She tried once to halt him. Squinting through the tall trees, Regan determined that the sun had risen high overhead. There was no mistaking the bright blood leaking through the dirty gauze that bound his wound. "Please stop," she pleaded, stumbling to her knees. Taz retraced his steps and sniffed her bent head. Uttering soft, guttural sounds in his throat, he slowly eased down next to her.

Using the small scissors from her first-aid kit, Regan cut an uneven six-inch strip from the bottom of her shirt—it hung in tatters, anyhow—and wrapped his worst injury again. They shared a miserly taste of the life-sustaining hoard of water. She worried. What would they do when it was gone? At times she feared the dog had lost his instincts and led them farther astray.

AT ELEVEN-FORTY-FIVE, Ethan, who'd made his way to the observatory instruments on the mountain and then back to camp without finding Regan, suffered a sinking sensation in his stomach at the scene that greeted him. The mood of the men and women who cleaned and packed their search gear was somber. One of defeat.

Ranger Murdock, a mobile phone to his ear, met

Ethan's eyes, then turned away to finish his conversation. Clicking off, he sighed. "Dammit, Knight. Quit looking at me like I kicked your dog. We've had a major rock slide over near the Girl Scout camp. It's blocking the road, and we have thirty kids stranded up there. I've got to pull my rangers from here. We're spread thin as it is."

"I understand," Ethan said, downing a swig of water. "Speaking of my dog, where is Taz?" Ethan's gaze roamed the group of all-terrain vehicles parked at odd angles near the ranger's forestry rig.

Murdock wiped a hand over eyes reddened by a lack of sleep. "I haven't seen him. Not since he tore out of here ahead of you last night. Hey," he called, catching the attention of searchers who still milled about, "anyone see Ethan's dog come in for food or water?"

No one had. They all looked blank.

"That's odd." Ethan picked up the pack he'd dropped moments earlier and shrugged into the straps again. "Whether or not Taz found Regan, he ought to be back. He's trained to check in every three hours. It's automatic with him."

Murdock appeared thoughtful. "Maybe he found the woman and she's hurt and can't walk out. Would he stay with a victim?"

Ethan considered Regan's aversion to dogs. "He's trained to get help. I can't see any reason why he'd break routine. Look, Murdock, we've got five hours of daylight left. Last week's rain left the mountain muddy enough for me to follow Taz's prints."

"Sure, Knight. I don't like to end a search prematurely, either. But don't you go out there and get lost. Stick to marked trails. Whistle for your dog. I don't want another disaster. You know as well as I do that the woman's been without food and water for two hot days and two cold nights. She could've died from dehydration. I won't stop a friend from continuing the search, but officially I have got to call it off and report that to my superiors.''

Ethan let the chill from the ranger's words run through his body before he ground his teeth and answered. ''Till dark today is all I'm asking.''

''You've got it. I know you have a two-way in your gear. Whatever the outcome, I'll expect a call from you by sunset. Replenish your supplies before we close up here.''

Ethan didn't waste any time. He restocked his water first. Although he didn't think he could stand to eat another energy bar, he stuck two in his pack. He'd worn out his flashlight during the night, so he reloaded it with new batteries and replaced the bulb—despite the fact that Murdock had ordered him to wind up before dark.

Taz's prints began exactly where Ethan expected. He lost them plenty of times, though. At approximately three o'clock, he hit a clearing where dog's tracks crossed bear tracks. Ethan's heart skipped wildly. Gouged trees, spattered blood and broken saplings told a grim story. He sank to his knees beside the shredded remains of a honey-oat bar wrapper and a mangled strap from a backpack.

Regan's pack? Please, no!

Standing on shaky legs, Ethan followed the waffle prints of a small hiking boot. They stopped at a sturdy tree. Dried blood dotted broad-leafed plants around the base. ''God!'' he exclaimed. ''No one thought about bears.'' For a minute he thought he'd be sick. He barely managed to pull himself together and act like the search-and-rescue professional he was.

Ethan read signs pretty well. Once he'd absorbed the initial jolt, he went over the area. He found indications that both woman and dog had bedded down among the rocks, apparently after the bear fled. News that should have delighted Ethan sent icy blood racing to his brain. He'd seen the scars from Regan's dog attack. How in hell had she survived this ordeal? Or had she?

Terror wasn't an emotion Ethan could afford to fall prey to, yet fear gripped him. He tasted it in the sweat that beaded his upper lip. Afraid he'd find Regan and Taz dead, he almost couldn't make himself search for their bodies. But dragging in one deep breath after another, his training took over. He searched methodically by grids. On the verge of giving up, he ran across deep boot tracks that led into the woods. No dog prints. Did he follow Regan's tracks or go back over an area he'd already searched, where he must have missed Taz?

Ethan shut his eyes briefly and blotted damp cheeks with a shirtsleeve. *Damn, he loved that dog.* For some time thereafter, his vision blurred and he could no longer see Regan's boot prints.

The sun had sunk well into the west, and Ethan's watch said four, straight up, when it dawned on him that the jumble of boot tracks once again mingled with paw prints. Two sets of prints, hours fresher than the ones near the tree where he figured Regan had taken refuge and Taz had engaged the bear.

Ethan felt the vise around his heart loosen as he all but ran along the trail. He yelled for Regan and Taz until he was hoarse.

It was sheer dumb luck that he found them shortly after dusk had blanketed the forest. He stumbled over them, to be exact. Because by then, even with the flashlight, Ethan had lost all tracks on a thick bed of pine needles.

He couldn't begin to express the joy he felt at seeing Regan and Taz huddled together under a tree. Regan's arms were looped completely around Taz—a sight beyond Ethan's wildest expectations.

For a charged moment, he and Regan stared mutely at each other, and Ethan was afraid he'd wanted to find them so badly he'd simply conjured them up.

Regan had similar thoughts, although she finally gasped out his name. "Ethan. Oh, Ethan, is it really you?" The broad beam of his flashlight formed a halo around her dirt-matted hair and revealed her badly scratched legs as she struggled to get up, holding the heavy dog.

Taz's yelp of pain spurred Ethan to move. "Stay there, Regan," he said in a husky voice that was more like a croak. "There's fresh blood on your shirt. Did the bear…? How bad…?" He cupped her face, but his voice failed completely.

"It's Taz," Regan cried, tears clogging her throat and eyes. "He saved me, but the bear got him twice. I can't stop the bleeding. How close are we to help? He needs a vet, Ethan. I lost my way so many times—oh, this mess is all my fault."

Ethan tried hugging her and Taz together. Regan aimed joyful kisses at Ethan's mouth, and Taz licked his hand.

At eighty pounds Taz was a deadweight in Regan's slender arms. Ethan relieved her of her burden, recognizing it as a miracle that she'd lifted, let alone carried, the dog at all. Yet the tracks indicated she'd done exactly that.

"Can you walk another mile?" he asked. He clutched his aching throat. "I called your names for hours."

"I'm able to walk," Regan said stoically. "Do you have water? We ran out—I don't know when." She reached out to touch Ethan, mainly to prove he wasn't a mirage. "My watch stopped yesterday. Oh, Ethan, say you're here because Odella made it out of the woods, not because her husband reported us missing."

"Odella's hobbling, but she's okay." Ethan kept walking. He carried Taz and urged Regan along after directing her to the bottled water in his backpack. She tried to hurry, but her knees were knocking.

"I couldn't bear it if Odella suffered on my account. Taz is bad enough."

Taz's bandage was blood-soaked. From the unsteady rise and fall of his chest, Ethan knew his injuries were serious. "My vet isn't far from the base of the mountain," Ethan said. "If our luck holds, I can drop him off in a little over an hour and take you on to the hospital. Or I can radio Mitch to meet us, and he can take you to the hospital."

Though panting to keep up, Regan gave a negative shake of her head.

"Don't tell me no. You're covered in scratches, Regan. Even if none of them are serious, you may be suffering from hypothermia. Look at you, still wearing shorts! There's a thermal blanket in my pack. Tie it around your waist."

"I'm fine. I'm going with you to the vets."

There was such determination in her voice Ethan only muttered, "People who operate under extreme duress are capable of Herculean feats—often followed by a big letdown. You must admit this has been quite a feat for you. How in God's name did you...?"

Regan hugged herself and shivered. Bit by bit, her story unfolded. She told him about her encounter with the bear and Taz's intervention. "You and my therapists said I needed to face a dog to deal with my fear. Until last night, nothing and no one could have convinced me it would help." Haltingly she explained how, at first, she'd been physically ill. Reaching around Ethan, Regan stroked the dog's ears. "Now we're kindred spirits, Taz and I."

Ethan hoped Regan's feelings lasted. He longed to take her in his arms and just hold her tight. Given all she'd been through, she was the bravest woman he knew.

Regan made it back to where the car was parked under her own steam. She even helped Ethan prepare a blanket bed on the back seat of the Honda for Taz. But before Ethan finished reporting in to Murdock, she was asleep, huddled in his leather jacket. And she slept like the dead all the way down the mountain to the veterinary clinic.

Ethan didn't break any speed limits, although he was sorely tempted. The clinic stayed open until seven. He rolled in at five to.

Regan woke up when his car door slammed. She'd been dreaming about being in a hot bath...with Ethan. It took her a second to realize where they were. She knew she must look a sight as she climbed, half-asleep, out of the vehicle, and opened the clinic doors for Ethan, who was carrying Taz.

A cacophony of muffled barks greeted them. For a moment Regan's stomach thrashed and she dropped back, hovering in the entrance.

"Ethan? Oh, what's happened to Taz?" exclaimed a young woman whose brown hair was scraped back into a ponytail. She spared a furtive glance for Regan's disheveled state before murmuring, "A car accident? Has Taz been hit? I'll page Dr. Adams. I was closing the office. He only just drove away."

Ethan obviously knew his way around the clinic. He thrust open a door that disclosed an examining room. "Jenny, tell Dr. Adams that Taz tangled with a bear. It's been...how many hours now?" he asked Regan as he heaved the whimpering animal onto a shiny metal table.

"Last night...late," Regan said, biting her lower lip. "The moon was fully up. I don't know the exact time." She overcame her panic to go and soothe Taz.

The doctor's assistant, Jenny, punched a series of numbers into the phone and soon relayed their message. "Dr. Adams is turning back," she announced as she hung up. She pulled open drawers and laid out an array of instruments, but her interest settled on Regan. "Are you the lost hiker all the newscasters are talking about? At noon a ranger announced that the search was suspended."

"You mean they stopped looking for me?" Regan's haunted gaze sought Ethan's.

"Volunteers often carry on after a search is officially canceled. Regan, why don't you have a seat? Better yet, let Jenny roust Mitch. You need those scrapes tended."

Jenny again reached for the phone. Regan stopped her with a shake of her head. "I'm fine," she declared, drawing Ethan's oversize jacket around her shoulders. "Where is that vet?"

"There," Jenny said brightly. "He's driving in now." She approached Ethan and laid a tanned hand—ring-free, Regan noticed—on Ethan's arm. "If you have to leave Taz overnight, I'll keep an eye on him, Ethan. I don't mind staying here. I often do. Infection from wild-animal bites can be dangerous."

Regan didn't know why she suddenly felt so possessive about both Ethan and Taz. "He wasn't bitten. The
bear clawed him," she informed the two who stood
shoulder to shoulder across the table. "And we'll take
him home to do our own nursing, won't we, Ethan?"

Regan saw him start and stare at her in surprise. She'd
surprised herself using that forceful *we*. There was really
nothing at all between her and Ethan except one night
of fantastic lovemaking and a lot of unresolved conflict.

"Yeah." Ethan relaxed. His slow smile was agreement enough for Regan. "I'd rather take him home. People and animals heal faster in the care of loved ones. By
the way, Jenny, have you met Regan Grant? She's the
supervisor who replaced Anna Murphy at CHC. Regan,
Jenny Scopes. She's assisted Dr. Adams for three or four
years now."

"Six," Jenny inserted smoothly as she barely acknowledged meeting Regan. "You've only been bringing Taz in for three years. I've watched him grow from
a pup." Jenny made the last remark staring at Regan, as
if laying some special claim to Taz. Regan was far too
exhausted to sort out what it meant, or if it meant anything.

Dr. Adams bustled in then and took over, flushing
Taz's wounds with saline and sewing up the worst of
his cuts and shooting him full of antibiotics. Afterward,
on the drive through town, Regan's fuzzy brain returned
to Jenny Scopes. "Are you and Jenny dating?" she
asked Ethan directly.

"Me and Jenny?" His eyes shifted from the rearview
mirror where he'd been checking on Taz. "No. Why do
you ask?"

"I don't know." Regan yawned. Her entire body had
begun to ache. "I started out thinking about what she

said. If the rangers called off the search at noon and you continued…oh, Ethan.'' Her eyes darkened. ''I don't know how I can begin to thank you.''

Ethan shrugged as if he'd done nothing.

All at once the enormity of everything that had happened hit Regan hard, and she started to shake. ''Uh…can you drop me off at my apartment? Somehow I don't think I'll be much help tonight in taking care of Taz. Maybe you should ask Mitch. Or Jenny. I'm sure she'd come if you asked.'' Her shivering escalated.

''Hey, don't fall apart on me now.'' Ethan reached across the seat and clasped her fingers tight. ''I'm either taking you to the hospital or you're going home with me. I won't leave you to fend for yourself after all you've been through. So, what'll it be?''

Regan shifted to face him. ''I hate to impose, but hospitals are about my least favorite places.''

''I should insist.'' They crossed under a street light, and his voice softened as he caught a glimpse of her tired features.

''My muscles are weak, but they'll recover with sleep.'' At the very word, her eyes began to close.

''It's no wonder you're weak, Regan. You walked miles. Do you know you traveled eighteen miles from the Butterfly Trail where Odella said you were hiking?''

''Eighteen? Boy, I screwed up big-time. I thought I might be a mile or so off course. Next time I'd better take a compass.''

''Next time stay with your partner.''

''That was my first mistake. I'm sorry I caused so much trouble for you and the others who had to hunt for me, Ethan. 'Thank you' seems…inadequate.''

He started to answer, but pulling into his driveway,

he saw a couple of TV vans and cameramen camped out. Two succinct curse words left his lips, instead.

"What is it? Who are those people?" Regan asked, clutching Ethan's jacket.

"Reporters. There's probably a matched set at your place."

Regan's face appeared pinched and white in the flash of their cameras. "I don't want to talk to them, Ethan. Please." She sounded almost frantic.

Separating a house key on his key ring, Ethan shoved it into her hand. "Go open the front door," he said. Climbing out of the Honda, he answered questions tossed at him from shouting reporters.

"Ms. Grant is safe. My dog, Taz, found her. He had a run-in with a bear, so please step aside and let me get him into the house. I promise I'll answer your questions tomorrow."

Regan, who'd slipped from her side of the car unnoticed, heard them bombarding Ethan with words like *hero*. She didn't turn on any lights but held the door for Ethan as he lugged Taz inside.

She shut the door fast and locked it. Then she snapped on a light and pulled a lap robe from the couch to make a bed on the floor for Taz.

"Thanks," Ethan murmured. "The press can be a pain. You go shower, Regan. There are clean T-shirts in my top dresser drawer. Feel free to nab one. I'm going to get Taz a drink. Dr. Adams said he could eat a little if he's hungry. Hey! You must be starved, too." His lashes lifted and he studied Regan's shaky appearance.

"Frankly, I'm not sure if my hunger outweighs my exhaustion or vice versa." She draped Ethan's jacket over a chair.

Still on his knees next to Taz, Ethan curved a hand

around Regan's ankle. "You've got a lot of deep scratches. There's antibiotic cream in my medicine cabinet."

Regan's skin quivered from the gentle exploration of his fingers. A ribbon of heat wound its way up her spine. She stood, with jumpy stomach, gazing down on his dirt-streaked face and thick dark hair. "I owe you everything," she whispered. "I heard a reporter out there confirm that everyone but you stopped searching." She swallowed, unable to go on.

"Shh." Ethan rose nimbly. He took her fully into his arms, something he'd longed to do since luck had led him to her and Taz. He crushed her against his chest and then, afraid of hurting her, allowed her space to catch her breath. "I'd never have given up. Others would have joined me. I'm just glad it didn't come to that." His fingers flexed in her torn sweatshirt, then in her hair.

Regan smelled the sharp scent of pine. Self-conscious, she wrinkled her nose and eased out of his arms. "I'm a mess. Pine and pitch is my new perfume."

"You think I care? I was so damned happy to see you in one piece. From the minute Odella confirmed you were lost, I...I..." His voice gave out and Regan cut in to cover his show of emotion.

"Odella's husband will never let her hike with me again."

Recovered, Ethan said gently, "You did what you thought was best for her. By the way, Roger met the chopper that flew Odella off the mountain. He told the ranger her ankle was only sprained."

"Thank God it wasn't any worse."

"Yes," he said, sending her a serious look that held more than casual interest. "I could say the same thing about you. Now, I assume you want to clean up before you do anything else. Let me see to Taz, grab a shower, and then if you're not dead to the world, I'll scrounge up something to eat.''

Regan let him point her toward the master suite. The interior of the house was as she'd imagined. Warm and rustic. She entered his bedroom; his bed and chest of drawers were fashioned from the spines of saguaro cactus. Colorful Native American rugs dotted tile floors. Painted pots and woven baskets nestled in the corners, and Southwestern artwork graced the walls. It wasn't a totally masculine room, which surprised Regan. His king-size bed called out to her, but she resisted.

Stripped naked, enjoying the sting of hot water against her battered flesh, Regan's mind wandered away from what she'd endured. Her thoughts centered on whether or not she and Ethan would share his big bed tonight or any other night. The looks and touches he kept giving her said they would. If only her boss hadn't sent that letter…

She'd missed Ethan terribly in the week since that blissful night they'd made love at her place. Until now, she hadn't allowed herself to dwell on how *much* she'd missed him. If not for Taz, she might never have had an opportunity to right things with Ethan.

She hurriedly finished her shower, then donned his T-shirt and a terry robe she found hanging in the bathroom.

Taz raised his head and barked once as Regan rushed into the living room, intent on clearing the air. The dog tried to get up, but Regan knelt beside him. The hand she extended toward his ears curled into her palm twice before she managed to pet him. ''Good dog,'' she murmured, recognizing that such gestures still didn't come easily to her.

While she struggled to conquer old feelings, Regan heard a shower running in another part of the house. "Looks like Ethan fixed you up and now he's taking care of himself. Maybe I'll go see what I can find in the kitchen." Taz lay back contentedly. Rising, Regan washed her hands before she rummaged in Ethan's cupboards.

She had a vegetable-and-cheese omelette sizzling in a pan and bagels browning in a toaster oven by the time he reappeared, looking damp but handsome and refreshed.

"Hey, I said I'd do that," he scolded, snatching the spatula out of her hand.

She snatched it back. "If you want to make yourself useful, set the table."

He started to reach into the cupboard above her head, then stopped, slid his arms around her and nuzzled her neck. "I like how you look in my robe...and in my house." He pressed a lingering kiss into the hollow below Regan's jaw. "Um, the pine scent is gone. Why is it that after three days in the woods and a shower, I can still smell your perfume?"

Laughing, she twisted out of his hold. Giddy from his kisses, she tried to flip the omelette. Surprisingly it turned. "You must have a supersensitive nose."

Shrugging, Ethan got out plates. "Taz is the one with the nose. Odella gave me your down vest. One whiff, and Taz took off like a shot. By the way, I called her to say you'd been found. She said, and I quote, 'Praise the Lord. And you tell Regan I don't want to see her skinny butt in the office for the rest of the week.'"

Regan laughed again. "She forgets which of us is the supervisor. Of course I'll go to work. As it is, our caseworkers probably think I'm sandbagging to get time off."

"I doubt it. You've been headline news for three days."

"Great. All the more reason for me to return quickly. Before Nathaniel decides I'm gone for good and hires someone else." As Regan cut the omelette in two and slid the pieces onto their respective plates, she stammered, "Ethan...I...I didn't write the letter of reprimand that went to your boss."

He almost dropped the bagels he'd removed from the toaster. "But your name..."

"...was typed by Nathaniel's secretary." She waved the spatula as she dumped the pan into the sink. "After the way you and I had been...together, how could you think I'd do such a thing?"

"I saw your name there in black and white." Ethan took the spatula from her hand, clasped her shoulders and turned her around. "Yes, we had a great night. But that letter was a powerful eye-opener. And just what would *you* have thought if it were the other way around?"

Regan wadded his shirtfront in both her hands. She blinked back tears. "I assumed I knew the kind of man you are, Ethan. I must not be so easy to read if you believed for a minute that I'd stab you in the back after...after...the way we made love."

"I wanted to call you and straighten things out, but the chief ordered me not to have any contact with you or CHC. If he knew we were together now..."

Regan let go of his shirt. She ate a few bites and watched him pick at his omelette. But clearing the air took precedence over eating. "Listen to us. My boss contacted your boss and set us against each other. The thing to do, Ethan, is to keep our jobs separate from now on. Our jobs, not our private lives.''

"You've got that right. I agree our jobs are the problem. But as far as our private lives are concerned, I can't seem to keep my hands off you.'' Leaning forward, Ethan kissed her on the mouth. He loved how Regan's slender frame flowed into his, proving she felt the same. When forced to surface for air, he only half regretted letting their food get cold. "You said you were starved,'' he murmured reluctantly.

"Nourishment comes in many forms.'' Regan's eyes told him eloquently that she wanted to be held and loved by him.

Ethan swept her into his arms. He carried her down the hall into his room, where a low light burned beside the bed. As he placed her there and divested her of the terry robe and T-shirt, which had never looked as good on him, the lamp's glow highlighted new scrapes, as well as old scars.

Ethan proceeded with caution. If she so much as winced, he'd call a halt to their love-making, no matter how much he wanted her. But Regan didn't; she welcomed him with a generous smile and open arms. Ethan was lost—they both were lost in a matter of seconds. There was no haste to their loving tonight, only tenderness.

Some time later, Regan fell asleep telling Ethan what a wonderful lover he was. His heart full to overflowing, he eased a sheet over her flushed naked limbs. "Sleep tight,'' he murmured, kissing the tip of her nose.

They'd talked little after entering the bedroom, but Ethan felt they'd made important promises with their bodies. He intended to book a meeting with Chief Wellington to set him straight about the letter. And he'd make clear that all bets were off when it came to his fraternizing with Regan Grant—outside of work hours, anyway. Satisfied with those decisions, Ethan slid out of bed, pausing to bestow a loving kiss on the woman he planned to fraternize with a lot. He hated to leave her, but it was time to check on Taz.

REGAN OPENED her eyes. The smell of coffee enticed her from a very pleasant dream involving Ethan Knight. Recognizing her surroundings, she realized her dream was more truth than fiction. Tossing covers aside, she crawled out of bed. Inside she felt young and alive. Outside, she felt ancient. Regan was determined to ignore all her feelings except the good ones.

"Hi, sleepyhead." Ethan beamed at her as she appeared in the kitchen doorway. "Taz is looking better today. I was about to leave you a note. I'm on duty in forty-five minutes."

"Oh, gosh. My car's outside, but I have nothing here to wear to work."

"Yes, you do. I woke up early and figured you'd need some things, since you insist on going in to work. I hope you don't mind that I let myself into your apartment. I grabbed the suit you had on the day we met. It's hanging in the bathroom, along with some underwear and stuff." He kissed her softly, then slid back a cuff and checked his watch. "If you can be ready in fifteen minutes, I'll drive you to the office. That would give us a chance to coordinate our stories for the press, too. I just watched the local news and they're blowing my role in finding you all out of proportion. They're making me out to be some damned hero."

Regan grinned and mumbled around the bite of toast she'd popped into her mouth. "You *are* a hero, Knight.

My hero.'' She batted her eyelashes and rubbed against him, knowing precisely the reaction she'd cause.

"Taz is the hero," he reminded her, giving her a tame swat on the backside. "Give credit where credit's due."

"I know what I know. I couldn't have carried Taz another step. He found me and saved me from the bear, but you got us both out of the woods." Leaving Ethan sputtering, Regan sped from the room. She showered in record time and dressed. As she applied light makeup, she wondered how many men would have remembered a woman's need for cosmetics. Ethan was more than a hero.

He dismissed her compliment when she rejoined him. "No man alive would have forgotten that perfume," he murmured as they left the house. "I'm not surprised it's called Romance. Speaking of romance," he said, grinning, "my place or yours tonight?"

"Yours. Taz looked so sad when we left. I'll fix a pot of spaghetti for dinner."

"Will you make enough to feed Valetti, too? He's always accusing me of dating women who can't cook Italian."

Regan would have liked Ethan to herself, but she knew how close partners on the police force were. Like brothers. "You can't cook just a little spaghetti. The more the merrier," she lied gracefully.

REGAN WAS LATE reaching her office. Only because so many of the caseworkers had heard about her rescue on the morning news and stopped her on the way in. She got tired of relating her escapade.

Piggot rarely, if ever, visited subordinates in their offices. He always called them into his. Regan was surprised to find him seated behind her desk.

"Close the door," he said before offering any other greeting.

Regan did and then stood awkwardly. "I feel good enough to be at work today, Nathaniel." She supposed that might be what was on his mind.

"I released a statement to the press on your behalf. They're making a big deal out of that cop finding you. And his department's damn quick to claim the glory," he said with a sniff. "My statement went a long way toward neutralizing that bastard's role."

"Ethan did find me!" Regan burst out. "Everything they're saying is true."

"Be that as it may, we can't have your names linked. Knight has run roughshod over this agency for too long. I expect you to refuse comment on this incident. And I want you to sever all contact with Knight. I've told Chief Wellington we'll deal with other members of the force, all by the book. Wellington says Knight already knows the score."

Regan thought of the night she'd spent in Ethan's bed and of the many nights she hoped to spend. "I spoke with Ethan," she said. "He promised he'd follow our rules from now on."

"Harrumph." Piggot cleared his throat, stood and straightened his tie. "I'm glad to hear you took the initiative, Regan. But I'll hold you accountable, the first stunt he pulls."

Regan watched her boss heave his bulk from the chair and waddle out. In a weak moment Ethan had agreed not to interfere with agency affairs. But what right did Nathaniel have, anyway, dictating whom she could or could not see outside work? How long, she wondered next, before the internal affairs review board acted on her complaint against Piggot? Perhaps she should send an addendum on his latest directive involving Ethan.

Throughout the day Regan caught herself daydreaming about Ethan. He'd seemed as anxious as she to expand their fledgling relationship. Men didn't invite their best friends to meet a woman unless they were pretty serious. Now that she'd conquered her fear of dogs—well, of Taz, at least—there was nothing to stand in the way of—

"Oh." Regan clapped a hand over her mouth. She'd never explained to him that the dog's attack had left her barren. She would. The moment an opportunity presented itself.

CHAPTER TWELVE

TAZ RECOVERED SLOWLY as days became weeks. He ran with Regan most mornings from early April through most of May. His presence kept other dogs at a distance. For that she was thankful. Yet she continued to have reservations. She wanted to accept him, and Ethan thought she had. The real truth was that any time Taz appeared suddenly or unexpectedly, Regan's throat constricted and a pervasive chill marched up her spine. It was an immediate visceral response, one she had trouble controlling.

During the days, Regan focused on her job. She hadn't received a reply to the letters she'd sent to the state review board for CHC. Her letters amounted to whistle-blowing, and Regan knew what she'd done was risky. While prepared to accept any consequences, she found the silence unnerving.

She sometimes felt as though she was trying to be two separate people. Outside work she and Ethan spent several evenings a week together. They stayed away from the usual haunts frequented by work pals who might carry tales back to either of their bosses. As a couple, they often joined his large family for Sunday barbecues. Regan enjoyed swimming in an environment where no one asked about her scars. She supposed Ethan had protected her by warning his family about her self-consciousness. He was the most considerate man she knew.

Professionally they kept their distance. Many nights Regan wanted to discuss a particular case with Ethan—like Mavis Shiller's continued hostility and refusal to meet with her. Then she'd catch herself in time to switch subjects. It was the same with him. He went about his detective work, never crossing into Regan's territory. As a result of their mutual discretion, Ethan didn't know she'd sent complaints about Piggot to head office. Likewise he knew nothing of the ultimatums issued to Regan by her boss.

Regan sometimes felt she was holding too many secrets inside—secrets that could damage her growing relationship with Ethan. She still hadn't told him about her infertility. Each time they made love, the words hovered on the tip of her tongue. Even in the cozy aftermath, Ethan seemed content to remain as they were. Friends and lovers. He made no mention of marriage, and until he did, Regan felt odd, presumptuous even, about introducing the topic of having babies. Or rather, her inability to have his babies.

Watching Ethan interact with his many nieces and nephews caused a searing pain in Regan's heart. He loved kids; any fool could tell. She ought to just do it. Tell him. Lay her cards on the table.

Unfortunately, and she didn't know how or when it had happened, she'd fallen in love with him. She couldn't bring herself to risk losing him.

By June his closest friends on the force had met and accepted Regan as Ethan's ''significant other'' in the words of some, his ''girlfriend'' in the language of others. They acted married, except Regan kept her apartment. She moved nothing but bare essentials into his house, even though she arrived there first most evenings and prepared their dinner. One weekend she attended another Schutzhund and actually sat through the entire competition. On rare occasions Ethan had to work all night. Those times, Regan went home to dust and care for neglected plants.

Mitch Valetti spent quite a few of his free evenings with Ethan and Regan. They generally played cards or assembled puzzles. Sometimes he brought a date, but generally he showed up alone. Regan came to trust Mitch. He was funny and he was honorable. Nothing like Jack's friends.

As the idyllic days of June gave way to the smoldering heat of summer, Ethan and Mitch's workload increased. "I hate summer," Ethan told Regan one night as they lay on top of the cool cotton sheets, their limbs pleasantly entangled.

"Why? Sunshine's good for body and soul."

"The excessive heat we have in Desert City drives some people over the edge. Besides, school's out so kids have nothing to do but hang out on the streets and cause trouble. Drug peddlers get bolder." He shook his head. "It seems as though every degenerate develops a hair-trigger temper."

"Are you trying to say I'll be spending more nights at my apartment?" Regan propped her arm on his chest and lifted herself to gaze over his chin.

"If we got married, Regan, my house would be yours. I wouldn't have to call three places to locate you if I'm running late. There would just be work and home. Our home."

Regan sat up. Her heart skidded around inside her chest.

"What's the matter?" Ethan bolted upright, too.

"You can't be surprised. All the guys at work keep asking when's the wedding. So does my family. Mom, especially." Ethan kissed Regan's shoulder, letting her feel his smile.

"I...we..." Regan gulped. "Wow, your proposal came out of left field. Isn't it customary to exchange a few *I love you*s first?"

"What have the last few months been about if not love? I sure feel in love. Don't you?" He snapped on the bedside lamp and frowned at her.

Regan dragged her knees to her chest and hunched over them, looping her arms around her ankles. Her hair fell across her face, hiding her alarm.

Ethan ran a hand along her back. "Are you saying I dreamed you whispering *I love you* these last few weeks when we made love? If I was too far gone to answer, I'm sorry. I love you, Regan. Will you be my wife and have my babies?" He tugged her around so he could see her face and drew one hand tenderly along the hollow of her cheek. The other hand spanned the soft flesh of her stomach. "These last few nights we haven't been very careful. Not that I'd mind starting out with a new little Knight." Grinning, Ethan feathered kisses from Regan's ear to her collarbone.

She closed her eyes to block his loving gestures. A cry welled up as she climbed out of bed. Her fingers gone numb, she badly fumbled pulling on her jeans.

"Regan?" Ethan watched her frantic efforts with a puzzled expression.

"I haven't told you the whole story, Ethan. About the attack."

"So tell me now."

Regan slid her feet into loafers and rummaged in her

purse for the keys to her car. She acted like a woman possessed. Her lips were white and her gestures jerky.

Ethan threw back the covers. The golden blush of the bedside lamp was kind to him in his nakedness. His arms were roped with muscles. His hips were slim, his legs tanned and sturdy. Not in the least abashed by his lack of clothing, he grabbed Regan and hugged her. "Talk to me. Whatever it is, we'll work it out together."

"I've been unfair," she said. "Selfish. I've known all along that you want a large family. You said as much right after we met. I should have been honest with you the first time we made love. I can't have children, Ethan. I lost internal organs in the dog attack. Spleen and appendix are of little consequence. But my uterus was so damaged the surgeon had to remove it."

Shock and something akin to disbelief washed over Ethan's face as the truth sank in. He released her, raised a hand, then let it fall limply to his side. His throat constricted when he tried to force words. Nothing came out.

Unable to face him after the hurtful blow she'd dealt him, Regan issued a last disjointed apology and blindly fled.

Taz loped down the hall to investigate the source of unusual night noises in his house. As she ran past the dog, Regan heard Ethan shout for her to wait. Then his bedside phone rang. Of course—he was on call. The drive to meet Mitch would give him time to digest her news.

She'd save him the trouble of ending their relationship. This time she wouldn't make the mistake of leaving anything behind for him to hold over her as Jack had done. Not that Ethan had a vindictive bone in his body. But she'd seen his shocked expression. Even if she hadn't, she couldn't expect him to forgive her deception.

Regan drove down the street and parked. She waited until he left, then she returned to the house to gather her few possessions.

It was too easy, stripping Ethan's house of all signs of her existence. Well, maybe she'd left a trace of her perfume on his sheets and in his bathroom. But by the time she closed car trunk, not so much as a teabag remained as tangible proof that she'd been in his life.

The kitchen clock in her apartment read 3 a.m. when Regan carried the last load into her apartment.

She'd barely made it to bed when her telephone rang. Ethan must have gotten home. The cop in him probably wanted to make sure of her safety. "Too bad," she muttered, yanking the phone cord from the wall. "I'm not strong enough to hear your voice tonight, Ethan. Maybe tomorrow."

IN THE MORNING, Regan dragged herself out of bed. She ached all over, and her head pounded mercilessly. Her face was blotchy from crying into her pillow. For the first time in her life, she couldn't muster the will to go into work. She phoned and left a message with Nathaniel's secretary that she was sick. And she crawled back into bed.

She was still there at four in the afternoon when her boss beat on her front door, demanding loudly, "Regan, open up this minute!" She recognized his nasal twang even through the haze caused by excess sleep.

Her feet were bare, her hair a mess and her terry robe tied askew when she released the dead bolt and opened the door. The anxiety in his voice had registered, but not why he was pacing outside her door.

"Nathaniel? What on earth?"

"So you are sick? No matter. I'm holding you directly

responsible for the mess that damned cop has created for CHC. Consider yourself fired, Ms. Grant. I've made out the paperwork. We'll call this your exit interview.''

"Fired? I assume you mean Ethan. But I haven't the foggiest idea what he's done.''

"No?'' Sweeping her aside, Nathaniel stormed into her apartment and slammed the door. "Get dressed and I'll tell you. Or turn on the TV and you'll see. Once again he's being proclaimed a hero while we look like bumbling fools.''

Regan couldn't imagine how Ethan had accomplished all that in a few short hours. Her curiosity piqued, she rushed to her room and threw on jeans, a T-shirt and her hiking boots. They lay on top of the heap of clothing she'd brought from Ethan's.

"Now,'' she said, returning to the living room where Piggot had turned the TV to a local station, "could you start at the beginning?''

Piggot huffed a few times. "If you really don't know... Ethan Knight jailed one of Mavis Shiller's clients last night. A single mother, for God's sake. He implied to the media that Mavis was negligent in her handling of the case. Reporters got her out of bed. And they've hounded me all day.''

Mavis again. Regan had left several messages on Mavis's desk that she wanted to see her, but the woman claimed a too-busy client schedule as a reason to postpone the meeting. A couple of caseworkers said Mavis seemed stressed out and was maybe doing too much, but Regan had never dreamed the woman would be negligent. "Did something tragic happen to the woman's child? It must have. Why else would Ethan be so upset with Mavis?''

"Not *a* child. *Quadruplets.* Mavis arranged for a decent apartment, set the mom up with day care and a job. All on the proviso that the current boyfriend, a real hothead, stay away. Mavis swears everything was hunky-dory at her most recent visit.''

"Oh, no! This is about the four babies? When did Mavis see them last?''

Nathaniel faltered for the first time. "Uh…in June, I believe. The day the babies turned five months old.''

"She hasn't visited them in a *month?* Nathaniel, you know as well as I do that a young single mom with four babies ought to have once-a-week follow-ups.''

"The girl lied to Mavis. Neighbors told the cops the boyfriend moved in soon after Mavis left. They described hearing loud arguments. One or two said the babies cried incessantly. But does anyone call us? No, they wait until the situation deteriorates—and then they phone the police.''

Regan didn't have to ask any more questions. The news broadcast came on and suddenly flipped to pictures in a hospital. A camera zoomed in on three of the battered quads. "Oh, my word!" Regan cried. "The boyfriend struck those infants and the mother just stood by? Nathaniel, how can you blame Ethan for interceding? How could Mavis not catch such obvious signs of abuse?''

"The girl is old enough to trust. She's twenty-one. Her folks emancipated her at fourteen. And Mavis swears Serena Trejo—that's the mom—was getting her act together.''

Regan clenched her fists. "According to the news, she and her boyfriend went out at night and left the babies unattended. They bought booze with money meant to feed the kids. How *dare* you be mad at Ethan! Those poor children belong in foster care. That mom and her boyfriend belong in jail. Is he the father, by the way?''

"Probably not. I'm ticked off at Knight because he demanded we find one foster home to take all four kids. Half the city backed him. Intake claims we haven't got anyone available. So we promised four good homes. That didn't suit Ethan Knight. Oh, no. He informed the press that he was licensed to give care and said he'd take a leave from his job to foster them himself.''

"Yes. That sounds like Ethan." Regan smiled. "I agree they should stay together. It sounds like they've suffered trauma enough.''

"At their age, you can't tell me they'll know if they're apart or together.''

"Of course they will,'' she said calmly. "Repeated psychological studies have proved it's unhealthy to split multiples. Furthermore, our own agency handbook urges counselors to keep families together at all cost.''

"Then you get down to the office right now and find a foster family who'll take all four kids. You have a week. I'm told three of them will be hospitalized that long.''

"So I'm not fired?''

Piggot sputtered. "Mavis insisted you were living with Knight. She thought you'd engineered this fiasco to get *her* fired. She's obviously wrong. Your paperwork wouldn't have gone out today at any rate.''

"Are you asking me to take this case away from Mavis and handle it myself?''

"Yes. Yes. That's what I want.''

"Do you remember telling me to let Mavis do her job and stop breathing down her neck? This was one of the cases I tried to follow up.''

"Uh...so do it now. I'll tell reporters I've put my top

supervisor on the problem. Assure them we're pulling out all stops to find adequate shelter, but that our aim is to return the children to the natural mother as quickly as possible.''

''I'll only take the job if I'm given free rein to handle it as I see fit. By that, I mean I want time to interview Serena and her boyfriend. I want to talk with her neighbors and her employer. Did you see the size of those babies's bruises? And the smallest girl has two broken limbs, the doctor said. The third may have brain damage. Maybe the mother can't handle raising four babies.''

''Then find a nice childless couple who'd like to adopt a big family. Do you have any idea how much it costs our agency to foster four kids indefinitely?''

''We aren't the pound seeking homes for abandoned kittens. I'm aware of the cost. And the entire community is aware that it's our responsibility, Nathaniel. This case is already in the public eye. Can we afford not to cover every base?''

''No. Thanks to that meddling cop. I don't care how, I want you to get those kids away from him. I won't have him rubbing our agency's nose in this…this debacle.''

Regan sighed. ''I'll do my best. He and I aren't on the best of terms. I don't see how he can be serious about single-handedly caring for them long-term, though. Ethan loves his job. And how much leave can one man get?''

''Find out. Even a week is too much.'' Nathaniel stalked across the room and jerked open the door. ''By the way, you don't look ill. What's wrong with you, anyway?''

Regan shrugged. ''A twenty-four-hour bug? I feel better. Good enough, I think, to burn some midnight oil at the office.''

''That's the spirit. I told Mavis you were too smart to get involved with the likes of Ethan Knight. I'll go collect the case files from her and drop them off on your desk.''

The door slammed, and every nerve in Regan's body tightened. If she was so smart, why did the thought of losing Ethan's love cause her so much pain?

Before she left the house, she tried phoning him; she wanted to hear his side. He must have taken his phone off the hook. Sighing, Regan left a message at the station, asking Mitch to call her at work.

True to his word, Nathaniel had left the file on her desk. There were pictures of the babies at birth. Two boys and two girls. Sweet kids. Regan touched the little faces reverently. For quads they'd had good birth weights. The boys, Marco and Rico, weighed five pounds and five-one, respectively. The girls, Angela and Cara, were smaller, four-two and three-twelve. Three had gone home on schedule, Cara two weeks later. The boyfriend, Tony DeSalvo, was not, according to Mavis's notes, the children's father. He was a small-time hood who probably provided Serena with alcohol and drugs, although the girl had been clean when the babies were born. Serena and Tony both had police records. At twenty-five, Tony would most likely face prison time if he was convicted.

Her phone rang and Regan snatched it up. It was Mitch. ''Yes, I know it's after work hours, but I'm working. I've taken over the quadruplets' case,'' she said, not giving him a chance to comment. ''I need to reach Ethan. He's apparently unplugged his home phone.''

She listened and her tension grew as Mitch fumbled

for words to tell her that Ethan might not welcome talking to her. "Hey, he was vague, Regan. Said you walked out on him. On the one hand, he's pretty broken up. On the other, he's up in arms over your agency's handling of these kids. If he has his way, Serena will lose the quads permanently, and she and Tony will both go down."

"I know, Mitch. The original counselor believed Serena had quit seeing Tony. I don't want to fight with Ethan, but I'm responsible for finding the babies temporary foster care."

"Ethan's family took him a bunch of baby stuff. His mom plans to give him a hand once they're all out of the hospital. Ethan doesn't believe DeSalvo will walk—I hope he's right. The dude is dangerous. If what I think matters, the kids will be safest left with Ethan."

Regan frowned. "I don't understand. Why are they in danger?"

"I shouldn't talk so freely about an open case, Regan. Word on the street is that Tony offed Benny Cruz, the kids' dad, in a drive-by right before they were born. Serena used to be Tony's girl. Rumor has it she met Benny on the sly. Serena swears not. Various members of Benny's gang say she's lying. Tony's a real bastard. A whole bunch of folks are afraid of him. Rightfully so."

"Goodness, isn't all that enough to hold him in jail?"

"Depends on how important he is to the local drug lord. His bail hasn't been set yet. One of Ethan's snitches thinks it's just a matter of time before he's sprung."

Regan pinched the bridge of her nose. Once again she was caught between Ethan and Piggot. Her boss had ordered her to find alternate housing for the quads. How could she, in good conscience, place a foster family in possible jeopardy? "I've worked with some unsavory characters over the years, Mitch, but this new violence we're seeing is beyond my comprehension. Um, could you just tell Ethan he'll be dealing with me as far as the babies are concerned?"

"I won't pry into what went on between you two. I wish you'd patch things up."

"I doubt that's possible. And I take full blame. I hope we're both adult enough to ensure that our breakup doesn't interfere with a job it appears we'll be sharing."

"Guess that's up to you. I don't know anybody more professional than Ethan."

Regan fought an urge to defend herself. Mitch had made it abundantly clear whose corner he was in. "My priority is the welfare of these babies. Goodbye, Mitch." She pushed the disconnect button, but held the receiver for some time afterward.

When she was finally able to disassociate her feelings for Ethan from the case, Regan downloaded a list of all eligible foster families. Despite her reservations and her fears for everyone's safety, she made calls until 9 p.m., then decided no one would welcome hearing from her any later. She'd made a huge dent in the list. No one felt capable of handling four babies, especially when three had medical problems. Regan had no reason to believe that anyone left on the list would feel differently, especially since all the remaining families already had one or more foster children.

Steeling herself, she closed her office and decided to pay Ethan a visit. He had an uncanny knack for scaring up suitable foster homes. Why couldn't he do it again? Considering his job and his personal circumstances, Ethan's own situation as a caregiver had to be extremely short-term.

Half an hour later, Ethan answered her knock. Taz poked his muzzle out through the crack left by the chain and barked so loudly that he drowned out Regan's attempt to explain her visit. For a minute she and Ethan stared at each other through the gap. At last he shushed Taz and unchained the door. "Mitch phoned," he said without preamble. "I didn't expect you to show up until tomorrow."

Regan stepped into the familiar entryway. It felt strange when Ethan didn't invite her further. Taz continued to bark, obviously confused. Inside, a baby wailed.

"Dammit, Taz! You woke Rico. I told you you'll have to bark softly. You'd better learn to mind your manners before we pick up the others." Turning to Regan, Ethan threw up his hands. "Come in. It took me an hour to get Rico asleep. Who knows how long it'll be this time? We can talk while I hold him."

Regan trailed after him, stopping in the living room to set her notebook and case folder on the coffee table.

Taz led the way down the hall, bounding exuberantly into the baby's room. Though he didn't bark, he thrust his nose between the crib slats and whined, a low throaty sound.

Regan blanched, seeing his big nose and teeth so close to the infant. "Make him stop," she told Ethan faintly.

He misunderstood. Picking up the wide-eyed dark-haired infant, Ethan joked grimly as he raised the boy to his shoulder. "Give me a break, Regan. I haven't been playing dad long enough for Rico to recognize me the minute I walk into the room. It takes time to develop a bond. We're getting better, aren't we guy?" The baby drew up his legs and wriggled before he buried his red face in Ethan's neck. Though his sobs lessened, they didn't stop. "Would you hold him?" Ethan asked abruptly. "My mother has better luck calming him. The poor kid is scared of a male voice. You're the psychologist, Regan. I know he's not even six months old, but could he already be afraid of men—because of the way Tony knocked him around?"

She accepted the bundle Ethan handed her. "Babies are smarter than most people give them credit for. They're sensitive to voices from birth. They feel tension when parents argue, for instance." Regan almost dropped the baby when Taz nudged her leg.

"Ethan, please take Taz out. He's probably jealous. Anyway, you shouldn't give him free access to this room."

"Jealous? He's a worrier. Taz knows something's wrong when Rico cries. Like you, he wants the crying stopped."

"That wasn't what I meant when I said make him stop." Regan swayed gently, patting the baby's back. "Taz had his nose shoved in Rico's ear. If nothing else, dog slobber can't be healthy."

Ethan rolled his eyes. "Taz lives, eats and sleeps with me. I doubt he has any germs I don't have. What's with you all of a sudden, Regan? Surely you aren't afraid of dogs again."

Regan said nothing. She *was* afraid. Not for herself, but for the babies. Taz was big and boisterous. She'd seen how he attacked the dummy of a full grown man during his Schutzhund. Ethan's friend had explained that the figure being attacked represented a burglar, but Regan had never understood how a dog could know the difference between friend and foe. What if Ethan put the babies down on a blanket and the dog mistook a thrashing infant for an enemy? She shuddered, picturing the outcome.

Ethan was smiling at her, and Regan had been so lost in thought she didn't know why.

"You have the magic touch. The woman's touch. Our little buddy is sawing logs again. I'll go fix tea and bring a plate of my mom's cookies out to the living room. See if you can get Rico back to bed without waking him. You and I need to talk."

Regan rubbed her cheek against the baby's soft hair. "It shouldn't be hard—he's limp as a noodle. You'll take Taz with you?"

"Come on, Taz. Regan thinks we're in the way. I'll get you a doggie treat." Ethan eyes held something back.

Regan waited until she could no longer hear Ethan's footsteps or Taz's pad, pad, pad down the hall, then she placed the baby on his back in the crib and covered him with a pale blue blanket. Mitch had been correct in saying that Ethan's family had come to his aid. Four cribs sat side by side, and a monitor was attached to the wall behind them. The closet was stacked with packages of diapers. Tiny clothing hung on small hangers. As Regan slipped out and pulled the door closed, she glanced into the room directly across the hall. It looked like a playroom in a day-care facility.

She certainly couldn't fault Ethan's preparedness. He wasn't in the living room, so she collected her notebook and went to join him in the kitchen. Actually the table there seemed a better place to conduct business than a couch where they'd often made love.

"Hey, you succeeded," he said. "The water just boiled. I'll have your favorite blackberry tea ready in a flash."

"How? I mean—" she gulped. "I—thought I to…took all the tea."

"You did. But you got me hooked on the stuff. I had Mom pick some up at the store when she shopped for baby stuff. In case you didn't notice when you left, my spare room wasn't stocked with diapers."

"A lot can change overnight. Mitch told you I've been assigned this case?"

"Yes." Ethan leaned against the counter and crossed his feet at the ankles. He hooked his thumbs in the waistband of low-riding jeans. "Can we talk about last night when you ran out on me?"

Regan turned to a clean page in her notebook. "I'm here to update agency records. Your application to provide foster care is out-of-date."

Ethan worried the inside of his mouth with his teeth. "Well, that's plain enough. Would you rather conduct this interview in the living room?"

"This is fine. It's only fair to tell you I'm looking for a two-parent family to take the babies."

"You think I didn't?"

"Records from Intake indicate you didn't give them enough time to do a complete search of our system."

"They're idiots. I tried to reach you from Serena's apartment. Your phone rang twice, then cut off. I tried later from the hospital, and this morning I phoned you at work, but Nicole said you'd called in sick. Believe me, Regan, I put the arm on every married couple I know. They'd all heard about the case on the news today and were sympathetic, but it's a lot to ask, even as a favor. Since my home is licensed, I decided to take them."

"For how long? How much leave can you get?"

"Enough. Mitch said he gave you some privileged information concerning Tony DeSalvo. For now, we've posted a guard outside the children's ward at the hospital. Once I get all four babies home, keeping them safe from DeSalvo will be easier.''

"He's still in jail, isn't he?''

"Sources tell me he's contacted a real iffy character, a lawyer known to help drug dealers. DeSalvo's bail is high. But someone could post his bond.''

"Why is he a threat if the babies are no longer with their mother? Isn't it more a case of the babies getting in the way of his fun?''

"You can never tell what the objective is with a twisted mind like Tony's. The guy is scum. Serena's a negligent mother, and he's cruel without conscience. You must've dealt with cases like this before.''

"Yes, but the caseworker said Serena was trying. She had a job. Tomorrow I'm planning to visit her place of employment and also talk with her neighbors. I may turn up evidence to recommend the court take her children away temporarily, rather than permanently. Our agency prefers keeping families together.''

"At the risk of the kids?''

"No. Don't be obtuse.''

"Serena didn't call the cops when Tony beat up her babies. The neighbors did. We're talking tiny babies, for crying out loud! DeSalvo's hand is almost as big as Cara's entire body. She's the smallest.'' Ethan set cookies and mugs of tea on the table, then slumped into a chair. "There are times I wish I didn't have to respect my badge,'' he muttered. "I itched to give that bastard a taste of his own medicine.''

"I'm sure he'd love to claim police brutality. His kind are really cowards who prey on the vulnerable—on people who aren't able to defend themselves.''

"That describes most child abusers. But I sensed something more lethal behind Tony's threats to kill me and the kids. No one thing I can point to. More of a gut feeling.''

Regan shivered. To ward off the chill caused by Ethan's words, she sipped her tea. ''When will you know if DeSalvo posts bail?''

''Soon. He was arraigned on assault and battery charges. If I could've made attempted murder stick, you can bet I would've gone for it. We asked Serena to sign a statement to that effect. She refused. I'd like to feel sympathy for her, but I'm not convinced she deserves it. She'll be charged tomorrow. I'm going to make it as tough on her as I can. Maybe if she sees she's going to the pen, she'll give us more on Tony boy. She could probably help us link him to the Benny Cruz shooting, too.''

''Who's going to watch Rico while you go to court?''

''My folks. Dad's on vacation. He just got back from taking Jeremy to see his mother.''

''Oh?'' Regan glanced up with interest. ''How did that go?''

''It was rough on the kid, but he handled it like a man. Dad's proud of him.''

''Any change in Jeremy's decision to keep his last name?''

''None. His mother promised not to interfere in his life if he turns down the chance to be adopted. He said keeping her name was the least he could do for her. He said she's really pathetic.''

''Don't you wonder why people bring kids into the world when they aren't prepared to do right by them?'' Regan sighed deeply.

''Children are a by-product of sex, and sex for many people is merely recreational.'' He raised his eyebrows.

"Surely you aren't planning to launch a crusade against having sex, are you?"

Regan shook her head. She drank her tea again to hide a smile. She choked at Ethan's next comment.

"That's right. We both enjoy sex. So I know you had ample opportunity to tell me you couldn't have children, Regan. Why didn't you?"

She leaped up from her chair and closed her notebook. "This interview is over."

Ethan stood, catching her wrist with one hand to keep her from leaving. "Is running away how you deal with everything you don't want to discuss? Didn't it occur to you that we could adopt? I'd have thought so since we both work with kids who need good homes. With kids who need good parents."

Regan pulled loose. "I...no, that didn't enter my mind. I've seen your family. They're proud of being Knights. I imagined you'd only want children of your own."

"If the court does declare Serena unfit, and if they remove the quadruplets permanently, they'll be eligible for adoption. Four is a nice-size family, don't you think?" This time Ethan rounded the table and placed a hand on either side of Regan's face. "What do you say? Will you marry me, help me go to bat for babies who need a loving caring mother to stand beside a humble hardworking dad?"

Regan jerked away from him. She knocked against the table and spilled the tea. Taz, who'd been napping underneath, exploded out from under it, snarling between yelps. Regan didn't realize the hot tea had dripped on the dog. In fact, she saw little beyond his bared teeth. "Look at him!"

"Come here, Taz. Regan doesn't realize she spilled

tea on you. Regan, look at his wet fur. You'll see he doesn't react without provocation.''

"You're splitting hairs, Ethan. I can't...*won't* recommend placing babies in a home where they may be mauled by a dog. You've seen what a dog did to me.''

"It was an accident, Regan. An isolated case. That dog was abused—and he wasn't trained.''

"I don't care. Technically I'm responsible for the safety of the babies. I'm not willing to put them at further risk. I'm living proof that owners aren't necessarily the best judges of their pets. I'm sorry, Ethan, my report will insist that you keep Taz separated from the babies.''

Ethan caught up to Regan at the front door. "That's hogwash! You all but lived with me and Taz. If you'd stop and think rationally, you'd admit Taz is harmless.''

Regan's voice held a hysterical edge. "I guess I'm not rational when it comes to dogs, after all, Ethan.''

He stared openmouthed at the door she slammed behind her. Sensing something wrong, Taz dropped to his belly and put his nose between his paws. He looked up with sad eyes. Ethan bent to tug his pet's ears. "Dammit, I thought we were past all that. What am I gonna do, boy?''

CHAPTER THIRTEEN

ON THE DRIVE back to her apartment, Regan worked to stifle the fear for those children that was on the verge of erupting. Half of her brain said Ethan was right—her feelings were illogical. If only she could stop imagining Taz's nose poked through the crib slats, his teeth bared as they'd been in the kitchen when she'd spilled her tea. Common sense told her Ethan had only taken the babies because there was no one else willing to keep them together. He'd said as much.

It was her job to find someone else.

Early the next morning Regan phoned the last group of families on her list. Not one of them could cope with four babies. Out of desperation she ran the standard newspaper ad, stressing the need for new foster families. She set it up to do the screenings herself.

Reporters previously camped on Ethan's doorstep somehow got Regan's name and phone number and they harassed her, as well. A few aggressive journalists delighted in pitting CHC against the Baby Cop, tactics that forced Regan to take a stand. CHC would find a safe and satisfactory home, she assured members of the press.

Ethan's friends, police associates and others in the community who knew his record for saving throwaway kids gave interviews. All heaped lavish praise upon him.

The day he took Marco, Angela and Cara home from the hospital, Ethan and Regan hadn't spoken for more than a week. She regretted that the media had under-mined her position as the babies' caseworker. Most of the articles twisted her words. Some took innocent re-marks out of context. She could only imagine how little Ethan must think of her after all was said and done.

She gave him a day to adjust to having four infants. Then, determined to outsmart the reporters, Regan parked a block from his house. She sneaked through neighbors' backyards and knocked softly on Ethan's kitchen door.

He glared at her through the screen, a crying baby cradled in each arm. "What do you want?"

"I'm doing my job, Ethan. It's my duty to see how the babies are getting along. Why are they so upset? Oh, you poor dears," she crooned, tapping on the screen.

"They're wet and hungry. My mom woke up with a head cold. She didn't want to risk infecting the kids. Anyhow, if I were really their dad, I'd have to learn to take care of them alone. So, come in or stay out. I'm busy." He unlatched the screen.

"Where's Taz?" Regan's gaze swept a kitchen that had shrunk considerably with the added presence of four high chairs.

"He's standing guard at the front door where those blasted reporters are making a racket. Don't start on me again about Taz."

"All I did was ask where he was! He's always at your heels."

"He's the only thing you didn't take issue with in any of those news stories, surprisingly enough."

"I, er, I've calmed down a lot from the other night. But about all these supposed comments of mine on the news—Ethan, I never said half of what's been reported.

Uh-oh. I hear more babies crying.'' She set her notebook on the kitchen counter. ''May I help?''

''If the offer's for real and not something designed to make me look incompetent, then sure. Grab a couple of bottles and follow me.''

Regan rinsed her hands, took the two bottles he'd left on the counter and hurried after him into the crowded nursery. Ethan allowed Taz to join them; he stood in the doorway, whining. If a dog could look worried, he did, until Ethan crooned to the babies and stilled their crying.

''When will doctors remove Marco's cast?'' Regan lifted the boy carefully from his crib. ''Oh, and Angela's poor face is still black-and-blue.''

''Cara's injuries are the worst. Will you feed her? She likes to be held by a woman.''

''Did Serena use bottles?''

''Yes, thank God. But the doctors don't think she held the kids. I doubt she has any maternal instincts at all.''

''Mmm. Ethan, what are your long-term plans for the babies? I know the court said the charges against Serena are serious. Her bail's impossibly high. I visited her this morning. Her tough-girl act isn't helping her. She spit on me and had to be restrained by a guard.''

''Personally I hope she's locked up for the maximum twenty-five years,'' he muttered. ''We suspect she and Tony sold drugs to kids no more than seven or eight. Add to that battery and neglect. I'll do my level best to make those charges stick. Maybe I should be asking what *your* plans are for the quads.''

Regan sat in an overstuffed rocker that had been added to the bedroom since her last visit. She stared at the babies, who gazed trustingly at her out of fathomless dark eyes. ''I'll be honest, Ethan. I haven't found a foster family who can take all four. Nathaniel's pressing me to split them up. He hasn't mandated it yet, but only because our guidelines say every effort should be made to keep families intact.''

"And how do you feel?" Ethan had finished changing Angela and Rico. He scrubbed his hands with an instant cleanser and sat in a wooden rocker across from Regan. Both babies reached for the bottles he juggled in one hand.

"At the moment I'm not sure. I'm reserving judgment until I see how you hold up as a foster dad." A tiny smile made its way to Regan's lips.

Her smile always had the same effect on Ethan. He shifted to ease the sudden tightness of his jeans. "Uh...you can visit me every day at feeding time, if you like. I'm organized, but I can't seem to feed all four at once."

"Have you tried using blankets and pillows on the living-room floor? Rico and Angela seem able to hold bottles by themselves. If you propped them between your legs on a pillow while you held Marco and Cara, it might work."

"It's not just bottles. The pediatrician said they should have started solid food last month. There were no baby-food jars in Serena's apartment. Today I introduced cereal. I got as much on my shirt as I did in their bellies."

Regan saw that was true. "I'll put them down for a nap while you shower."

"Thanks. I may have to hire help," he said forthrightly. "I'd hoped I wouldn't have to bring in an outsider, but..." He shrugged.

"I can lend a hand for a while. Until I finish my evaluation," she added quickly, careful to veil the eagerness in her eyes. Ethan already owned a piece of her heart; she couldn't let him see that the babies were fast claiming a portion, too.

"I don't suppose you'd consider sleeping over?" Ethan sounded wistful. "Last night they woke up crying every two hours. It made me realize how long and lonely nights can be."

"Ethan, I can't. We have to keep this professional for the sake of our jobs."

Reasons for why he didn't care if she lost her job ran through Ethan's mind. And yet, he knew that wasn't fair. Regan loved her work as much as he loved his. Furthermore she was good at it. He let the moment pass, saying nothing.

As she'd promised, Regan put the babies down while he showered. She was still in the nursery when he returned, his hair clean but still damp, his face smooth from a fresh shave.

She stammered out an excuse to leave. "I'll, uh, see if I can rearrange my schedule to stay longer tomorrow. Through dinner. To help, er, observe how well they take solid food. I'll go into the office early, and I'll bring home work for a while—to give me time with the babies. Now, is there anything you need from the grocery?" She released the catch on the screen door. "I pass a market on my way here from the office."

"As a matter of fact, apple juice is on the list the doctor gave me. Oh, and the small jars of peas and squash."

"Sounds yummy. How about adult food?"

"I haven't had a decent meal since you left," he blurted. "Uh…erase that. Yesterday Mitch brought cheeseburgers from Flo's. And my sisters stocked my freezer. Too bad the stuff doesn't jump out and heat itself."

"Why don't you invite Mitch again tomorrow night?" Regan's smile spread. "Tell him I'm fixing chile rellenos with rice and black beans. I've never seen a man put away Mexican food the way he does."

Ethan locked the screen after Regan stepped out onto the porch. "If you're using Mitch so you don't have to be alone with me, Regan, it's not necessary. I understand *no* well enough."

"That isn't why I said to invite him." She was genuinely flustered. "I thought you two might like an opportunity to discuss work. You must miss it."

"I do, as a matter of fact. Thanks." He studied her so seriously and for so long Regan almost tripped as she backed down the steps.

"By the way, I hope I don't hear what I said repeated on the nightly news. I'm committed to these kids, and I'm willing to make whatever sacrifices are necessary. Shoot me if I'm breaking one of your exalted CHC rules, but from here on, Regan, I'm calling the boys Rick and Mark. Rico and Marco are from another life."

"They aren't my rules. I'm sorry you have such a low opinion of me, Ethan."

"I didn't. Don't. It's the way you flip-flop that drives me crazy. I changed my sheets," he murmured, "but still smell your perfume when I wake up at night. Even Taz wanders the house looking for you. He got used to us being…well, us." Ethan opened the screen, reached out and brought Regan's palm to his lips for a kiss. He looked solemn when she jerked her hand away. "See, you're doing it again."

"That's the thing about children of trauma, Ethan. Even as adults there are no guarantees we won't backslide, or flip-flop as you call it."

"I've worked with enough victims of trauma to understand the problem. All I'm asking for is a chance to help you work out solutions. You and me together, Regan. Us.''

"There is no us, except for this professional association. And if my boss and yours had their way, they'd torpedo that.'' Regan left before her voice broke. Ethan was right; her views did flip-flop. So did her heart—and her stomach. She might have fewer concerns about Taz, but couldn't put aside her fears entirely. Plus, it was her job to remain distant while doing her utmost to be objective. She had to, for everyone's sake. Most of all her own.

THE NEXT DAY, Regan firmly affixed her professional demeanor when she went to Ethan's. She wore her pin-striped suit and never shed her jacket. She covered herself with a plain white apron when they fed the babies lunch and donned it again to prepare dinner for Ethan and Mitch.

Thank God for Mitch. The words became Regan's mantra throughout the meal. She hadn't imagined it'd be so hard to sit across from Ethan at a table. It *shouldn't* have been, but how could she sit and listen to him sing her praises?

"You should've seen Regan feed those kids their peas and applesauce,'' Ethan regaled Mitch with the incident for the tenth time. "She held two jars in one hand and worked her way around four high chairs like a pro. The kids mouths popped open like baby birds waiting for worms. I'd been trying to use a separate jar and spoon for each baby.'' Ethan toasted Regan with his water glass. Both men clinked glasses with hers.

"Stop! You guys are making me self-conscious. I called a parent who has triplets. She said multiples share germs, anyway. The object is for Mom to save steps and conserve energy. Uh, I'm not Mom, of course. She meant, the less time spent on chores, the more a caregiver has left to do fun things with the kids.''

Mitch twirled his glass. "Occasionally I think how my life would change if I had a child. One. Four at once boggles the mind.''

Regan glanced up with interest. "Building a family usually begins with marriage, Mitch. If you're thinking of fatherhood, does that mean you've settled on one of the women you've paraded through here?''

"Jeez, no! Don't either of you start a rumor like that. I take enough heat from my folks. My sisters are married with kids, but my dad's big on perpetuating the Valetti name.'' Mitch shrugged. "I've thought about settling down....''

"So what's stopping you?'' Regan teased.

Ethan answered for him. "He only dates airheads, that's what. When he stares into their eyes and comes up blank, it's no wonder he can't see himself growing old with them.''

"I've seen the way Mitch looks at your sister Amy,'' Regan said. "She's no airhead.''

Mitch groaned. "You saw me when? At the Schutzhund? I flirted with Amy to get Nicky Mason off my back. Brrr. That one's a little too possessive for me. Amy's...well, it's a damn shame she's stuck on our hotshot DA.''

"Really?'' Regan said. "I haven't met him.''

Ethan grimaced. "The family isn't encouraging that alliance. His name, Creighton Henner IV, is reason enough. We have backyard barbecues. Cray attends soireés at his club, if that tells you anything. When he does come to our dos, he's wearing tennis whites.''

"Your *family* isn't marrying him," Regan chided. "Does Amy play tennis?"

Ethan and Mitch nodded glumly.

Regan stood and began clearing dishes. "I see the real problem. Mitch is more serious about Amy than he cares to admit. And you Knights are probably all shoving him down her throat. Maybe if everyone backed off, she wouldn't run away so fast."

"A few years ago that might have been true," Mitch said. "Now she's had a taste of Henner's world. She won't even come out to the ranch to ride anymore. Claims she doesn't want to smell horsey." His voice was scornful. "Like Creighton's aftershave smells better."

"So what if Amy's a lost cause? There are other women in Desert City." Ethan brightened. "I read about a guy who made a list of all the things he wanted in a woman—a wife. Then, for every woman he dated, he checked them against the list."

"Sounds like work," Mitch muttered.

Regan jerked the water glass right out of Ethan's hand. "Sounds cold-blooded to me. What woman wants to be chosen by a scorecard—as if you won her at bingo?"

"No, no," Ethan interjected. "It's not hit and miss like bingo. More scientifically accurate. Compatibility is the whole basis."

Mitch leaned forward, clearly interested. "So looks don't play a part? And your method would rule out irritating stuff like baby talk, whining and putting on airs."

"That depends entirely on the guy setting the criteria. Clever, no?"

"Clever, yes." Mitch grinned.

Regan scraped plates and turned on the garbage disposal. It drowned out their nonsense. Immediately afterward she started the dishwasher. "I'm leaving," she announced. "Mitch, Ethan forgot to mention that his idea comes from a sixth grader," she added sarcastically.

The men ignored her. Shaking her head, Regan left.

The next afternoon she expected to hear more about Ethan's infamous plan for finding a wife. It didn't come up in the course of their conversation, and the hours she spent with him and the babies flew by pleasantly.

Every day she noticed that the babies seemed happier and more at ease. In the two weeks she'd been helping out, they'd stopped flinching when a door slammed or someone spoke loudly.

During lunch on Friday, Ethan coaxed noisy laughs from Rick and Angela. It stood to reason that Mark and Cara, the two who'd been most injured by Tony DeSalvo's loss of control, would take longer to trust again.

Regan slowly began to soften toward Taz. At first her heart had skipped a beat each time Ethan placed the babies on the floor and Taz came near. Soon it was evident that the little ones loved to touch his fur and he never seemed to mind. Taz was also quick to hunt down Ethan or her if a baby so much as whimpered.

After three weeks of hands-on observation, Regan sat in her office contemplating ways to give Ethan full agency approval to indefinitely foster the quadruplets. Once her report was finished, she hand-delivered it to Nathaniel.

"This is preposterous," he thundered once he'd read her summary. "Why haven't you placed those kids with a real foster family?"

"You mean besides the fact that the babies are thriving under Ethan's care? If you need additional reasons, the family-court judge asked that the babies remain where they are until Serena and her boyfriend's preliminary hearings. The bailiff said DeSalvo is actively trying to make bail. He's already threatened to kill the babies. Who better to keep them safe than a cop? Besides, there's no one else to take them. I'm sure you've seen articles to that effect in this week's paper.''

''Who's keeping this story alive in the media? Normally this wouldn't warrant a blip on the back page. Yet we're still front-page news.''

''Four battered babies are hard to forget. Everyone with children of their own wants justice for those poor little kids.''

''Yes, well, they've become the focus of an outpouring of rage against the Child Help Center. At our last budget meeting there was talk of withholding our funding until the state's assured we're doing a good job here in Desert City. I took it as a direct slap at my ability to run this office.''

''Why don't you tell the committee that the kids are fine where they are? On my last visit, Cara smiled. She's the one doctors feared had brain damage.''

Nathaniel flattened his hands on the desk. ''It's no secret that I'm adamantly opposed to Knight fostering these kids. But it wouldn't do for our advisory staff at the capital to get the idea I'm opposing him out of vindictiveness. I want you checking on those children every day.''

Regan had hesitated to tell Piggot how frequently she visited Ethan's home. The order to go daily shocked her. ''I'll put that in my schedule,'' she murmured.

''Turn some of your on-site duties over to Odella. I dislike that woman, but the other counselors seem to respond well to her. Triple your visits to Knight, if need be. I want him caught flagrantly disobeying agency rules. Meanwhile continue to interview other prospects. I'm releasing a public statement to that effect. To prove we're running the show.''

''You're ordering me to *spy* on Ethan?'' She sounded as horrified as the idea made her feel. Though reluctant to give Nathaniel any reason to restrict her visits to Ethan and the babies, she would not be a party to something so…so despicable.

''Spy has such a disagreeable connotation.'' Piggot bounced the tips of his pudgy fingers together. ''Let's just say I trust you won't forget who authorizes your paychecks.''

Regan wanted to tell him what he could do with her paycheck. She ought to ask to be taken off the case and have him give it to another counselor. But she wouldn't, even though logic said she was getting too involved. And she would add Nathaniel's latest transgression to the complaints she'd sent to the review board. Maybe they *had* listened if someone up there questioned whether Piggot was doing his job.

MITCH STOPPED to see Ethan after his shift, bringing pizza, beer and soft drinks. ''Where's the love of your life tonight, buddy?''

Ethan slid a piece of Flo's pizza from the box. ''If you mean Regan, she's probably poring over her rule book looking for reasons to take the kids away.''

''Aw, man. Why would she do that? She's been here every day, pitching in like a trouper. Don't tell me you haven't noticed those cow eyes she lays on you when she thinks you're not paying attention.''

''Huh? You're the one not paying attention, my friend. I've done everything but stand on my head and ride a pony backward to convince that woman to marry me. She's still afraid Taz is going to gobble up one of the kids.''

Mitch tore off a second slice of pizza. "Regan's had it rough from what you told me. Hang in there, Ethan. She'll get squared away sooner or later."

"I wish I could wait. The chief buttonholed me today. He said to get my butt back to work ASAP. Regan's agency thinks I'm on indefinite leave. Truth is, time's run out. I've got to find someone to help me care for the babies, or let them be separated. Hell, I'd like them permanently. You and I both know Serena's fighting a losing battle."

"So what are you saying?"

Ethan sighed and slapped his knees nervously. "I need a wife, buddy."

Mitch spewed a swig of beer onto his pant legs. "Just like that?"

"You think CHC will approve of me hiring a nanny?"

A piece of sausage fell off Mitch's pizza. He swore and tossed the meat to Taz. "I know you said you asked Regan to marry you and she turned you down."

"So?"

"So, maybe you oughtta ask again."

Ethan shook his head.

"I don't get you, man. You'd settle for second-best? If you love Regan, make her listen."

"How many times would you ask someone to marry you?"

"Well, hell. Once, I suppose."

"Yeah? I asked her twice. Bared my soul. She turned me down flat both times. Dammit, why am I explaining? *You* were the one, if I recall, who said that one person can't fix another's hang-ups."

The longer Mitch stared blankly, the more defensive Ethan became. "Angela, Mark, Cara and Rick deserve consistency. The morning paper said CHC is continuing to interview foster parents. Why? I'll just have to learn to put Regan out of my mind and find someone else who'll open her heart to four kids and a dog."

"Well, I wish you luck, I guess. Too bad you're nuts. When Regan hears this, she'll have you declared certifiable."

"Do you plan to run out and tell her?"

"No, but she's here all the time. When are you proposing to date anyone else?"

Ethan slumped into a corner of the couch and drained his soft drink. "Don't worry. The social psychologist in her will see merit in..." He frowned. "There's a word for what I'm doing. Can't think of it."

"Gigolo?" Mitch downed the remainder of his beer and stood.

"No!" Ethan shouted. "Marriage of convenience. That's the term."

Mitch hooted. "In America? Not since we fought and won the Revolutionary War. Anyway, women in love don't deal in logic, my man. I don't care how many degrees they have after their name. Mark my words, Regan Grant's in love with you." Mitch poked a finger at Ethan's chest.

For a moment Ethan sat gaping at his friend, until a baby started to wail at the other end of the house.

"I hear what you're saying. Wellington's ordered you back. Do yourself a favor and give this half-assed idea more thought. Juggle shifts for a while. Ask your mom or your sisters to help out." Mitch crossed to the door.

"Listen, I'm on shift. Gotta go, or I'd stay and help."

"Hey, thanks for listening. And thanks for dinner."

Ethan locked the door after Mitch left. He closed his eyes and massaged the back of his neck. "Okay, I hear them," he informed Taz, who appeared in the hallway to bark on behalf of the crying infants.

The rest of the night Ethan replayed various conversations he'd had with Regan over the past few of weeks. When morning arrived, he still hadn't discovered the slightest hint that she'd begun to reverse her position. Only a fool would stick out his neck a third time knowing it'd be lopped off.

So what if he married someone for the sake of the kids, and then Serena beat her rap and CHC gave the babies back?

That worry had no more than entered his head when Ethan received a telephone call from the courthouse—a clerk saying three psychiatrists had examined Serena. All had signed affidavits finding her incapable of caring for her kids. An additional bit of good news—DeSalvo hadn't dredged up bail.

But Ethan's next phone call came from Chief Wellington. "Knight," he growled, "you've got one more week off. One, that's it." *Bang* went the chief's receiver. Ethan felt the clock ticking down. If he wanted a shot at permanent custody, he needed a helpmate. And fast.

REGAN FOUND ETHAN distracted and moody that afternoon when she visited. "You've been cooped up too long. Let's take the kids to the park. I bought this really cool stroller with four seats. It's in the trunk of my car."

"You bought it or the agency did?"

"Me. Why?" She answered his frown with one of her own.

"No reason."

His terse response had her scratching her head. "If

you need time alone, Ethan, I'll take the babies by myself. I swear I won't steal them.'' She made an exaggerated *X* over her heart, shivering a little when Ethan continued to stare intently at her.

"Good idea," he said at last. "I could use a couple of hours to take care of some personal stuff. You'll bring Taz along to the park?"

Regan pictured the big dog running amok in a park filled with little kids. Her mouth opened to refuse. Only…what if Ethan was testing her? She consciously turned off old tapes dealing with old fears. "Um…sure, Taz can come. Go, Ethan. I'll change the babies, get their hats and fill their bottles with water. This August heat is murder."

Ethan kissed the babies. Regan thought he seemed reluctant to leave.

A short while later she dismissed him from her mind. She and the kids had a fine afternoon in the park. Taz stayed by their side, his behavior impeccable.

She was pretty smug about beating Ethan back to the house. She'd given all four babies their afternoon bottles by the time he wandered in.

Because he didn't seem to be in any better frame of mind, she gathered her things. "See you tomorrow, Ethan. I hope you have a good evening. I think the kids will sleep well after their outing." Troubled by his uncharacteristic moodiness she rose on tiptoe and kissed him on the cheek.

He reared back, nearly knocking her over. "What was that for?"

"Just because you're one good man, Ethan Knight." Calling herself all kinds of fool, Regan ducked her head and hurried out.

Ethan placed his palm over the spot she'd kissed. He

stared at the closed door until one of the babies—Angela, he thought from the cry—claimed his attention.

For the remainder of the week, the heat and humidity made the kids fussy. Soothing them kept Regan and Ethan too busy for chitchat. Just before she left on Friday, Ethan said, "Mom thinks we both need a break. She's offered to spell us this weekend—so we can get some adult time for a change."

Her heart pounding, Regan waited for Ethan to ask her out. All he said while she hovered in the doorway was, "Rest up. And don't get lost if you go hiking."

Disappointed, Regan merely nodded, telling herself that she needed to catch up on laundry and on office paperwork she'd let slide. Perhaps Ethan needed time by himself.

MONDAY MORNING, she stopped at the data center to drop off a batch of tapes she'd dictated. Nicole Mason and two caseworkers were huddled together at the counter. Overhearing Ethan's name, Regan stopped to listen.

"I have it on good authority," Nicole said, not exactly trying to keep her message confidential, "that Ethan Knight is shopping for a wife."

Regan was too shocked to speak. Not that she'd involve herself, in any event.

"The news came straight from his sister Amy," Nicole rushed to say. "I guess he wants someone hot rather than a cold fish." She slanted a quick glance at Regan.

Regan cursed the fair skin that let her cheeks flame so readily. She managed, she thought, to leave the room with a modicum of dignity. Which wasn't to say she didn't stew over Nicole's audacity all morning. More than once she reached for the phone, intending to ask

Ethan point-blank—for the sake of the babies. What did it say for her ability to choose a good foster home if he was trolling for a wife like a bottom feeder? What if the media got hold of such a rumor?

Eventually Regan decided Nicole had made the whole thing up for her benefit. So she didn't phone Ethan, but had gotten a lock on her jealousy by the time she left for her afternoon visit.

At Ethan's everything seemed status quo. "Did you read about the rescue mission Taz and I performed on Saturday?" he asked.

"No, I'm afraid I worked all weekend. Another hiker?"

"A child who wandered away from his parents in a wooded park. I've never seen happier parents. They promised Taz a year of rawhide bones."

Regan listened and was even more convinced that Nicole had deliberately lied. A little later, Ethan called from the babies' room. "I need Angela's pacifier. It's on my nightstand. Hers is yellow. Would you bring it, Regan? She's nearly asleep."

Regan raced into Ethan's room and found the pacifier. His bed wasn't made and a couple of dirty shirts lay where he'd dropped them. Dust had collected on his dresser. His room had been immaculate before the babies' arrival. Ethan clearly needed a housekeeper. *Or a wife.* The last pulsed in her head as Regan dashed down the hall and handed him Angela's pacifier.

"Thanks," he whispered, still rubbing the baby's back. Smiling up at Regan, he asked unexpectedly, "Have I said thanks for all your help? If not, I want you to know I couldn't have done this without you. I know I *said* I could, but I was wrong."

He looked and sounded so serious all Regan could do

was nod. She wanted to hug him and somehow wipe away the signs of fatigue she hadn't noticed until now. If only she could turn back the clock—to the last time he'd proposed. She'd accept as soon as he got the words out. The realization hit her like a load of bricks. She'd just admitted to herself that she wanted to marry Ethan Knight.

"Uh, no thanks necessary," she mumbled, backing from the room. "Bye. I'll see you tomorrow."

He answered with a two-fingered wave.

Regan let herself out. She started her car with an unsteady hand, reflecting that she'd lost Ethan through pure stupidity. Now it was up to her to win him back. Tomorrow she'd surprise him—send him out on some pretext so she could cook his favorite meal. She'd bathe and feed the babies and put them down a little early. Then she'd slip into the sexy black dress she'd bought on impulse last month. And…and…after that, she'd spend the rest of the evening seducing Ethan Knight.

Unlocking the door to her apartment, she thought about her plan for tomorrow night. And she danced around the floor, anticipating his pleasure.

THE NEXT DAY at the agency, she barely stopped fidgeting long enough to complete her work. Odella Price popped in just as Regan prepared to leave.

"I heard an odd rumor. That Ethan's talking to his preacher. What's wrong with you, girl? I've seen how that man looks at you."

"We had a falling-out, Odella. Totally my fault. I'm hoping to rectify my mistake. But it's true Ethan needs someone. The babies are wearing him out."

"Mmm. You're hooked on the four babies and not

him?'' Odella asked, narrowing her eyes as she walked with Regan out to her car.

"Oh, I'm very hooked on him. Odella…wish me luck in convincing Ethan that I'm the person he needs in his life. I'm going to lose my job, you know. This isn't for publication, but I blew the whistle on Piggot's ongoing feud with Ethan, in which he tried to involve me. And five minutes before you walked in, I faxed my final recommendations to the court and to the state. I'm circumventing Nathaniel and backing Ethan's bid to foster the babies.''

"Good for you. I hope they ax Piggot. It's long overdue. He stinks as a boss.'' Odella flashed Regan a thumbs-up as she climbed into her own car. "Hey, good luck doing you-know-what,'' she called, grinning as Regan drove off.

ETHAN ENTERED HIS HOUSE through the back door, thoroughly wet after washing his and Regan's cars. He'd started the project at her surprising insistence. The kitchen smelled of roast beef. A frosted chocolate layer cake sat on the counter.

He plunged to a halt outside the dining room, staring at a table set for two. Candles floated in a brandy snifter of water, ringed by a centerpiece of fresh flowers. *What the hell was going on?*

"Hey, Regan?'' Ethan called out. "Anyone?''

"Hey, yourself,'' Regan responded faintly from the vicinity of the babies' room. "You have time to shower before dinner, Ethan.''

He pursed his lips thoughtfully and glanced at the clock. Damn, he needed to clean up fast. This morning he'd taken the bull by the horns—he'd phoned Jenny Scopes, his veterinarian's assistant. Granted, she was quiet. But she was friendly and she loved Taz. Any time he'd taken the dog to be checked after his encounter with the bear, Jenny asked about the babies. So he'd invited her over for dinner. He'd figured on ordering something in. Give them time to talk and get to know each other.

Even under the hot spray, Ethan could smell the roast Regan had in the oven. Damn, Mitch had warned him he'd have to break the news sooner or later. And this was definitely sooner than he'd intended. *Why did she pick tonight to stay late?*

And that table! Gussied up. She did have a knack with stuff like that. Well, maybe she could take the flowers home so they wouldn't go to waste.

Dressed again, Ethan strode purposefully into the living room. The speech he'd prepared stuck in his throat. Regan stepped out of the kitchen wearing a short black dress that showed plenty of thigh and cleavage. Her perfume reached across the room and punched him hard, reminding Ethan that he was a man with sexual needs. Boy, was he ever, and he was sure it showed.

"Our little darlings are sound asleep." Regan's hips swayed sensually as she crossed the room to his small bar. "Dinner isn't quite done. We have time for a drink. What'll you have? The usual?" She glanced over her shoulder, innuendo in her smile.

The husky promise in her voice knocked all coherence from Ethan's head. If the sway in her walk hadn't done it her throaty growl had. Either way, Ethan was a goner. He barely avoided drooling on Regan when she brought him a cold sarsaparilla, his favorite soft drink.

He padded after her like a puppy.

With her glass of cola she curled into a corner of the couch not ten inches from where Ethan's rubbery legs deposited him. The remnants of lucidity left in his brain turned to pure lust.

Regan didn't appear bothered by his heavy breathing. She seemed content to smile and run one finger around and around the edge of her frosty glass.

For starters, Ethan itched to touch her hair. She'd fixed it differently tonight. Two sections were braided and scooped back with flashy doodads. A single curl escaped and clung to the corner of her mouth. He leaned over to free it.

Regan turned and pressed her lush red lips into his palm. Ethan's temperature spiked high enough to break a thermometer.

Snatching both drinks, he slammed them down hard on the coffee table—seconds before he dragged Regan onto his lap and into a crushing kiss. When he ran out of breath, he licked every tasty speck of lipstick off her lips.

"Ethan," she whispered. "I think dinner's ready."

"Who needs food when you taste so good?" Ethan had forgotten Jenny Scopes. Forgotten he needed to call her and beg off. When he was in the middle of unzipping Regan's dress and the doorbell chimed, twice in rapid succession he remembered. It rang a third time.

"Holy cow," he gasped, thrusting Regan away, clumsily trying to rezip her dress.

She surfaced through a fog. Enough to register his guilty-as-sin expression. "Are you expecting company? Is it Mitch?" With fumbling fingers, she wiped smudged lipstick from his face and tried to slip on the spiky heels she hadn't realized she'd lost.

"Not Mitch. Regan, I, uh… This is a hell of a thing to try and explain." Ethan grabbed Regan's hands, then dropped them as fast. "That'll be Jenny Scopes. Jenny, from the vet's office. You met her, remember?"

"Yes. Taz isn't sick, is he?" But no, he was at the door barking happily.

Ethan sprang up and hauled Regan from the couch. "I invited Jenny over for dinner," he said, knowing damned well he was doing a piss-poor job of clearing this up. "I had no idea you were going to..." He gestured helplessly toward the intimately set dining table and back to her dress. "I, uh, Jenny assumes she's my date."

"Your *date?* Fine." Regan sucked in a harsh breath. "That's just fine." Spots of red dotted her cheeks as she attempted to smooth the wrinkles out of her dress. "Well, don't just stand there, show your date in, Ethan. Tell her I'm the maid," she said tartly. Stalking across the room, she dug an apron out of a shopping bag. The doorbell chimed again as she pulled it over her head.

"What do you think you're doing?" Ethan hissed, walking backward to the door. "That apron is longer than your dress."

"Who cares? I'll dish up dinner before it dries out. No sense ruining a good standing rib roast."

"Regan, I can explain," he said desperately.

"No need." She waved him away. "I get the message. Please, let Jenny in before she wakes the babies leaning on that doorbell. Or Taz does, barking like that."

"You *don't* get the message, dammit. Oh, all right." He stomped to the door and yanked it open.

Jenny shifted from foot to foot. She peered nervously into the dimly lit room. "Oh, Ms. Grant is here. Uh...did I screw up? Do I have the wrong night?"

"Right night," Regan said from behind, mustering a generous smile. "Ethan ran late with chores. I was here checking on the babies and had time on my hands, so I threw together a little something for dinner.'' She didn't say it had taken her almost two hours of preparation. ''Come in. Take a seat at the table, please. I'll serve everything, then I'll run along.''

Ethan closed the door behind Jenny with a loud bang. ''Regan isn't quite giving you the correct story, Jenny. Truth is, I owe you both an apology. When I phoned today, Jenny, you said you thought Regan and I were an item. We were. Are,'' he firmly corrected. ''I'm, uh, still crazy about her. I made a mistake in thinking I could put her out of my mind. I hope you can forgive me.''

Jenny didn't seem to fully grasp his explanation. Regan did. Her gaze connected with Ethan's. Love softened both their expressions. ''Hey, really, I fixed enough food for a small army,'' she said quickly. ''Come on, Jenny, I'd hate for you to leave not only hungry, but thinking Ethan and I are total screwballs.''

Ethan supposed he deserved to face them both at once, but he felt like a fool as he pulled out a chair at the table for Jenny, with Regan bustling to and from the kitchen. Even after she'd served the luscious meal, talk remained stilted. Taz had presumably returned to watch over the babies, so even he couldn't provide a distraction.

During a patently awkward lull in the conversation, the telephone rang. Welcoming the excuse to extricate himself, Ethan jumped up to answer it. ''What?'' he yelped at Mitch, who was the caller. ''Tony DeSalvo overpowered a guard? Who authorized him to go to the clinic? Yeah, yeah, you're right. Probably no reason he'll show up here. Still, I'll get my weapon and have a look outside. What's your ETA? Ten minutes? Good!'' Hanging up, Ethan started to explain to the women.

Regan was already on her feet. ''Do what needs doing, Ethan. Jenny and I will stand guard over the babies. You'll be careful, won't you?'' She gave Ethan's arm a worried squeeze.

''It'll be okay. If Tony's headed here, Mitch will pick him up. If he should show his ugly face, the two of you lie low. I'll handle everything.''

Regan nodded. Jenny had turned white. Staring past Ethan and Regan, she uttered a bloodcurdling, hair-raising scream.

The couple whirled in time to see a man dressed in prison orange hurl himself through Ethan's living-room window. As glass shattered and flew, he rolled once and dove behind the couch, throwing off a gray blanket he had wrapped over one arm.

Ethan grabbed both women and shoved them into the hall. ''Regan, you two vamoose. I'll take care of De-Salvo.''

''Without a gun?'' Regan raised her voice to be heard above a squeal of tires out on the street. Down the hall Taz barked and a baby began to wail.

CHAPTER FOURTEEN

JENNY SEEMED ROOTED to the floor. Regan shook her and whispered, "Quick! Go down the hall to the first door on your left. Wait with the babies. I'll get Ethan's gun from his room and call 911. He'll have his hands full with that lunatic until Mitch arrives. Maybe the dispatcher knows when that'll be."

From the living room, Tony DeSalvo screamed obscenities, insisting he'd kill everyone in the house. Taz's barking sounded muffled, as if he'd gone outside.

Ethan had carefully positioned himself between the women and the intruder. He'd taken time to blow out the candles on the table. Lacking any other weapon, he grabbed the lead-crystal salt and pepper shakers and lobbed them over the couch. As they crashed, DeSalvo cursed louder.

"Regan, you and Jenny go in with the kids," he yelled. "Go! Leave this SOB to Mitch and me."

The intruder rose above the back of the couch and fired an automatic weapon at Ethan, who ducked and motioned the women down. "How in hell did he get a gun?"

Terror congealed in Regan's stomach. She was still the one closest to Ethan's bedroom and a phone. She crawled as quietly and as fast as possible. Her hands shook as she punched in 911. Holding the phone against her shoulder, she used her free hand to yank open the drawer where Ethan kept his service revolver in a locked box. Not knowing the combination, she took the whole box. It seemed like forever, but within seconds a dispatcher answered. Regan rattled off the situation and Ethan's address. "Please, tell them to hurry. The guy is off his rocker and he has a gun," she gasped, hanging up even though the dispatcher requested she stay on the line.

Uppermost in Regan's mind was getting the box to Ethan. But on her return, recent developments in the living room sent her heart to her throat. Over Ethan's shoulder Mitch climbed stealthily through the broken window. The frame still glittered with jagged glass. Regan stopped and held her breath.

Mitch proceeded slowly and of necessity, held his thirty-eight at an odd angle. He must have made a noise to attract DeSalvo.

Rising and spinning toward the window, DeSalvo pulled the trigger. Blood—Mitch's blood—splattered on the windowsill and the wall, smearing a piece of glass that remained intact. The force of the shots propelled him backward through the opening. He landed with a sickening thud in the oleander shrubs that ran the length of Ethan's house.

"Mitch! Mitch! Answer me, dammit!" Hearing no response, Ethan doubled a fist and struck the wall.

Regan closed her eyes and prayed. More shots erupted as she tried to cross the opening to reach Ethan. She hit something in the dark and almost lost her grip on the box. As her ears rang from DeSalvo's shots, it took Regan a moment to realize she'd tripped over Jenny.

"She's passed out, I think," Ethan muttered. "We've gotta move her."

"More help is on the way," Regan panted, shoving

the gun box into Ethan's hands. "I called 911 from your bedroom."

"I didn't know where you'd gone." Ethan stopped dragging Jenny's deadweight toward the spare bedroom. He clawed at the combination lock until the box lid sprang open. Regan shook Jenny roughly. Finally the woman's eyes fluttered open and Regan guided her across the hall. Jenny stumbled into the nearest bedroom and shut the door.

"Is Mitch is all right?" Regan's teeth chattered in Ethan's ear. He touched her face briefly.

"I don't know, but he's tough."

Another round of DeSalvo's sprayed overhead, chipping wood from the cove molding in the hallway. Ethan released Regan and crouched to load his weapon. "Mitch is probably looking for another way in. I want you to stay with the babies and don't come out until one or the other of us says it's safe."

Nodding once, Regan bent low and zigzagged along the hall to the babies' room. She opened the door and was mowed down when Taz exploded out. The door must have closed accidentally, shutting him in with the babies. Behind her she heard an exchange of gunfire. Ethan's single shot sounded futile against the automatic. Regan considered going back to make sure Ethan was safe, but knew that would be foolish. In the living room, she heard Tony swear and demand Serena's kids. The man was insane or else flying high on drugs. Either way he was dangerous.

Regan shut the door and locked it. As an added measure, she shoved a heavy chest of drawers against it. Frightened that Tony might get past Ethan and Taz, she spread blankets on the floor at the back of a walk-in closet. Her hands shook as she picked up the babies, then placed them on the blanket. She gave each a pacifier and curled around them, prepared to shield them with her body if necessary. She pulled the door shut even though she'd never liked the dark. To calm her own jumpy nerves as well as soothe the babies, she sang softly. Brokenly. For an interminable time.

ETHAN, WHO'D EXTRACTED his thirty-eight from the box, got off only one shot. Barely breathing, he held the pistol with both hands, pointing it at the ceiling. Flattened against the hall wall, he elected to let Tony make the next move. He cocked an ear, listening for Mitch. Where was he?

Taz flew past. "No, boy. Stay," Ethan hissed. In a rare act of disobedience, the well-trained dog ignored a command. Snarling, Taz leaped over the couch. Hearing a scuffle and wild curses, Ethan sneaked a peek.

DeSalvo was dancing in circles, swearing, attempting to dislodge Taz, whose teeth were sunk into the fabric of his prison jumpsuit.

"Dammit! No room to shoot." Inhaling, Ethan drew back. Amid the grunts and snarls, he dared a second look—in time to see DeSalvo's heavy boot connect with the ribs Taz had injured previously. The dog issued a sharp yelp and fell in a limp heap next to Ethan's recliner.

Concerned for Taz and really worried now about Mitch's continued silence, Ethan stepped fully into the doorway. Going down on one knee, he set both hands to take sure aim.

DeSalvo pulled his trigger first.

Ethan felt something sear his left shoulder. The impact slammed him into the wall. Blood ran down his arm onto his hand. It was only by a miracle that he maintained his grip on the revolver. He heard DeSalvo plunging toward him. Ethan forced his mind off the pain in his shoulder. Keeping his head low, he duck-walked down the hall, determined to stay between DeSalvo and Regan and the kids. He hoped to hell Jenny had sense enough to remain in the guest room.

INSIDE THE CLOSET, Regan stopped singing. That last series of shots unnerved her, and her heart bucked wildly. Thankfully the babies had been lulled back to sleep by a combination of the darkness and her presence. Regan struggled hard to stifle a resurgence of her fear. She did that by reminding herself she was responsible for four helpless babies who didn't need any more trauma in their young lives.

That same good sense told Regan to be quiet and keep hidden. However, an ever-growing concern, spurred on by the absence of Taz's barks—not to mention her desperate concern for Ethan's welfare—prompted her to creep out of the closet. As quietly as she could, she slid the chest of drawers aside. Enough to wriggle out for a quick look-see.

A heavy hand came out of nowhere, twisted in her hair and yanked her up on her tip toes. Tears sprang to Regan's eyes. She barely managed to muffle a cry of pain. Terror clawed at her throat. For a moment she was ten again and fighting off her neighbor's crazed poodle.

"Where are the kids, bitch?" Tony DeSalvo's rancid breath fanned Regan's face. Sanity returned, although she nearly fainted. She'd never be able to live with herself if she let him harm those babies. Gritting her teeth, she said nothing.

"Answer me," the furious man screamed in her ear.

Regan couldn't have spoken a syllable by then if she'd tried. Her silence further provoked DeSalvo. Jerking her by the hair, he flung her across the hall. She fell hard, and as she hit the floor, her teeth went through her bottom lip.

Regan scrambled to her knees. "Go to hell," she said, oddly enough no longer afraid. She was angry now. Furious. How dared this pitiful excuse for a human being come into her home and terrorize the occupants? In her fury, she forgot it was Ethan's home.

Behind the door, Ethan breathed in shallow spurts. The room was fading in and out. He heard distant sirens and hoped help arrived before the bastard finished him off and went looking for Regan and the babies. Over the sirens Ethan heard someone hit the floor—followed by a woman's voice.

Had Jenny somehow wandered into DeSalvo's path? Ethan took a firmer grip on the wavering gun and shook his head to clear it. Innocent panic-stricken Jenny? If she'd fainted, fallen out of his way, Ethan might get off a clear shot. He eased the door open a crack. His eyes had to adjust to a change in light. As they did, he saw Regan on the floor, blood trickling from her mouth. Enraged and heedless of his injuries, Ethan bellowed to draw DeSalvo's attention. Letting the door fly, Ethan sailed right over Regan and, surprise on his side, struck Tony low. The two men fell with a horrendous crash inches from Regan, still on her knees.

Down the hall a picture of Ethan's family tumbled off the wall. The glass frame shattered, along with Regan's nerves.

Then miraculously both men's weapons went flying as they grappled with one another. She scuttled around them, scooping up first one gun, then the other. Not trained to shoot, she ran blindly away. Her thought was to get the guns as far out of DeSalvo's reach as possible. But oh, how she wished she had the expertise to shoot straight. Her fury was unlike any she'd ever experienced.

Regan knew Ethan was in good shape, but DeSalvo fought with the strength of ten men. There had been blood on Ethan's shirt. On his face. Regan was frightened for him. And for the babies. Panic gripped her, checking her forward motion.

The welcome shriek of sirens just outside caused her to swerve toward the living room, even though her plan had been to hide the guns under Ethan's bed. Near the fireplace she tripped over an accent rug and screamed as Taz loomed up, blocking her path. He staggered, unsteady on his feet.

Regan teetered. "Oh, God. Taz, you're bleeding."

The dog shook himself solidly, whined and took off down the hall toward the babies and Ethan. She let him go, silently hoping he'd tear Tony DeSalvo limb from limb. Again her savagery shocked her.

Heavy fists pounded on the front door. A deep male voice gave an order to open up. Regan couldn't comply fast enough, even though her heart leaped into her throat when the door swung inward and five SWAT team members in full gear faced her with raised rifles. "Ethan's hurt," she gasped. "And Mitch. That's his blood." She pointed to the broken window and shuddered. The new arrivals split up. Three ran past her and two dashed outside to check for Mitch.

After that things happened so fast, Regan couldn't keep up. She directed the next emergency personnel— two paramedics outside to help with Mitch. Their partner she led cautiously into the hallway.

A grateful cry spilled from her lips when Ethan broke away from a circle of SWAT officers long enough to haul her into a bear hug.

He was alive. Regan paid no heed to the sticky blood Ethan dripped on her new black dress until the paramedic tried to part them so he could treat Ethan's wound. "I'll live," Ethan growled. "Find Mitch. He may be badly hurt. Then check Regan. That son of a bitch threw her into a wall. Oh, and there's a woman in the first bedroom off the hall. I expect she's in shock."

Jenny. Regan had forgotten her. She let go of Ethan and ran to check, finding the younger woman huddled behind the door, sobbing. "Oh, dear." Regan helped her up. "I'm sorry, Jenny. I know what it's like to be frightened out of your wits."

Jenny pushed Regan away. She was white and trembling. "Please, I just want out of here." She refused to let the paramedic touch her. "And I'm never coming back," she told Ethan in a shaky voice.

Snatching her jacket from an overturned couch, Jenny shook out the glass and all but ran through the front door. She squeezed past two officers who'd gone to fetch fresh evidence-collection bags.

"Sorry," Regan muttered to Ethan, raising one eyebrow. "I guess this scotches your best marriage prospect." Sidling around the writhing DeSalvo, she opened the door to the babies' room.

Ethan yanked her back against his chest with his good arm. "I'm glad you still have a sense of humor. A few years down the road, you'll need it even more. You, my love, are my most promising marriage prospect. Got that? The only prospect I want or need. I'll prove it after I help the sergeant take out this garbage"—he indicated

DeSalvo—"and we see how Mitch is doing." Ethan spared a glower for the shackled man, who continued to make ugly threats against everyone in the house.

Baring his teeth, Taz landed two front paws on DeSalvo's chest. Nose to nose with the trussed felon, Taz dripped saliva onto the man's chin.

Regan realized it was the first time she hadn't been terrified by the sight of bared canine teeth.

Rattling his cuffs, DeSalvo belly flopped away. "Somebody call off that mad dog! I've got rights, you know."

"Shut up," responded the sergeant. "If I had my way, I'd order Taz to sink his teeth into your jugular. The only right you have is to remain silent and to have an attorney present when we interrogate you. Hey," he said with an exaggerated shrug, "I can't help what happens if I leave to go see what's up with my buddies outside."

"Don't…leave me alone with this…wolf." Tony began to blubber.

"I never thought I say this, Ethan, but I wish Taz *would* go for DeSalvo's jugular." Regan shuddered and hesitated inside the door to the babies' room. "What'll happen the next time DeSalvo gets loose?"

"He won't get loose anytime soon," Ethan assured her. "Tonight he racked up enough charges to put him away until these kids are married with kids of their own. I'll go with you to look in on them, and then I've got to locate Mitch."

Regan opened the closet door. Ethan's arm circled her waist automatically as they gazed at the four babies who slept on, tiny arms stretched above their heads.

"They're so relaxed. It's as if they know their future's safe," Ethan whispered.

"I hate to disturb them. But a closet floor's hardly a proper bed—according to rule 504 in our handbook for housing foster kids." She rolled her eyes. "All we need is for a zealous reporter to snap a picture of this and plaster it on TV. Nathaniel would self-destruct. On second thought..." Regan offered a grim smile as Ethan lifted Mark and placed him in the crib. She repeated the process with Cara, then moved Rick and Angela together.

"Piggot can go to hell. After all we've been through, no dunce like him is going to take these babies away from us, Regan."

The *us* had a nice ring. She touched his bloody shoulder lightly. "I'll stay. You go see what happened to Mitch and have this wound seen to."

"Promise you won't take off while I'm gone?"

"I'm sure someone will need my statement. Anyway," she admitted, meeting his eyes, "I hadn't intended to go home tonight. Before Jenny, that is. This night turned out very differently from the one I planned. Believe it or not, I set out to have my wicked way with you, Ethan Knight. When you were too weak to fight back, I'd intended to beg you to marry me."

Ethan, who'd reached the doorway, stopped and stared at Regan out of eyes that smoldered. "Hold that thought. It's been my fantasy for weeks."

Regan nodded, her throat too clogged to respond. "Go." She shooed him out and stepped to the door to follow his progress down the hall.

Soon after, Cara, the only one of the quadruplets who still took a bottle in the middle of the night, woke up crying. Regan changed her wet diaper and carried the fussy baby into the kitchen to prepare a bottle. Crime tape crisscrossed the broken front window. Regan shivered. Thank goodness DeSalvo had been carted away.

Ethan didn't appear to be around. Only one officer remained, a woman who spoke into a handheld recorder. She glanced at Regan and the baby, then shut off the mike. "Hello. I'm Karen Miller, forensics specialist. You must be Regan. Ethan said not to disturb you."

"Where is he?" Regan took a bottle from the fridge and set it in the microwave. "And where's Taz?"

"Don't you know? Brian Fitzgerald took Taz to the vet's. And Ethan asked the sergeant to tell you he'd be at the hospital with Mitch."

Regan paused in the act of testing the warm milk on her arm. "Hospital?"

"Yes. Three slugs hit Mitch. I heard a paramedic say one bullet severed nerves in his left leg. I hope the doc can save it."

"Save his leg?" Regan's limbs felt weak. She pulled out a chair and sat to feed Cara. "If Mitch hadn't climbed through that window, DeSalvo would have killed Ethan and probably me and Jenny. And...and the babies. Mitch saved us. I can't bear to think of him...disabled." She swallowed a sob. "And poor Taz..."

"Don't dwell on the negative," the policewoman advised.

"Which hospital? I'll phone Ethan. He must be devastated. Mitch is like a brother."

The woman named the hospital, then fell silent.

"I have another question," Regan said. "I expected to be bombarded by press. Their absence is a pleasant surprise."

"You owe Ethan for that, too. He told them the real story was in the downed officer. They snapped pictures of Mitch and the broken window—and of DeSalvo as the team trucked him away. Ethan asked us to keep silent about the babies. He told reporters DeSalvo came after him because he was the arresting officer.''

''Bless Ethan. The babies have had enough trauma to last a lifetime. I'm sure some enterprising reporter will eventually remember they're here. By then we'll probably have things under control.''

The woman examined Regan. ''You're kind of amazing, you know. Ethan said you phoned for backup and brought him his gun. A lot of women would have gone to pieces.''

''Not long ago I probably would have,'' Regan admitted. ''Being in love with someone who's in great danger changes the picture dramatically.''

''I guess you mean Ethan.''

''Yes. And the babies.'' Regan brushed a cheek across Cara's soft hair. ''This one suffered horribly at De-Salvo's hands. I want to see her run and jump and play with her sister and brothers. And that's another thing that makes Ethan so special. How many men would step in to raise four kids who weren't his?''

The policewoman cocked a wry eyebrow. ''Not many. Gals all over town used to stand in line to date Ethan. When rumors started floating around recently suggesting that four babies were part of the package, they bailed out in droves. There are probably only a couple left who'll look at you with envy.''

''Are you one of them?'' The thought had just occurred to Regan.

The woman flashed a left hand sporting a twinkling diamond. ''Mercy, no.''

Regan blushed. ''Just thought I'd ask. Ethan and I...well, nothing's official.''

"Maybe not in your mind, but in his. I could tell from the way he barked orders before he left. You're real important to him."

"Mmm. That's nice. I've been taking care of myself for so long. It'll be nice having someone... Oh, look, Cara's fallen asleep." Regan eased the nipple from the baby's still-sucking lips. "I'll put her in her crib. Then if you don't need me, I'll try phoning Ethan."

"Our official chat can wait. I still have a couple of bullet holes to calculate angles on and such."

As bullets weren't anything Regan cared to be reminded of, she left the room with Cara.

She placed the call to the hospital from Ethan's bedroom. A switchboard operator transferred her to the surgery wing, where a nurse found Ethan pacing the hall.

"Hey," he said in a gravelly voice the moment he came on the line. "I was just looking for a pay phone to call you, Angel Eyes. I just heard from Brian. Taz, thank God, is okay—bruises but no broken bones. Brian took Taz to his place for the night. How's everything at home?"

"Fine. How's Mitch? A policewoman, Karen, said he might be badly injured."

"Yeah. I should've taken my chances with DeSalvo once Mitch didn't resurface."

"Ethan, you can't blame yourself! DeSalvo shot you, too."

"I know, but I should've taken time to phone dispatch and say my partner was down."

"I told a dispatcher DeSalvo was armed. It all happened so fast. Anyway, there's no going back. Not that I'd want to. Is Mitch still in surgery?"

"Recovery. They won't know the extent of the nerve damage to his leg for a few weeks. The good news is, he's alive. I tried to call his folks at their place in Palm Springs. A housekeeper said they're on a cruise. She has no idea how to reach them. I wonder...what do you think about inviting him to recover at our place?''

"It's your home, Ethan.''

"And it's going to be yours. Tell me I didn't dream that proposal.''

Regan felt a blush start at her toes. "I suppose I'll have to live with you crowing about that for the rest of my life.''

"Nope. Nary another word on the subject if you promise to marry me soon.''

"Before Mitch gets back on his feet? Won't he want to be your best man?''

"Things are moving faster than I expected, Regan. I don't like having this conversation on a public phone. With Mitch out on medical leave, the chief ordered me back PDQ. Dammit, I feel like I'm hustling you to the altar. I'd hoped we could figure a way to split our work hours in order to juggle child care.''

"Why can't we? Ethan, we're practical adults, not crazy-in-love kids.''

"I *am* crazy-in-love with you, Regan. I hope you feel the same about me. And Taz. I take it you've decided to share a house with Taz?''

"Yes...to both. I just meant we aren't going to be the average newlyweds. We've got a complete family *before* marriage.''

"Are you all right with that? Damn, I'd rather have you in my arms when I'm asking stuff like this.''

"Me, too.'' Regan sighed. "We are going about this backward. But, Ethan, it can't be helped. There'll be time for us later. I want the babies. And we have to take care of Mitch for however long he needs it.''

"I love you, Regan. For more reasons than I have time to list."

"And I love you. I've known for weeks that I'd made the biggest mistake of my life refusing you. Taz won't hurt the babies. I'm so sorry I overreacted."

"All of that said, I'll hurry home as fast as humanly possible. Right after they move Mitch into a private room and I see him settled in."

"Ethan, before we leave the subject of marriage, do we need my salary to make ends meet?"

"No. I have substantial savings. I own the house and I make enough to feed us and buy shoes for the kids."

"I don't plan on being out of a job that long. But it'll look better to Family Court if one of us is home full-time. Plus, Mitch will need tending at first. Besides, I left Nathaniel a note more or less telling him to stuff the job."

Ethan laughed. "Oh, Regan, I do love you."

"You make me feel cherished, Ethan. No one's ever done that before. On that note, hadn't we better hang up? Do hurry home."

"Wild horses won't stop me. Change into something comfy," he growled softly.

AS IT HAPPENED, all four babies were awake demanding to be fed when Ethan dragged his tired body home. He still wore the shirt with the bullet hole in the sleeve and blood-spattered pants. Regan's "something comfy" turned out to be jeans and one of Ethan's shirts.

"Sorry to be so late," he told Regan, gathering her and the two babies she held into his arms. "Mitch was in recovery longer than expected. He was stable when I left, but I had to swing by the jail and dictate an arrest report on DeSalvo. This time he's being held without bail. The guard he overpowered died. Tony's going down on a murder rap."

"I can't say I'm sorry—except for the guard. Anyway, that news should speed Mitch's recovery. You know, Ethan, I've always wanted a brother. Do you suppose I can adopt Mitch?"

"I think he'd like that. He agreed to stay here until he's well enough to go back to his ranch. He may quit the force and raise saddle horses. This is his second serious injury. It takes time to build a profitable ranch, though. Might've been the pain medication talking, but he said maybe he'll supplement his pension by doing a little private-investigation work on the side."

"I'm licensed to provide private counseling. After Mitch leaves, perhaps I'll set up an office in the back bedroom. Odella said the city needs more good child psychologists. I could work part-time while the babies are little and work with the schools once they start kindergarten."

"What about Cara? Won't she always need home care?"

"This morning she rolled onto her side and tried to lift her head. We'll help her, Ethan. Over time, I believe she'll catch up with her siblings."

Ethan kissed Rick and Angela, the babies in Regan's arms. Then he lavished attention on her, leaving her breathless and weak-kneed when he'd finished.

"Mitch is glad we've made up. What would you say to having our wedding ceremony in his hospital room? That way he can still be my best man."

"That's perfect, Ethan. Do you think your mother would let us have our reception in her backyard? I want your family to share in our happy event.'' She grinned mischievously. ''And that way, we won't have to get a sitter for the babies.''

''I doubt it'll be the wedding you've always dreamed of, Regan.''

''It's exactly what I want, Ethan. I mean it.''

''Okay. My mom and sisters are old hands at planning and decorating for community shindigs. Shall I turn them loose on this?''

''Oh, yes.'' She kissed him on the lips. ''This will be a wedding to remember.''

AND IT WAS. Those who couldn't squeeze into Mitch's hospital room for the ceremony two weeks later, lined both sides of the hallway to catch a glimpse of the bride and groom. Regan wore an ivory dress that one of Ethan's sisters had worn at her own wedding. Ethan even agreed to a black tux and a teal cummerbund. Several nurses stopped what they were doing to watch him walk into Mitch's room.

Mitch was no slouch in hospital white, his leg elevated and immobilized. A flirty little brunette nurse even slipped him a glass of champagne to toast the happy couple, for which he kissed her.

Jeremy handled the rings. He was dashing in a new tan suit. He blushed when Regan told him he'd be fighting off girls by the score if he showed up at the reception looking like Mr. Cool.

The only blight on Regan's happiness occurred the evening she phoned her dad with the joyous news. He was, of course, too busy to attend. But he wired money. Lots of money. Hurt for her, Ethan wanted to send it back. ''No,'' Regan said, ''We'll start a college fund for the babies.'' Besides, not everyone in the family had disappointed her; Blair, her sister, had squealed with delight. She'd laughed and cried with Regan, and made her promise to send pictures. She also swore that, one way or another, she'd visit when school let out next summer.

Regan and Ethan sealed their vows with a long-drawn-out kiss and left the hospital, followed by their guests. All streets leading to the elder Knights' home were blocked with cars.

''No wedding reception in Desert City has ever been so well attended,'' Odella's husband, Roger, said as he stopped to congratulate the newlyweds.

''My mom and dad placed an open invitation in the newspaper. They said the whole town backed me in the matter of the babies. They thought it was a fitting way to thank everyone and introduce them to the kids. If Serena's convicted or committed, and there's little doubt that one or the other will occur, Regan and I plan to try and adopt the babies. We may need the whole town in our corner.''

Roger Price grinned. ''Your mom thinks like my wife, who's over there spoiling a couple of those babies. If you don't watch out, Regan, that woman will be camped out on your doorstep.''

Regan glanced across the yard at Taz, who was keeping a watchful eye on the babies. ''I hope so, Roger. Last week I asked Odella to leave the agency and come into private practice with me. With Ethan working the streets and Odella and me handling counseling, maybe we'll decrease the need for foster care in Desert City. That's my hope, anyway. For kids like the quads and Joey Hawkins.'' She turned to her husband. ''Ethan, I may have forgotten to tell you that Joey's back with

Maddy and Greg. Her mom fell off the wagon big-time. She was also caught selling cocaine. She's going up the river for at least five years.''

"Yeah," Brian Fitzgerald piped up, Dani beside him. "Without your tip, that powder would've blanketed the city.''

"What'll you and my wife do when you work yourselves out of a job?'' Roger asked Regan. "Oh, I guess you could run what's left of CHC. Since the state is investigating Piggot's handling of internal affairs—thanks to you, Regan—there's a ninety percent chance his job'll be up for grabs.''

Regan curved into her husband's side. "Couldn't happen to a more deserving guy.''

"There's something else,'' Ethan said after stealing a kiss from Regan. "Did you hear Mitch say I was the luckiest man alive? Well, he asked if you'd be on the lookout for a woman for him. Someone just like you.''

"If he's serious, I may. We owe him for stopping bullets meant for us, Ethan.'' She laughed, but the face she turned up for Ethan's second kiss suggested the wheels in her head were already turning.

Ethan's sisters, Erica and Jenny, murmured that Mitch Valetti should be careful what he wished for. Several of his former fellow officers dug in their pockets and anted up for a pool on picking a month Valetti would lose his bachelor status.

Ethan was so busy kissing Regan that a friend, a sergeant, helped himself to Ethan's billfold and drew out a twenty-dollar bill. Chief Wellington plucked it out of the sergeant's hand and slapped Ethan on the back. "The bigger they come, the harder they fall,'' he said. "Don't tell Mitch I'm holding the kitty. And I'm doubling Ethan's bet. My money's on his wife. Anyone who can rid a town of a jerk like Nathaniel Piggot is bound to have the Cowboy hitched and hogtied before those babies start crawling. Mark my words.''

* * * * *

Will Mitch Valetti fall in love? Read
LOST BUT NOT FORGOTTEN
to find out! Available at retail stores
in September 2001.

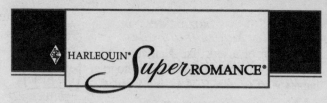

HARLEQUIN *Super* ROMANCE

To celebrate the
1000th Superromance book
We're presenting you with 3 books
from 3 of your favorite authors in

All Summer Long

Home, Hearth and Haley
by **Muriel Jensen**

Meet the men and women of Muriel's
upcoming **Men of Maple Hill** trilogy

Daddy's Girl
by **Judith Arnold**

Another **Daddy School** story!

Temperature Rising
by **Bobby Hutchinson**

Life and love at St. Joe's Hospital are as feverish
as ever in this **Emergency!** story

On sale July 2001
Available wherever Harlequin books are sold.

HARLEQUIN®
Makes any time special ®

Harlequin truly does
make any time special. . . .
This year we are celebrating
weddings in style!

To help us celebrate, we want you to tell us how wearing the Harlequin wedding gown will make your wedding day special. As the grand prize, Harlequin will offer one lucky bride the chance to **"Walk Down the Aisle" in the Harlequin wedding gown!**

There's more...

For her honeymoon, she and her groom will spend five nights at the **Hyatt Regency Maui.** As part of this five-night honeymoon at the hotel renowned for its romantic attractions, the couple will enjoy a candlelit dinner for two in Swan Court, a sunset sail on the hotel's catamaran, and duet spa treatments.

A HYATT RESORT AND SPA   Maui • Molokai • Lanai

To enter, please write, in, 250 words or less, how wearing the Harlequin wedding gown will make your wedding day special. The entry will be judged based on its emotionally compelling nature, its originality and creativity, and its sincerity. This contest is open to Canadian and U.S. residents only and to those who are 18 years of age and older. There is no purchase necessary to enter. Void where prohibited. See further contest rules attached. Please send your entry to:

Walk Down the Aisle Contest

In Canada	In U.S.A.
P.O. Box 637	P.O. Box 9076
Fort Erie, Ontario	3010 Walden Ave.
L2A 5X3	Buffalo, NY 14269-9076

You can also enter by visiting www.eHarlequin.com
Win the Harlequin wedding gown and the vacation of a lifetime!
The deadline for entries is October 1, 2001.

HARLEQUIN®
Makes any time special ®

PHWDACONT1

HARLEQUIN WALK DOWN THE AISLE TO MAUI CONTEST 1197
OFFICIAL RULES
NO PURCHASE NECESSARY TO ENTER

1. To enter, follow directions published in the offer to which you are responding. Contest begins April 2, 2001, and ends on October 1, 2001. Method of entry may vary. Mailed entries must be postmarked by October 1, 2001, and received by October 8, 2001.

2. Contest entry may be, at times, presented via the Internet, but will be restricted solely to residents of certain geographic areas that are disclosed on the Web site. To enter via the Internet, if permissible, access the Harlequin Web site (www.eHarlequin.com) and follow the directions displayed online. Online entries must be received by 11:59 p.m. E.S.T. on October 1, 2001.

   In lieu of submitting an entry online, enter by mail by hand-printing (or typing) on an 8½" x 11" plain piece of paper, your name, address (including zip code), Contest number/name and in 250 words or fewer, why winning a Harlequin wedding dress would make your wedding day special. Mail via first-class mail to: Harlequin Walk Down the Aisle Contest 1197, (in the U.S.) P.O. Box 9076, 3010 Walden Avenue, Buffalo, NY 14269-9076, (in Canada) P.O. Box 637, Fort Erie, Ontario L2A 5X3, Canada.

   Limit one entry per person, household address and e-mail address. Online and/or mailed entries received from persons residing in geographic areas in which Internet entry is not permissible will be disqualified.

3. Contests will be judged by a panel of members of the Harlequin editorial, marketing and public relations staff based on the following criteria:

   - Originality and Creativity—50%
   - Emotionally Compelling—25%
   - Sincerity—25%

   In the event of a tie, duplicate prizes will be awarded. Decisions of the judges are final.

4. All entries become the property of Torstar Corp. and will not be returned. No responsibility is assumed for lost, late, illegible, incomplete, inaccurate, nondelivered or misdirected mail or misdirected e-mail, for technical, hardware or software failures of any kind, lost or unavailable network connections, or failed, incomplete, garbled or delayed computer transmission or any human error which may occur in the receipt or processing of the entries in this Contest.

5. Contest open only to residents of the U.S. (except Puerto Rico) and Canada, who are 18 years of age or older, and is void wherever prohibited by law; all applicable laws and regulations apply. Any litigation within the Province of Quebec respecting the conduct or organization of a publicity contest may be submitted to the Régie des alcools, des courses et des jeux for a ruling. Any litigation respecting the awarding of a prize may be submitted to the Régie des alcools, des courses et des jeux only for the purpose of helping the parties reach a settlement. Employees and immediate family members of Torstar Corp. and D. L. Blair, Inc., their affiliates, subsidiaries and all other agencies, entities and persons connected with the use, marketing or conduct of this Contest are not eligible to enter. Taxes on prizes are the sole responsibility of winners. Acceptance of any prize offered constitutes permission to use winner's name, photograph or other likeness for the purposes of advertising, trade and promotion on behalf of Torstar Corp., its affiliates and subsidiaries without further compensation to the winner, unless prohibited by law.

6. Winners will be determined no later than November 15, 2001, and will be notified by mail. Winners will be required to sign and return an Affidavit of Eligibility form within 15 days after winner notification. Noncompliance within that time period may result in disqualification and an alternative winner may be selected. Winners of trip must execute a Release of Liability prior to ticketing and must possess required travel documents (e.g. passport, photo ID) where applicable. Trip must be completed by November 2002. No substitution of prize permitted by winner. Torstar Corp. and D. L. Blair, Inc., their parents, affiliates, and subsidiaries are not responsible for errors in printing or electronic presentation of Contest, entries and/or game pieces. In the event of printing or other errors which may result in unintended prize values or duplication of prizes, all affected game pieces or entries shall be null and void. If for any reason the Internet portion of the Contest is not capable of running as planned, including infection by computer virus, bugs, tampering, unauthorized intervention, fraud, technical failures, or any other causes beyond the control of Torstar Corp. which corrupt or affect the administration, secrecy, fairness, integrity or proper conduct of the Contest, Torstar Corp. reserves the right, at its sole discretion, to disqualify any individual who tampers with the entry process and to cancel, terminate, modify or suspend the Contest or the Internet portion thereof. In the event of a dispute regarding an online entry, the entry will be deemed submitted by the authorized holder of the e-mail account submitted at the time of entry. Authorized account holder is defined as the natural person who is assigned to an e-mail address by an Internet access provider, online service provider or other organization that is responsible for arranging e-mail address for the domain associated with the submitted e-mail address. **Purchase or acceptance of a product offer does not improve your chances of winning.**

7. Prizes: (1) Grand Prize—A Harlequin wedding dress (approximate retail value: $3,500) and a 5-night/6-day honeymoon trip to Maui, HI, including round-trip air transportation provided by Maui Visitors Bureau from Los Angeles International Airport (winner is responsible for transportation to and from Los Angeles International Airport) and a Harlequin Romance Package, including hotel accomodations (double occupancy) at the Hyatt Regency Maui Resort and Spa, dinner for (2) two at Swan Court, a sunset sail on Kiele V and a spa treatment for the winner (approximate retail value: $4,000); (5) Five runner-up prizes of a $1000 gift certificate to selected retail outlets to be determined by Sponsor (retail value $1000 ea.). Prizes consist of only those items listed as part of the prize. Limit one prize per person. All prizes are valued in U.S. currency.

8. For a list of winners (available after December 17, 2001) send a self-addressed, stamped envelope to: Harlequin Walk Down the Aisle Contest 1197 Winners, P.O. Box 4200 Blair, NE 68009-4200 or you may access the www.eHarlequin.com Web site through January 15, 2002.

Contest sponsored by Torstar Corp., P.O. Box 9042, Buffalo, NY 14269-9042, U.S.A.